BRIAN FLYNN

THE EBONY STAG

With an introduction by
Steve Barge

DEAN STREET PRESS

BRIAN FLYNN
THE EBONY STAG

BRIAN FLYNN was born in 1885 in Leyton, Essex. He won a scholarship to the City Of London School, and from there went into the civil service. In World War I he served as Special Constable on the Home Front, also teaching "Accountancy, Languages, Maths and Elocution to men, women, boys and girls" in the evenings, and acting in his spare time.

It was a seaside family holiday that inspired Brian Flynn to turn his hand to writing in the mid-twenties. Finding most mystery novels of the time "mediocre in the extreme", he decided to compose his own. Edith, the author's wife, encouraged its completion, and after a protracted period finding a publisher, it was eventually released in 1927 by John Hamilton in the UK and Macrae Smith in the U.S. as *The Billiard-Room Mystery*.

The author died in 1958. In all, he wrote and published 57 mysteries, the vast majority featuring the super-sleuth Antony Bathurst.

INTRODUCTION

"I believe that the primary function of the mystery story is
to entertain; to stimulate the imagination and even, at times,
to supply humour. But it pleases the connoisseur most when
it presents – and reveals – genuine mystery. To reach its full
height, it has to offer an intellectual problem for the reader
to consider, measure and solve."

Brian Flynn, *Crime Book* magazine, 1948

BRIAN Flynn began his writing career with *The Billiard Room Mystery*
in 1927, primarily at the prompting of his wife Edith who had grown
tired of hearing him say how he could write a better mystery novel
than the ones he had been reading. Four more books followed under
his original publisher, John Hamilton, before he moved to John
Long, who would go on to publish the remaining forty-eight of his
Anthony Bathurst mysteries, along with his three Sebastian Stole
titles, released under the pseudonym Charles Wogan. Some of the
early books were released in the US, and there were also a small
number of translations of his mysteries into Swedish and German.
In the article from which the above quote is taken from, Brian also
claims that there were also French and Danish translations but to
date, I have not found a single piece of evidence for their existence.
The only translations that I have been able to find evidence of are
War Es Der Zahnarzt? and *Bathurst Greift Ein* in German – *The
Mystery of the Peacock's Eye*, retitled to the less dramatic "Was It
The Dentist?", and *The Horn* becoming "Bathurst Takes Action" –
and, in Swedish, *De 22 Svarta*, a more direct translation of *The Case
of the Black Twenty-Two*. There may well be more work to be done
finding these, but tracking down all of his books written in the original English has been challenging enough!

Reprints of Brian's books were rare. Four titles were released
as paperbacks as part of John Long's Four Square Thriller range in
the late 1930s, four more re-appeared during the war from Cherry
Tree Books and Mellifont Press, albeit abridged by at least a third,
and two others that I am aware of, *Such Bright Disguises* (1941)
and *Reverse the Charges* (1943), received a paperback release as

part of John Long's Pocket Edition range in the early 1950s – these were also possibly abridged, but only by about 10%. They were the exceptions, rather than the rule, however, and it was not until 2019, when Dean Street Press released his first ten titles, that his work was generally available again.

The question still persists as to why his work disappeared from the awareness of all but the most ardent collectors. As you may expect, when a title was only released once, back in the early 1930s, finding copies of the original text is not a straightforward matter – not even Brian's estate has a copy of every title. We are particularly grateful to one particular collector for providing *The Edge of Terror*, Brian's first serial killer tale, and another for *The Ebony Stag* and *The Grim Maiden*. With these, the reader can breathe a sigh of relief as a copy of every one of Brian's books has now been located – it only took about five years . . .

One of Brian's strengths was the variety of stories that he was willing to tell. Despite, under his own name at least, never straying from involving Anthony Bathurst in his novels – technically he doesn't appear in the non-series *Tragedy at Trinket*, although he gets a name-check from the sleuth of that tale who happens to be his nephew – it is fair to say that it was rare that two consecutive books ever followed the same structure. Some stories are narrated by a Watson-esque character, although never the same person twice, and others are written by Bathurst's "chronicler". The books sometimes focus on just Bathurst and his investigation but sometimes we get to see the events occurring to the whole cast of characters. On occasion, Bathurst himself will "write" the final chapter, just to make sure his chronicler has got the details correct. The murderer may be an opportunist or they may have a convoluted (and, on occasion, a somewhat over-the-top) plan. They may be working for personal gain or as part of a criminal enterprise or society. Compare for example, *The League of Matthias* and *The Horn* – consecutive releases but were it not for Bathurst's involvement, and a similar sense of humour underlying Brian's writing, you could easily believe that they were from the pen of different writers.

Brian seems to have been determined to keep stretching himself with his writing as he continued Bathurst's adventures, and the ten books starting with *Cold Evil* show him still trying new things. Two of the books are inverted mysteries – where we know who the killer is, and we follow their attempts to commit the crime and/or escape justice and also, in some cases, the detective's attempt to bring them to justice. That description doesn't do justice to either *Black Edged* or *Such Bright Disguises*, as there is more revealed in the finale than the reader might expect . . . There is one particular innovation in *The Grim Maiden*, namely the introduction of a female officer at Scotland Yard.

Helen Repton, an officer from "the woman's side of the Yard" is recruited in that book, as Bathurst's plan require an undercover officer in a cinema. This is her first appearance, despite the text implying that Bathurst has met her before, but it is notable as the narrative spends a little time apart from Bathurst. It follows Helen Repton's investigations based on superb initiative, which generates some leads in the case. At this point in crime fiction, there have been few, if any, serious depictions of a female police detective – the primary example would be Mrs Pym from the pen of Nigel Morland, but she (not just the only female detective at the Yard, but the Assistant Deputy Commissioner no less) would seem to be something of a caricature. Helen would go on to become a semi-regular character in the series, and there are certainly hints of a romantic connection between her and Bathurst.

It is often interesting to see how crime writers tackled the Second World War in their writing. Some brought the ongoing conflict into their writing – John Rhode (and his pseudonym Miles Burton) wrote several titles set in England during the conflict, as did others such as E.C.R. Lorac, Christopher Bush, Gladys Mitchell and many others. Other writers chose not to include the War in their tales – Agatha Christie had ten books published in the war years, yet only *N or M?* uses it as a subject.

Brian only uses the war as a backdrop in one title, *Glittering Prizes*, the story of a possible plan to undermine the Empire. It illustrates the problem of writing when the outcome of the conflict was unknown – it was written presumably in 1941 – where there seems little sign of life in England of the war going on, one character states that he has fought in the conflict, but messages are sent from Nazi conspirators, ending *"Heil Hitler!"*. Brian had good reason for not wanting to write about the conflict in detail, though, as he had immediate family involved in the fighting and it is quite understandable to see writing as a distraction from that.

While Brian had until recently been all but forgotten, there are some mentions for Brian's work in some studies of the genre – Sutherland Scott in *Blood in their Ink* praises *The Mystery of the Peacock's Eye* as containing "one of the ablest pieces of misdirection" before promptly spoiling that misdirection a few pages later, and John Dickson Carr similarly spoils the ending of *The Billiard Room Mystery* in his famous essay "The Grandest Game In The World". One should also include in this list Barzun and Taylor's entry in their *Catalog of Crime* where they attempted to cover Brian by looking at a single title – the somewhat odd *Conspiracy at Angel* (1947) – and summarising it as "Straight tripe and savorless. It is doubtful, on the evidence, if any of his others would be different." Judging an author based on a single title seems desperately unfair – how many people have given up on Agatha Christie after only reading *Postern Of Fate*, for example – but at least that misjudgement is being rectified now.

Contemporary reviews of Brian's work were much more favourable, although as John Long were publishing his work for a library market, not all of his titles garnered attention. At this point in his writing career – 1938 to 1944 – a number of his books won reviews in the national press, most of which were positive. Maurice Richardson in the *Observer* commented that "Brian Flynn balances his ingredients with considerable skill" when reviewing *The Ebony Stag* and praised *Such Bright Disguises* as a "suburban horror melodrama" with an "ingenious final solution". "Suspense is well maintained until the end" in *The Case of the Faithful Heart*, and the protagonist's narration in *Black Edged* in "impressively nightmarish".

It is quite possible that Brian's harshest critic, though, was himself. In the *Crime Book* magazine, he wrote about how, when reading the current output of detective fiction "I delight in the dazzling erudition that has come to grace and decorate the craft of the *'roman policier'*." He then goes on to say "At the same time, however, I feel my own comparative unworthiness for the fire and burden of the competition." Such a feeling may well be the reason why he never made significant inroads into the social side of crime-writing, such as the Detection Club or the Crime Writers Association. Thankfully, he uses this sense of unworthiness as inspiration, concluding "The stars, though, have always been the most desired of all goals, so I allow exultation and determination to take the place of that but temporary dismay."

In Anthony Bathurst, Flynn created a sleuth that shared a number of traits with Holmes but was hardly a carbon-copy. Bathurst is a polymath and gentleman sleuth, a man of contradictions whose background is never made clear to the reader. He clearly has money, as he has his own rooms in London with a pair of servants on call and went to public school (Uppingham) and university (Oxford). He is a follower of all things that fall under the banner of sport, in particular horse racing and cricket, the latter being a sport that he could, allegedly, have represented England at. He is also a bit of a show-off, littering his speech (at times) with classical quotes, the obscurer the better, provided by the copies of the *Oxford Diction-ary of Quotations* and *Brewer's Dictionary of Phrase & Fable* that Flynn kept by his writing desk, although Bathurst generally restrains himself to only doing this with people who would appreciate it or to annoy the local constabulary. He is fond of amateur dramatics (as was Flynn, a well-regarded amateur thespian who appeared in at least one self-penned play, *Blue Murder*), having been a member of OUDS, the Oxford University Dramatic Society. General information about his background is light on the ground. His parents were Irish, but he doesn't have an accent – see *The Spiked Lion* (1933) – and his eyes are grey. Despite the fact that he is an incredibly charming and handsome individual, we learn in *The Orange Axe* that he doesn't pursue romantic relationships due to a bad experience in his first romance. We find out more about that relationship and the woman involved in *The Edge of Terror*, and soon thereafter he falls head over heels in love in *Fear and Trembling*, although we never hear of that young lady again. After that, there are eventual hints of an attraction between Helen Repton, but nothing more. That doesn't stop women falling head over heels for Bathurst – as he departs her company in *The Padded Door*, one character muses "What other man could she ever love . . . after this secret idolatry?"

As we reach the halfway point in Anthony's career, his companions have somewhat stablised, with Chief Inspector Andrew MacMorran now his near-constant junior partner in investigation. The friendship with MacMorran is a highlight (despite MacMorran always calling him "Mr. Bathurst") with the sparring between them always a delight to read. MacMorran's junior officers, notably Superintendent Hemingway and Sergeant Chatterton, are frequently recurring characters. The notion of the local constabulary calling in help from Scotland Yard enables cases to be set around the country while still maintaining the same central cast (along with a local bobby or two).

Cold Evil (1938), the twenty-first Bathurst mystery, finally pins down Bathurst's age, and we find that in *The Billiard Room Mystery* (1927), his first outing, he was a fresh-faced Bright Young Thing of twenty-two. How he can survive with his own rooms, at least two servants, and no noticeable source of income remains a mystery. One can also ask at what point in his life he travelled the world, as he has, at least, been to Bangkok at some point. It is, perhaps, best not to analyse Bathurst's past too carefully . . .

"Judging from the correspondence my books have excited it seems I have managed to achieve some measure of success, for my faithful readers comprise a circle in which high dignitaries of the Church rub shoulders with their brothers and sisters of the common touch."

For someone who wrote to entertain, such correspondence would have delighted Brian, and I wish he were around to see how many people have enjoyed the reprints of his work so far. *The Mystery of the Peacock's Eye* (1928) won Cross Examining Crime's Reprint Of The Year award for 2019, with *Tread Softly* garnering second place the following year. His family are delighted with the reactions that people have passed on, and I hope that this set of books will delight just as much.

Steve Barge

Chapter I
MR. BATHURST BURNS HIS FINGERS

THE October wind whipped the fallen leaves into a whirling scurry. At intervals, too, as the wind died down after fiercely spending itself on the passive foliage, the rain came into its kingdom and lashed savagely on the glass of windows.

Anthony Bathurst listened to these sounds of wind and weather almost curiously, drew his arm-chair nearer the fire, and poked the flames to a more generous glow. It was apparent that his two guests appreciated the results of his action as keenly as he himself did. The dismal conditions outside only served to accentuate the snug comfort of the room. In fact, Sir Austin Kemble, Commissioner of Police, New Scotland Yard, permitted himself to move his chair also and to hold his hands closer to the blaze.

"Autumn has come on us quickly," he declared. "Before we know where we are, we shall be talking in terms of Christmas. Dear, dear, almost incredible. In my opinion, the character of the weather has altogether changed since I was a boy, I really think so. It used to be much hotter and the heat would last for a much longer time. Sometimes we had really marvellous spells! I remember sitting for exams when I was a boy at school, for weeks at a stretch, in my shirt-sleeves, because the weather was so damned hot and I was so damned uncomfortable."

"I agree, Sir Austin," remarked the third member of the company, "I can recall that I had much the same experience. You have probably heard that the latest idea of the scientists is that the change in conditions is due to that inconstant lady, the moon."

Major Marriner, having spoken, rubbed his hands and followed the examples of his host and fellow-guests by drawing his chair towards the welcome warmth of the fire.

"Change of weather," said Mr. Bathurst cheerfully, "is believed to have been the primary cause of the decay of Xibalban culture and the ultimate fall of the Maya Old Empire. So that your adolescent shirt sleeves, Sir Austin, were not unworthy participators in what may be termed a Grand Procession."

"Er . . . quite so, Bathurst," returned the Commissioner. "Er . . . exactly."

Anthony continued. Sir Austin Kemble in this mood and under these conditions never failed to entertain him.

"Although I must admit that other causes are considered by different authorities to have been equally as active. Causes such as the exhaustion of the soil, due to wasteful agriculture, false direction from the priests in fulfilment of ancient prophecies, and even—quite sensibly—to the onset of malaria, itself due to the increased rainfall. Thus we can visualize the drift into Yucatan."

Major Marriner intervened with a degree of impatience.

"I think, Mr. Bathurst, that we may reasonably leave these Mayan problems for an inspection of the one that has brought Sir Austin and me here to see you."

In addition to the impatience there was a tinge of cynicism in his tone. Anthony Bathurst—smiling inwardly—was not slow to notice it.

"I am at your service, Major Marriner; forgive me for the digression. Will you, or Sir Austin here, tell me the story? I promise you that I shall listen with commendable patience. Start at the beginning, please, and don't omit the most seemingly unimportant detail. But forgive my mentioning that—I should have remembered! The Chief Constable of Remenham requires no insistence from me on that point. My profound apologies."

Major Marriner glanced sharply at the Commissioner, evidently seeking a lead. Sir Austin Kemble nodded his acquiescence without the slightest hesitation.

"Mr. Bathurst," said Major Marriner, "it is no wish of mine that you are being troubled with regard to this recent murder down at Upchalke. I have approached Sir Austin Kemble—I felt, indeed, that I must—and he is entirely responsible for the case being brought to you. Believe me, had it lain with me I should not have worried you."

"My dear Major Marriner," said Anthony, "please don't apologize. It won't assist matters at all. You are here. Command me. Just make yourself happily comfortable and tell me the full story of the crime."

Major Marriner coughed. "Very well, then, I will."

"I understand exactly how you feel," murmured Anthony lazily, "and no doubt my blood *will* be on my own head. Proceed, Major Marriner, will you, please?"

Major Marriner sought words. "Robert Forsyth was murdered on the evening of October the 3rd. According to the medical evidence, his death occurred at approximately ten o'clock. He had met his death as the result of a weapon of some kind having been plunged through his chest. A great gash just above the breast-bone was ample evidence of what had taken place, and death must have been almost instantaneous. He was seventy-three years of age at the time of his death and had resided in the village of Upchalke for the last couple of years. I should tell you now that Forsyth was a retired rate-collector, having left the service of one of the London Borough Councils at the age of sixty-four. He was unmarried—as far as I know, he had never been married. His nephew's wife kept house for him, a woman in the late thirties. By name, Winifred Forsyth.

"She had been out during the best part of the evening. Went out, according to her own story, directly after she and Forsyth had finished their tea. That would be—also according to her story—about a quarter to six. She returned to the bungalow about half past ten, and when she got in, found her uncle, as she habitually calls him, dead in the little living-room where she had left him. He had fallen forward and his head was resting on the table in front of him, with the place a veritable shambles. His arms were stretched in front of him, and his face, when his head was lifted up by the doctor, bore a look of contorted horror that for the peace of one's mind is best forgotten. It was twisted like a lost soul in torment, showing an agony almost indescribable.

"Every article of furniture which was anything like near the dead man, parts of the table itself on which his head lay, and even the floor and the hearth, all were bespattered with Forsyth's blood. As I said, the place was a shambles. His mouth had been cut also, and so severe had been the blow that one of his front teeth was hanging from the gum. Mrs. Forsyth showed more courage and clear-headedness, perhaps, than most women would have done, caught in a similar set of circumstances. Directly she realized that her uncle was dead, she ran out into the road and found assistance. In quite reasonable time there arrived an Inspector of Police from Chalke, the town within two miles of Upchalke, accompanied by the Police doctor, Dr. Thorold. I have already told you with some detail the general conclusions to which Dr. Thorold came."

Major Marriner paused, fingered his trim dark moustache, sat silent for a moment or so, and then turned impulsively towards Anthony Bathurst.

"There you have what I will call the main outline of the crime, Mr. Bathurst. If you are satisfied with what I have already told you, I will continue with the more intricate details of the affair. You will find them decidedly interesting, I can assure you. You see what I am doing, Sir Austin?"

The commissioner nodded impressively. "Yes . . . yes . . . quite so . . . excellent idea. I'm sure Bathurst will appreciate it."

Anthony Bathurst interposed. "Thank you, Major Marriner. May I ask a question or so affecting—to use your own words—the main outline of the crime before you come to give me the lesser details? I feel that it will help me considerably."

Major Marriner moved stiffly in his chair.

"Certainly. I will answer any questions you care to ask with the greatest pleasure. Will you ask them now?"

"I take it, then, Major Marriner, from your description of the room in which Forsyth was murdered, that the Forsyth dwelling-place was a small one. Yes?"

The Major nodded. "Oh, undoubtedly. A small bungalow in the village of Upchalke. I am told by the niece that Forsyth's pension was about four pounds a week."

"Any dwelling-houses near?"

"Yes, there are other bungalows scattered about within, say, fifty yards of each other."

"Where had the niece, Winifred Forsyth, been during the evening?"

"To a meeting of a Bazaar Committee that is connected with the church which she attends, St. Veronica's, Chalke. That has been verified. Upchalke, as you doubtless know, is a suburb of the seaport of Chalke. I think I previously stated that they are about a couple of miles apart. The little River Chal winds its way from Upchalke to the sea."

"Thank you, Major Marriner. All this information is helpful. There are other questions for me to ask you, but I think that I will keep them until later. Now let me have what you have described as your more intricate details."

Major Marriner nodded his understanding and complied with the request.

"In many respects, Mr. Bathurst, they are most remarkable. I beg of you to listen to what I am about to say with the utmost care. I told you that Mrs. Forsyth sought assistance. This is what occurred. It was the custom of Mrs. Forsyth, whenever she went out for any length of time which meant leaving the old man at home, to slide the bolt of the front door of the bungalow and to go out by the back door, which old Forsyth, as a measure of safety, would immediately lock behind her as he saw her off the premises. Are you following me?"

Major Marriner put the question almost anxiously. The two others signified that they were. Major Marriner, therefore, continued his story.

"Now this is the almost inexplicable position which confronted Mrs. Forsyth when she returned to the bungalow in the neighbour-hood of half past ten. She knocked, as was her invariable custom, on the back door for her uncle to come out of the living-room and let her in. There was, of course, no answer. She then tried the front door, thinking that he might have gone to bed and unbolted it for her. However, she found that the front door was still bolted as it had been when she left the bungalow at a quarter to six in the early evening.

"Mrs. Forsyth has been closely interrogated on this point and states that her next reaction was to think that her uncle must have fallen asleep in the living-room over a book, perhaps, so she returned to the back door and knocked again—hard. But still nobody came, although she knocked several times. Mrs. Forsyth, as you may well understand, was now in a quandary. But close to the back door is the small window of the scullery, which was partly open. Mrs. Forsyth, racking her brains for a way out of her difficulty, then remembered that the small son of the people living in the next bungalow might not yet be in bed, so she went quickly to the bungalow in question and eventually, having told her story, Jimmie Ward, the small boy referred to, accompanied her back to her own place and, assisted by her, managed to get in through this partly opened scullery window. But again they were faced with a difficulty."

For the second time that evening Major Marriner paused dramatically.

"What do you think that difficulty was?" he demanded.

Sir Austin Kemble remained silent. Anthony Bathurst smiled and shook his head.

"I can think of several that might reasonably fill the bill, but I won't venture to suggest any. Please tell me."

Major Marriner permitted himself a half-smile.

"*The key had gone from the back door and the bolt was also shot.* Note what that means. Although the door was still locked, the key was not there. You see the point?"

Anthony rubbed his hands. "If anything, your problem grows in interest, Major Marriner. I find it approximating definite attractiveness. Please go on."

"Well, the boy, Jimmie Ward, called out to Mrs. Forsyth, still standing outside the back door, that he couldn't let her in that way, as she had told him to, because the door was locked and there was no key in the door. When she heard this surprising news Mrs. Forsyth realized, of course, that there must be something seriously wrong and began to wonder what she had best do. At the same time, she had a thought for the boy whose help she had enlisted and for his feelings, as he stood there inside the bungalow. He was only a kid, remember.

"So she called out to him: 'Jimmie! I'll go round to the front door again. You go up to it along the passage, draw the bolt and then let me in that way, will you? Don't be frightened. Just ran up the passage as I say. When I get in, everything will be all right. There's a good boy. Do just as I tell you.' Jimmie Ward did as he was told, went up the passage to the front door, drew the bolt, and let Mrs. Forsyth in as he had been instructed. Then Mrs. Forsyth, still mindful of the boy's feelings, told him to wait by the front door and set about finding out where her uncle was and the real reason behind all this trouble. From the passage she called out to her uncle two or three times, and then, obtaining no reply to any of her calls, went into the living-room and, to her horror, found her uncle dead in the conditions that I have already described to you. You know the rest."

Major Marriner concluded his recital and pushed his chair back from the fire. There came a silence to the room. Outside, the rain beat harder than ever on the window-panes. The silence was eventually broken by the Commissioner of Police.

"And that's the problem, Bathurst, that the local authorities have brought to Scotland Yard and which I have brought round to you. You would oblige me tremendously if you would have a look at it. MacMorran is at work on the Paddington poisoning case and both Copeland and Tait have their hands full. So have a look at this for me, will you?"

Anthony Bathurst deliberated. "You say that the murder took place on October 3rd. Today is the 25th. More than three weeks have elapsed. To be exact, twenty-two days."

Major Marriner shrugged his shoulders at Mr. Bathurst's statement.

"I am aware of that, but, as things have gone, the delay was inevitable."

Anthony countered at once. "I commend your phrase, Major Marriner, 'as things have gone'. I am wondering what vitally important things there were that may have gone, never to return."

"Scotland Yard has resources that are much greater than ours at Chalke." Major Marriner defended his position.

"I am not denying that. I realize your handicaps. I am merely pointing out that the scent which I am being asked to follow up is more than cold. I should say that it's several degrees below zero."

Again the room knew silence until the Commissioner coughed. Suddenly Anthony Bathurst swung round on to Major Marriner.

"What is the population of this village of Upchalke—approximately, that is?"

"Under a thousand. The burgess roll is 650."

"Had Forsyth any definite circle of acquaintance in the village?"

"Oh yes, from what I can gather. For a Local Government officer he was a fairly well-read man. He had the knack, I should say, of making friends quickly. Jovial man and good-tempered. Had a fair number of interests in his life too. Oh, I suppose that I ought to tell you this. When he first came to live at Upchalke he was offered and accepted a post on the *Chalke Daily Gazette*. He became what is known as a district reporter. He used to look after the Upchalke and Chalcombe districts. You know the idea of these local reporters. Local news, weddings and funerals, bazaars, concerts and flower-shows, local sport, cricket and football matches. Forsyth did very well at it. The locals liked him. The news that he scooped was only important to them. But a month or so ago he gave up the job. 'Got too old for it' he said."

"All that activity," remarked Anthony, "would tend to *increase* the circle of his acquaintanceship. On that account, it may conceivably make our task more difficult. Now tell me this. Had Forsyth any *close* friends? Friends, say, who were in the habit of visiting him either frequently or even regularly?"

"We have, of course, given keen attention to that point. Mrs. Forsyth, the niece, has been questioned closely on it. And when I pass on to you her answers, I will divide the names that she gave me into two categories. Firstly, those whom Forsyth might have called his 'cronies'. Secondly, those who occasionally visited him and who might be classed as just ordinary friends and acquaintances. Do you get the idea?"

Anthony Bathurst nodded. "Yes, I understand what you mean. Please give me the names."

Major Marriner produced a slip of paper from his pocket.

"Robert Forsyth had three intimates. In the neighbourhood they have been described to me by the term 'old chinas'—if that phrase conveys anything to you."

Anthony's eyes showed Major Marriner his understanding. The Major continued.

"The names of these three people are as follows: Randolph Skipwith, Leonard Burns, and Andrew McCracken. They are all three middle-aged men, you will observe. Skipwith is, like Forsyth himself, a retired official. He had done much the same kind of work as Forsyth, which fact, I understand, was the link which brought them together in the first instance. Burns is a retired motor engineer, who made his money in the Birmingham district some years ago and retired to Upchalke with a comfortable sum of money behind him at a comparatively early age. McCracken, the third man, is considerably easier to describe. He seems to have joined the Forsyth-Skipwith-Burns group a few months or so back. He is a veterinary surgeon from Edinburgh and one of the most popular men in the district. Anyhow, Skipwith, Burns, McCracken, and Forsyth used to visit each other frequently and have a hand at cards together. They were also frequent visitors to an inn known as the 'Tracy Arms'."

Major Marriner paused for a moment and then contributed a further explanation.

"Time hangs a bit, you know, in these 'bungalow retirement' communities, and companionship that is congenial is welcomed by the inhabitants and valued exceedingly."

Sir Austin Kemble chuckled rather noisily.

"I know all about that. A pensioned existence isn't all honey. I've told dozens of my chaps that when they've cleared out from the Yard. It doesn't turn out anything like the majority of 'em expect it will, not by a long chalk. And why? Do you know why, Bathurst?" The Commissioner almost thrust the query at Anthony.

"Tell me, sir."

"Because retirement for most people means that they've got half their usual money to get along with and all day long to spend it in! That's why," concluded Sir Austin triumphantly. "If you don't believe me, work it out for yourself."

Major Marriner nodded. "No doubt there's something in what you say, sir. But I feel that you need to be superannuated yourself to realize the position as it actually is." He continued. "I will now come to the people who visited Robert Forsyth occasionally. Those whom we called just now his friends and acquaintances. One—his doctor, although Forsyth was a healthy man for his age and rarely needed, I'm told, medical attention. Dr. Innes of Chalke. Two—the Vicar of St. Veronica's, the church which Mrs. Forsyth attended. Forsyth himself hardly ever did. The Reverend Charles A. Sellon. Three—a young journalist, happy in the possession of a private income, who shared with Robert Forsyth an interest in and a liking for amateur-dramatic work. By name, Cyril Mulrenan. Lastly—a middle-aged woman whom, so I am told, Forsyth had known for years—a Mrs. Margaret Swan. According to the information that I have gleaned, she used to visit Forsyth about once a month. Certainly not more, and probably, I should say, less. Her last visit took place about a week before the murder. There, Mr. Bathurst, you have the information that I said I would give you—Forsyth's chosen friends and his mere acquaintances. I'm afraid that you won't find it to be of very much assistance to you."

Anthony considered for a moment before replying.

"Well, there is this to it—I know more than I did. To effect anything, I *must* have certain knowledge. In that respect alone, you have helped me considerably. I am in your debt."

Major Marriner waved a deprecating hand.

"I have done my best. In all other respects, you must blame the Commissioner. He warned me on our way here that I should have to be extremely careful."

Anthony smiled. "One more question before we turn to the more comfortable things and those kindly fruits of the earth which Emily will shortly be bringing in to us. Was there anything stolen from the Forsyth living-room, or from any part of the house?"

The Chief Constable of Remenham shook his head.

"As far as we can trace, acting entirely upon what Mrs. Forsyth has told us, nothing—nothing at all."

"Or anything disturbed anywhere?"

Major Marriner leant forward impressively in his chair. At the same time he lowered his voice.

"Yes, Mr. Bathurst, there *was* something disturbed. I have kept this fact until the last. On Forsyth's mantelpiece there used to stand the carved figure of a small imitation ebony stag. This ebony stag had been knocked down and—well—very much more than broken."

Major Marriner paused again. Mr. Bathurst was in the act of applying a lighted match to a cigarette. He stopped and looked up at the Major, with the burning match held between thumb and finger.

"How do you mean—more than broken?"

Major Marriner answered with deliberate emphasis.

"This carved stag had been struck with a heavy object and smashed into—well, smithereens. Almost, if I may use the word, vindictively."

"Certain of that?"

"As far as one can be, yes."

"Curse it," said Anthony, as the flame of the match that he had forgotten to extinguish licked his fingers.

"Not knocked down, not trodden on in a struggle as might reasonably have been expected, but smashed of malice aforethought. Smashed to smithereens! I wonder!"

Chapter II
DEEP WATERS

AGAIN there came a silence.

"Do you know what I find intensely interesting?" eventually declared Anthony. "That blow that you say Forsyth had in the mouth. I think you remarked, Major Marriner, that its force had been such that one of the dead man's front teeth was loosened . . . yes?"

"That is so, Mr. Bathurst. One of the teeth in the upper jaw right in the front of the mouth. A terrific blow from somebody or something, without a doubt."

"Were there any other signs of a struggle?"

"No, none."

"The blow, then, may have taken Forsyth by surprise. It may well have been the start of the whole business. He wasn't expecting trouble, got a temporary knock-out, and then the *coup de grâce* through his chest. Yes—that certainly looks like it to me."

"That means that you're already believing in a quarrel? That Forsyth had a row with somebody and then this other fellow finished him off?"

"Well, it certainly looks like it, doesn't it? But I admit we can't pin anything on to anybody."

"All Forsyth's intimates have been well looked at, I can assure you. Their movements on that particular evening and so on. As far as we have been able to find out, there's nothing suspicious about any one of them."

"What about the others—the occasionals?"

Major Marriner shrugged his shoulders. It was evident that he considered the question a foolish one.

"You can ignore the doctor and the vicar, I presume, the insurance agent happened to be in another place, and as for Mrs. Swan, whose visits are no more than monthly ones—well, I can't see that she can have had anything to do with it."

Anthony Bathurst made no reply. This statement of Major Marriner's was so obviously open to critical attack that Anthony judged it prudent to keep silent. Instead, therefore, of discussing the terms of Marriner's reply, he headed in a fresh direction.

"Another question I'd like to ask you. The dead man, Forsyth, you say, has been living at Upchalke for about two years. But you also said that his retirement covers a period of nine years. Where did he live before he came to Upchalke—any idea?"

Major Marriner nodded. "Yes, I made similar inquiries, thinking on the same lines as you. He lived on the south coast. At Lanning—in Sussex."

"Lanning, eh? Charming little place—I know it well. Why did he move away from there—any idea?"

Major Marriner shook his head. "I'm afraid I can't answer that question."

"Would you say that Lanning is a more attractive spot than Upchalke? If my memory serves me correctly, the coast-line beyond Chalke is wild and rocky, surely?"

"Oh, quite. But Upchalke itself is an entirely delightful place that nestles behind the headland and escapes the full force of the gales. Hence its popularity as a place for retirement. This fact, added to the attraction of the little river that runs to the sea. The walk alongside the Chal all the way into Chalke itself must be actually taken for its beauty to be thoroughly appreciated. It's utterly charming. Mere description of it is hopelessly inadequate."

Anthony Bathurst pursed his lips. "So that, on the score of attractiveness, one place may be said to have nothing in hand of the other. A man can be happy with either. I see."

He leant forward in his chair, his finger-tips pressed together, and stared into the heart of the fire. Outside, the wind's fury grew and the windows continued to resist noisily the persistent onslaught of the rain. Sir Austin Kemble frowned and poured himself out yet another helping of Scotch. As he reached for the siphon, Anthony Bathurst spoke quietly.

"A most unusual and interesting case, Major Marriner. With at least three most remarkable features. A locked door minus the key that must have been used to lock it. A most extraordinarily terrible wound through a dead man's chest. And finally a carved stag smashed to smithereens on the floor of the room where its owner died. Why?— to all three of them."

Major Marriner blew his nose. "Your second point is perhaps the most eloquent of all. The process of elimination arises from it so beautifully. Forsyth died as the result of a terrific blow. Which means, happily for us who investigate, that ninety per cent of ordinary people can be ruled out at the very start of the investigation. Decidedly useful that, my dear Bathurst, as you yourself must admit."

The Major turned in his chair and eyed Anthony Bathurst shrewdly. Anthony countered.

"Of *ordinary* people, yes. But in the course of my investigations I may come up against a number of extraordinary people. And then, *ipso facto*, the percentage of elimination may turn out to be considerably smaller."

The Commissioner of Police drained his whisky-glass. His face showed a certain satisfaction.

"You will give me a hand then, Bathurst?"

"I think so, sir. Quite frankly, the case attracts me. It's definitely removed from the commonplace. If it weren't, I'd turn it down without a second thought."

"When can you start?"

"At once, sir. I must! I've already lost far too much time as it is."

"You will come down to Chalke?" inquired Major Marriner.

"Tomorrow morning, Major. How far is the place from London?"

"A hundred and fifty-five miles. Will you travel by train or by road?"

"Oh, train, I think—yes, train tomorrow. What's a good one?"

"The 11.22 from Waterloo," returned Major Marriner. "Change at Hatchett. You will have about ten minutes' wait there for the local train to Chalke. I'd accompany you but for the fact that I came up by car and shall return the same way tomorrow morning. I prefer the road myself."

Anthony demurred. "I do sometimes. But, you see, I want to think—and I can think better sitting in a train than when I'm driving a car." He smiled at the Chief Constable of Remenham. "But there's this. Can you recommend me an hotel?"

"At Upchalke itself? Or Chalke? Where do you intend to stay?"

Anthony considered the question. "Keep it dark who I am and why I'm down there, and I'll put up at Upchalke itself. If I stay there, I shall be right in the heart of things. Not too bad for an investigator, that! Where can I go?"

"The only possible place for you will be the 'Tracy Arms'. You'll find it quite good. Nothing to worry about at all. It is situated a couple of miles or so from Chalke station on the Hatchett road. You can get a taxi up, or there's a bus service of sorts. Don't rely on it too much. The bus runs about once an hour."

"Good. Is this 'Tracy Arms' outfit on the telephone, do you know?"

"It is. What's more, I can give you the number. Chalke 222. I've often rung them myself. Fentiman's the name. Very decent chap he is, too. Tom Fentiman."

"Chalke 222," repeated Anthony. "I'll remember that and get on to there before I go to bed tonight. I hope they can fix me up. And not a word to any of your people, Major Marriner, as to my whys and wherefores. I shall start then with a fair chance."

"Rely on me. I promise you that I'll be discretion itself."

Anthony Bathurst gave expression to what appeared to be an afterthought. "The ebony stag that you spoke about, Major Marriner, the broken ebony stag. I take it that the pieces, such as they were when picked up, have been preserved? I feel that I should very much like to have a look at them."

"Oh yes, I have them at Chalke. You can examine them whenever you choose to, although I'm afraid they won't help you."

"Thank you, Major Marriner. I am very much obliged to you. Do you mind if I put one more question before you go?"

"You have but to ask it, Mr. Bathurst."

"Do you happen to know the name of the borough where Forsyth was employed as a rate-collector before he retired to Lanning?"

"Yes, I can claim to answer that, Mr. Bathurst. I made inquiries about it. Forsyth had been in the service of the County Borough of Easthampton. I made general inquiries as to his career there. He entered on his duties at Easthampton in 1889 and retired in the

June of 1929 after forty years' service. As a matter of fact, I've been in correspondence with the Borough Treasurer there with regard to the point and he has satisfied me. Is there anything else?"

"I think not, Major Marriner. You may expect me at Upchalke some time tomorrow."

"Thank you, Bathurst," declared Sir Austin Kemble. "As I am situated at the moment, your help is most timely. Believe me, I appreciate it. I may even come down to Upchalke myself and give you a look in later on. I'll let you know."

Mr. Bathurst rang. Emily brought in refreshment. Mr. Bathurst and Major Marriner discussed Rugby football. Eventually the three men shook hands; the Commissioner of Police and the Chief Constable of Remenham took their departure. Anthony Bathurst looked at the time. It was a quarter to ten.

"Chalke 222," he murmured, "and the comfort of the 'Tracy Arms'."

As he did so, his own telephone bell rang. Slightly puzzled, he walked across to it and picked up the receiver. From the delay that took place he knew that he was being called from a public call-box. He waited in patience for the speech that was to come. At length he was rewarded. A woman's voice, clear and silver-toned, greeted his ears.

"Is that Mr. Anthony Bathurst?"

"Yes," he replied. "This is Anthony Bathurst speaking. Who are you?"

"I cannot give you my name," came the altogether unexpected and amazing reply. "But you may regard me as your friend. *Entirely* your friend. I am speaking to you now to warn you, and for God's sake, *please* do not neglect the warning, because I am sending it to you at great risk to myself. Have nothing whatever to do with the Forsyth murder case—nothing at all, do you hear? If you *do*, you will find yourself in deep waters. Deeper waters than any in which you have previously found yourself. Your life will not be worth a minute's purchase. Your operations will be hampered at every turn. Please believe me! I assure you that I am speaking the truth."

The voice ceased as suddenly as it had started to speak.

"Please tell me who you are," returned Anthony, "and then perhaps we can discuss things."

"Good-bye," came the reply, and Anthony was left standing there with the receiver in his hand, contemplating the more material possibilities of television. He replaced the receiver and frowned over the act. Then he walked slowly back to his arm-chair and stretched out his long legs to the comfort of the blaze. Thoughts rioted through his brain. "So there's a woman in the case after all, with a voice worthy of an angel. And Forsyth was three years past his allotted span. There is only one explanation. Marriner must have been followed from Chalke and watched all the way here. Deep waters, indeed! Well . . . I'm very much obliged to you, my fair and unknown informer, but there is still the desirable haven of the 'Tracy Arms', despite the sticky end that you vaticinate for me." Mr. Bathurst thought a minute and then returned to the telephone.

"Give me Trunks," he said quietly, and then eventually, "Chalke 222, please."

As Major Marriner had indicated, Tom Fentiman seemed a very genial host indeed.

Chapter III
THE "TRACY ARMS"

Mr. Bathurst left Waterloo punctually at 11.22 on the following morning and noted with satisfaction that the train's one stop was at Salisbury. He arranged that he enjoyed a corner seat of a first-class compartment and placed several packages upon the rack. After the rain of the previous evening, the morning had turned out to be one of late October's best. The sun was comparatively strong for the time of the year and the air had that champagne-like quality which always makes one feel thankful for the gift of life. Anthony, from his corner seat and for reasons of policy, carefully watched the various people who came down the platform. With the mysterious telephone message of the night before still fresh in his mind, he was taking no chances. If his movements were to be hampered at every turn as had been promised, it might well be that the opposition campaign would start at once. But he saw nothing that excited either his interest or his suspicions.

An elderly man, who suggested that he might have been an officer in the Army, came into the compartment and took the corner seat diagonally opposite to Anthony Bathurst. He placed a heavy travelling-rug on the seat, twirled his moustache, selected a cigar from his case, and settled himself down to travel his journey in comfort.

Anthony and he were alone in the compartment until the time came to within a minute of the train's starting. Then, rather surprisingly, from the point of view of their outward appearance, two people entered, with a black spaniel on a lead. As they came into the compartment, Mr. Bathurst looked up and saw a middle-aged couple of the artisan class. The man was thin, tall, and spare. He wore glasses and his most prominent feature was a high-bridged nose. There were patches of high colour on the points of his cheek-bones which contrasted sharply with his pale face. The woman was short and very stout. She talked quickly, continuously, and loudly. To Mr. Bathurst, next to whom she seated herself, the October morning became by no means so attractive. The black spaniel took a somewhat embarrassing liking to his left shoe, and just as Anthony was considering the idea of changing his compartment, the whistle blew and the train started. This was the signal for the woman to talk more loudly and then produce a bottle of beer from a basket.

The journey, however, proved uneventful. Delays at Woking and Bisley made Salisbury, with its gossamer-spired cathedral, the third stop instead of the first and only, as had been announced at Waterloo. The military-looking man showed signs of annoyance. The thin man left the compartment at Salisbury and had not returned by the time that the train restarted. A few minutes later, the stout lady, accompanied by her spaniel, also went out, presumably to look for the man who had left her.

Mr. Bathurst had not seen them again when Hatchett was reached. Hatchett was where he had to change for Chalke. After an annoying wait of several minutes, the local train ran in at the far-side platform. Anthony found a compartment. From the window through which he looked he saw the main-line train, which had also been held up, continue its journey west. There was no sign of either the man or the woman on the platform at Hatchett. So far, so good, reflected Mr. Bathurst. The Chalke train started and after a journey through some most delightful country, Anthony came into the station at Chalke, where the clock showed the time at half past two. A quick get-away and a taxi brought him to the "Tracy Arms" within ten minutes.

As he alighted, he turned round and then looked right across the valley of the placid, smoothly running Chal. Truly a fair and lovely country! Forsyth had not left Lanning for anything other than sheer beauty. To meet murder on his way!

The "Tracy Arms" stood in a good position on the main road from Chalke to Hatchett, and Fentiman, the landlord, made Anthony welcome at once. To him, Mr. Bathurst amplified an explanation that he had given on the telephone on the previous evening, when he had booked his apartment. This representation to Fentiman was that he was an artist hoping to execute two or three picture commissions during his stay by the waters of the Chal. His parcels contained his stock-in-trade. Fentiman listened and after a time contributed enthusiasm.

"Why, sir," he said in his curiously lilting drawl, "you'll be able to paint here to your heart's content. And some beautiful views at that. The old water-mill. The view down Repton Straight. The corner where the old 'Mutiny' public-house used to stand. Plenty of places, too, along the banks of the Chal. The hill where the Monmouth rebels were hanged. We're well known down here. There never is a time when we haven't a few ladies and gentlemen down here painting something—or trying to," he added with a dry touch.

Anthony at once felt the man's attraction. He was tall and lean-jawed with blue eyes that held a fund of kindness. If anything, the many crows'-feet round his eyes only served to emphasize the cordiality that looked out of them.

"We're a bit famous, too, down here these days," he went on to say. "I don't know as you've heard about it, sir, but we had a murder done here gettin' on for a month ago."

"A murder?" Anthony made consideration obvious. "Oh yes, I fancy I remember something of it now that you mention it. An old pensioner living down here, wasn't it?"

Fentiman nodded. "Yes. Mr. Forsyth. Knew him well I did. Used to come in here regular, he did. It was a rare shock to all of us when we heard of his death, I can tell you. His bungalow isn't above a quarter of a mile from here, if you'd be carin' to take a walk one day to have a look at it."

"Well, now, that's most interesting, Fentiman. When I'm thinking of going, I'll ask you the way. But I don't suppose it will be for a day or two, you know. I must settle down first. And I'll tell you something else. I'm doing no painting for at least a week. A rest first—for me."

But Fentiman was not to be denied. Cicerone he would be. He pointed out of the dining-room window.

"If you take that turning to the left there, just opposite the butcher's, and carry on down the road past the church, it's the third bungalow on the left-hand side. You can't miss it. There's a big thatched cottage just beyond it, belongs to a sister of Rear-Admiral Ranger."

"I see. When I go, I'll look out for it as you say."

Then Fentiman said something more which made Anthony Bathurst sit up and take notice.

"The name of poor old Forsyth's bungalow is on the front gate. If I tell you, it will help you. 'The Antlers', it's called."

The name, with its obvious association, stung him. He translated some of his interest into immediate words.

"'The Antlers'! That's an unusual name for a house, isn't it? What was the connection?"

The landlord of the "Tracy Arms" shook his head.

"I couldn't say what it was, sir. Bit of a fancy like, I suppose, on the part of the late Mr. Forsyth. After all, what's in a name? You can never tell what's behind the name of a house."

"Exactly, Fentiman. That was the idea behind the question I put to you. The name was so unusual that I wondered what had prompted the late Mr. Forsyth's fancy. Still, it's of no importance. Just a piece of curiosity on my part."

Fentiman dismissed the matter with his next remark.

"You'd best come and have a bit of lunch, Mr. Lotherington. Mrs. Fentiman's cooked you a nice chicken. She thought it 'ud be a bit safer like than a duck. A duck, she finds, isn't to everybody's taste. It runs a bit fatty and we find that it isn't everybody that can take it."

Anthony smiled. "Mrs. Fentiman need have no fears on my account. You can tell her that. I'll promise you that I'll eat all the ducks that she, from the goodness of her heart, sends me. Show me to the dining-room, Fentiman, will you, please, even though there's foul play on this occasion."

When Anthony had finished the repast that Mrs. Fentiman had set in front of him he knew that, from one point of view at least, his stay at the "Tracy Arms" would be entirely satisfactory. He took his time over his meal and at four o'clock set out for the Forsyth bungalow. He was careful to see that when he left the house of the Fentimans he was unobserved. He arranged that neither Fentiman nor his wife saw which direction he took. But all the same he realized that it was going to prove an extremely difficult matter for him to keep his real mission secret for any length of time. He would speak to Marriner again about it. All that he intended to do today, as far as Forsyth's bungalow was concerned, was to look at it from the outside in order that he might get the lie of the land. He thought of the name again. "The Antlers"! Extraordinary thing, that! Surely there must be a significance about this name which, if he could but find it, would assist him to an appreciation and understanding of the truth.

Already he felt inclined to readjust his ideas. For this reason. He had imagined, in the first place, when Major Marriner had informed him of the broken stag found on the floor of the dead man's room, that the carved figure had been broken because it had served as a place of concealment. In other words, that it had been deliberately smashed for the sake of what it contained, or was supposed to have contained. But now it seemed to him, bearing in mind this fresh piece of evidence concerning Forsyth's bungalow being known as "The Antlers", that the true significance might lie in the fact that the carving was in the shape of a *stag*.

What in the name of goodness could this significance be? According to what Major Marriner had said in his flat, the figure of the stag was a small one. Anthony felt positive that "small" was the adjective which the Major had used. There were obvious limitations, therefore, on the score of size, as to what the carving might have contained.

As he walked on that October afternoon, Anthony turned many things over in his mind. He refused steadily to overlook two most important points with regard to the Forsyth murder. One—there was the distinct possibility that the murderer might still be in possession of the key to the bungalow's back door, and two—that if the murderer were a strong, powerful man, as the death-blow seemed to prove conclusively that he must be, it would have been a physical impossibility for him to have escaped from the bungalow by climbing through the scullery window! And, conceding this, how then had he made his departure? That was one of the crucial points.

Anthony wanted to look at the building carefully in the hope that his survey might bring him a more reasonable answer to this question. He passed the trimly kept churchyard leading up to a Norman-towered church which to a walker in the road below appeared to be perched precariously at the top of a slope, and began to look out for the third bungalow on the left-hand side of the road which Fentiman had described to him. From what he could see as he approached, it would probably stand a little way back from the roadway.

Anthony walked on steadily. The countryside was entirely unspoiled, with footpaths and bridle tracks branching off in almost all directions. Anthony stopped and looked back. From where he was he could see a line of white cliffs and a fir-topped hill. On every side of him in the lanes grew countless ferns and the adjacent gorselands were stretches of blazing glory. It was difficult indeed to associate this place of charm and beauty with the sense of evil and violent death.

Anthony walked on again. As he came nearer to the Forsyth bungalow, he saw that the road rose considerably and that within his vision came the white sweep of the foam-lined coast. He paused in front of "The Antlers". From its outward appearance it seemed to be unoccupied and Anthony concluded that Mrs. Forsyth, the dead man's niece, had found temporary accommodation elsewhere. If this were a fact, it suited his book. He skirted the bungalow on its right-hand side and came round to the back. It was quite accessible, he found. There was a back gate which was obviously customarily kept open. Anthony pushed this gate, which yielded to the impetus, and found himself standing in the garden of "The Antlers". "If Fentiman could see me now," he said to himself, "he'd pour himself out another double brandy and port." He walked quietly up to the back of the building. He could see plainly now how Mrs. Forsyth had stood there on the night of the murder and how Jimmie Ward, the neighbour's son, had made his somewhat belated entrance through the scullery window. Certainly no full-grown man could have got in that way, and even Ward, the boy, must have been, Mr. Bathurst thought, considerably smaller than the average.

Anthony took stock of his surroundings. The quietness that pervaded the place was extraordinary, and if conditions were like this at this time of the day Anthony could well imagine what it would be like at night. A man could be murdered here in broad daylight and nobody be any the wiser, let alone under conditions of night with its attendant darkness.

Anthony walked across the garden towards the scullery window. It was low, he saw—considerably lower than is usual with scullery windows in bungalows of this size. Had the window been open instead of fastened, Anthony, using his height, would have been able to have seen into the scullery. Any comparatively tall man in the region of six feet would be able to. Anthony fell to thinking. Why had the murderer locked the back door as well, shooting the bolt, and, in that case, how had he got out? There was surely no need for him to go to the trouble that he had, if his sole desire were to obtain possession of the back-door key. And how *had* he got out? Most puzzling, that. There was one question that he *must* ask either Mrs. Forsyth or Master James Ward as soon as he could get to grips with one of them.

Suddenly Mr. Bathurst had an idea. His grey eyes gleamed, for the idea had definite possibilities about it and pleased him. He looked round the garden of the bungalow. In the far corner there stood a small tool-shed. Mr. Bathurst went towards it. The door was open. Anthony went in. Within the shed was the usual array of gardening and domestic appliances. A mangle, several deck-chairs, a number of boxes, a length of hose-pipe on a wheel, twine and rope, a pair of steps, a rake, spades, a gardening-fork, two hoes, a trowel, with various cans and empty bottles. Anthony noted these contents with extreme satisfaction. First thing tomorrow he would see Major Marriner and arrange to look over these premises. No! More than that. He would get into touch with Marriner when he got back into Upchalke without the people at the "Tracy Arms" being aware of the fact, and ask him to bring Mrs. Forsyth from wherever she might be over to the bungalow.

He carefully looked round the tool-shed again, noted where the various articles were, then closed the door behind him and came out. The idea that had recently come to his brain was already in the process of definite development. An interesting problem—undoubtedly. He was glad that he had promised to look into it—if only for the fact that the investigation had brought him to Upchalke. From the shed he walked across to the back gate, and just as he came to it he heard, to his surprise, the sound of footsteps.

He had taken the risk of coming here, of course, and, in that respect, had but himself to blame, but despite this Mr. Bathurst had a feeling of irritation. He had no wish to be associated with the Forsyth murder case quite as early as this. He waited by the gate, therefore, in the hope that the walker would pass by, but within a second of his stopping a young man came through the opening.

Mr. Bathurst perceived that the young man was not an ordinary young man. Both the pattern and the creases of his striped trousers were distinctly pronounced. The set of his white collar was impeccable. His tie was artistry itself. His black hat, black overcoat, rather long white cuffs and silk handkerchief protruding most correctly from the breast pocket of the overcoat were all that they might or even might not be. The high polish on his shoes reflected the sunshine. As this young man saw Anthony Bathurst standing there, he raised his hat with a gesture that was correctness itself, and Anthony noticed that not a strand of his plentiful jet-black hair, brushed flat back from forehead to the nape of his neck, could justly be said to be out of place.

"Good afternoon, sir," he said with what seemed to Anthony a strange, almost intimate, eagerness. "Am I right in assuming that this is the bungalow where the late Mr. Forsyth was killed? Or perhaps I should more correctly say—murdered?"

At once he gave the impression of being absorbed in what he had said. Even his smile exuded the same sense of intimacy.

"This is the late Mr. Forsyth's bungalow. Yes."

"By Jove," the young man answered, "life's pretty grim—what? A here-today-and-gone-tomorrow sort of business if ever there were one. Don't you agree, sir?"

"I suppose it is." Anthony was a trifle curt. For one thing he was on his guard, and for another he was just a little puzzled. He was unable to place the man to his own satisfaction.

"I suppose I couldn't look over the place, could I? You see, it's like this. I used to know old Bob Forsyth pretty well in the old days. Used to work with him up at Easthampton."

This explanation cleared the air considerably. Anthony saw the position more clearly.

"Oh, really! I see. Well, I'm afraid you won't be able to look over the place—it's locked up and there's nobody here. I strolled in here myself with much the same idea. I happened to be passing, but, as I say, I was destined for disappointment."

The stranger's eyes flashed understanding.

"Oh, I say! What a pity! Perhaps we could manage it another time. We'll try to fix things up, shall we? Are you walking back?"

"Well, I suppose I am."

"I'll walk with you, then—if you don't mind. I feel that I ought to make you an apology. You know—that I ought to explain myself and my presence here a bit more fully. I'll wager that you're thinking all these things, even though you won't admit that you are. Come now, you are, aren't you?"

Anthony smiled as they retraced their steps along the road that he had recently covered.

"Tell me," he said with simple directness.

The young man at once gave him smile for smile. Anthony assessed his age at anything between twenty-five and thirty-two.

"My name's Wilfred Hatherley. I am chief Audit Clerk to the County Borough of Easthampton. It's a pretty responsible job, you know. I have a staff of seven under me, apart from a comptometer operator. Of course, I'm a fully qualified man. One day I hope to be Borough Treasurer."

"Why?" demanded Anthony Bathurst.

Mr. Hatherley unhappily missed the point.

"Oh—because there's quite a reasonable chance of it."

"I see," murmured Mr. Bathurst. "That makes a difference, I admit."

Hatherley commenced to splutter again.

"I'll tell you all about it. Poor old Bob Forsyth used to be a rate-collector at our place when I was a junior clerk. I knew him well. Even when I was a junior—and I wasn't a junior very long, let me tell you—I was thought a great deal of. I made a special study of Income Tax. I was always more like a private secretary to the chief than an ordinary junior. Yes, I was thought a great deal of."

"And about, I expect," interposed Anthony.

Hatherley again paid no heed to the remark. Oozing self-confidence, he rattled on unconcernedly.

"Well, old Bob Forsyth took a violent fancy to me, and when the time came for him to retire some years ago I was damned sorry to lose him, I can tell you. I used to chaff him that he'd live to be ninety and on several occasions visited him when he was living at Lanning. As far as I knew, he had no relations living, and I was quite surprised to read that his niece by marriage was residing with him down here at Upchalke. I happened to read that in the newspapers, you see."

He cocked a critical eye at Anthony almost as though he desired him to challenge the veracity of the remark.

"I presumed as much," declared Mr. Bathurst.

"Well, to cut a long story short, the news of poor old Bob's murder came as a rare shock to me and to all of us who knew him in the Easthampton service, and as I still had two or three days leave, due to me" (he pronounced it "leaf") "I thought I'd pop down here, have a look at things generally, and in doing so pay a sort of last tribute to the dear old boy's memory."

Anthony demurred a trifle. "In that case, might I suggest, Mr. Hatherley, that you have left this duty visit of yours rather late? It's over three weeks since your old colleague was murdered. It was on October 3rd, to be exact."

But Wilfred Hatherley was far from being dismayed at Mr. Bathurst's statement.

"I know," he cried, "none better. But you see, sir—you haven't told me who you are yet, by the way—on October 3rd I was away on my annual summer leave. I was in Madeira—I went on one of the special cruises—and never troubled to look at a newspaper. When I got back to the Town Hall on Monday, that's the Easthampton Town Hall—I did tell you that I was at Easthampton, didn't I?—I was met with the terrible news of poor old Bob Forsyth's murder. Now do you see, sir?"

For the time being, at least, Anthony ignored the broad hint that had come from Hatherley concerning the question of his identity. Hatherley, however, didn't seem to notice the omission, for he continued to talk.

"As it was, the accounts that I got of the affair, from the various people in the service at Easthampton, were more or less garbled, as you might say, and really unreliable, and beyond the fact that Bob Forsyth was found stabbed or something by this semi-niece of his, one evening, in his room way back there, I know very little. Tell me, sir, did the poor fellow suffer much, do you think?"

Anthony thought that Hatherley appeared to be genuinely concerned over the ex-rate-collector's fate.

"We will trust not," said Anthony Bathurst gravely. "From the accounts that I read in the various papers, there seems to have been a short, sharp struggle in the room and eventually Forsyth was killed by a weapon of some kind being thrust through his chest. When that took place, I should say that there's little doubt his death must have been almost instantaneous."

Hatherley screwed up his eyes as though querying something that Mr. Bathurst had said.

"I am sorry to hear what you say. A struggle, eh? Do I take it that the police found definite evidence in the room that pointed to a struggle?"

Anthony nodded acquiescence. "Oh yes, there's no doubt on that point either. I understand too, from two or three of the newspaper reports of the case that I read, that the old man's mouth had been rather badly cut—by a heavy blow of some kind evidently. Possibly from the murderer's fist. In fact, this blow was so severe that one of Forsyth's front teeth was loosened and was actually hanging from the gum when Mr. Forsyth found him."

Hatherley, to Anthony's intense surprise, stopped dead in his tracks and turned towards him with sharp abruptness. There was a strange, almost fierce, look in his eyes.

"What?" he cried. "Say that again."

Anthony, mystified in the extreme by Hatherley's action, repeated his previous statement. Hatherley's eyes still shone with bright excitement.

"I must take a grip on myself," he cried, almost wildly, "or else I shall begin to lose control. But there's a screw loose somewhere in this story that you've just told me, and a very serious screw at that, sir. *Because my old colleague, Bob Forsyth, hadn't a natural tooth in his head. I know for a fact that he had his teeth extracted two or three years before he retired."*

CHAPTER IV
THE PLAYERS ASSEMBLE

SOMETHING seemed to be stretched taut in Mr. Bathurst's brain. This audit clerk from the County Borough of Easthampton had been sent to him, he concluded, from heaven above, as manna from the very skies. For the moment he was still undecided as to whether to declare his real identity or not. He came to a rapid decision to continue to hold his incognito. He also, by a strong effort, collected his thoughts, which had bolted in many directions. If this man Hatherley had stumbled into an even more mysterious problem than he had hitherto anticipated. Mr. Bathurst decided to finesse.

"I am afraid that I don't quite follow you, Mr. Hatherley," he contented himself with saying. "If you imply that this dead Forsyth cannot be the Forsyth whom you knew—well, it's manifestly impossible, isn't it? Or is it?"

Hatherley's face showed that his mind was working with quick emotion.

"That's just what I'm trying to work out," he answered. "I'm as bewildered as you are. Don't you understand that as Chief Audit Clerk to the Easthampton Authority it touches me professionally? I can tell you at once that to my way of thinking the whole affair's damned serious."

"I agree," returned Mr. Bathurst dryly. "Especially for the unfortunate Forsyth."

Hatherley muttered strange and uninteresting words to himself.

"What puzzles me," Anthony heard him say—"what puzzles me is the matter of the Life Certificate. How in the name of goodness—" He paused abruptly.

Anthony began to see light. "Yes, I fancy I see what you mean, Mr. Hatherley. Quite a number of interesting possibilities are beginning to be opened up, aren't they?"

Hatherley turned on him again with swift insistence.

"Tell me, please, can I see a photograph anywhere of this dead Forsyth of Upchalke?"

"It shouldn't be difficult. Perhaps one of the local papers published one at the time of the murder—it's quite likely. We shall have to scout round and see what we can find out. How long are you staying down here?"

"Till the end of the week. I must be back at the office on Monday— haven't any more leave owing, that's the trouble. Wish I had. Especially seeing the turn that the case has taken. My blood's sort of 'up'. I expect you can understand how I'm feeling."

"Very well indeed," returned Anthony. He went on: "Let me take you back a little, Mr. Hatherley, to a remark that you made a moment ago. I fancy that I was able to see what was puzzling you. I'll endeavour to prove it to you. I think you mentioned the words 'Life Certificate'. What steps does your authority take to be assured that a superannuated officer or employee, who is not seen regularly, is still living?"

Hatherley was in like a flash. "You're right—absolutely right. That's just the point I was after! Every person in receipt of a super- annuation allowance who is not seen regularly has to present a signed Life Certificate at the commencement of every quarter. One of my own duties is to see that these are received and are properly filled up. They're O.K. too—every one of 'em. I know that all right. And that's what's puzzling me."

Mr. Bathurst reflected. "Signed? Signed by whom?"

"By a responsible third party. These people are specified on the form. My authority is satisfied with the signature of a doctor, a clergy- man, a justice of the peace, or say, a solicitor. The certificate that we issue takes this form." Hatherley passed his hand over his brow and quoted from memory. "'I hereby certify that I have today seen Mr. Blank and testify that he is alive.' No loophole there, surely?"

Anthony thought carefully over what Hatherley had said. "How many of these forms of Life Certificate would one of these pensioned people have in his possession at any one time?"

"One, and one only," returned Hatherley with emphasis. "A certificate is sent out to him at the commencement of each quarter, and it's the recipient's duty to get the form signed and then to return it to us immediately. That's watertight all right. What's wrong with it?"

They had by now turned into the road that led to the "Tracy Arms".

"So that there could be no question, for instance, of anybody having several of these certificates in hand, as it were, to last him over a number of years?"

"None whatever," replied Hatherley firmly. "You may take it from me as a certainty that more than one is never sent out. That's our invariable system, and up to the present it's always worked out satisfactorily."

"As far as you know," said Anthony quietly.

"As far as we know," repeated Hatherley.

"These signed certificates that you received regularly from Forsyth, supporting the fact that he was still in the land of the living—by whom were they signed, can you remember?"

Hatherley furrowed his forehead. "Yes, I can answer that question here and now. I can remember Forsyth's certificates. They were signed by a 'Clerk's Holy Orders'. That was the exact designation that he gave himself. Let me think now for a moment and I'll give you the man's full name. It was the Reverend Charles Ashmore Sellon, M.A., Vicar of St.—" Hatherley paused. "The name of his church was unusual. Not one of the—what I'll call common-or-garden saints. Now what was it? Let me think. I know—St. Veronica's. Vicar of St. Veronica's, Chalke. That was the name of the church. Yes, I'm positive of it. I should think that I've had about half a dozen certificates signed like that."

"St. Veronica's, Chalke," thought Anthony. "That's a coincidence. I've heard the name of that church before in connection with this case. It seems that I must establish that association before this Mr. Hatherley and I proceed any further. I've got it! Mrs. Forsyth had been to a meeting of a Bazaar Committee (horrible thought!) to do with this church of St. Veronica's, Chalke, on the evening that Forsyth, her uncle, had been murdered. Strange!"

He turned towards his companionship, Hatherley. They had come to within a hundred yards of the "Tracy Arms".

"Where are you staying, Mr. Hatherley? Anywhere near here?"

Hatherley's reply somewhat surprised him. "At the 'Tracy Arms'. That's the place, just a few yards from here. I booked up there this afternoon just before I walked out and met you." He pointed up the road.

"Coincidence number two," murmured Mr. Bathurst. "I happen to be staying there myself."

"Say! Is that so? Oh, good. I'm pleased. Well, then, I'm damned glad that I met you, Mr.—You know, you haven't told me your name yet."

"My name's Lotherington," rejoined Anthony, taking the bull by the horns. "I'm an artist and this part of the country attracts me tremendously. We must see more of each other during the time that you stay here, Mr. Hatherley. And if it isn't trespassing on your kindness, I should like to know how you settle this Forsyth identity problem."

"Sure, I'll let you in on it, never fear."

They came to the front entrance of the "Tracy Arms". A sturdy, flaxen-haired man of middle height, wearing a naval uniform and a small beard, whom Anthony hadn't seen before, was standing on the step. He nodded to Hatherley as Anthony and the latter entered. They passed into the lounge, which faced the bar and was situated on the right-hand side of the main passage.

"Who's your friend the sailor?" queried Anthony carelessly.

"Captain Falk Stromm," replied Hatherley. "From Sweden. There's a Swedish timber ship put in at Chalke this morning, the *Vaar*. There was a crowd down at the harbour when I came through. She was unloading. He's made the voyage as a holiday and is staying here a month, until she comes back again. Says he's always wanted to have a look at England. Then he returns to Sweden. Very charming man. It's his first visit to this country. Used to be in the Swedish Navy."

Anthony turned the details of the information over in his mind. It seemed to him that the "Tracy Arms" had suddenly achieved an abnormal popularity. He himself, Hatherley from Easthampton, and now a Swedish naval officer (retired). Who else was to follow?

The thought had scarcely been born in his mind when he heard the sound of a car stopping on the crest of the road outside the "Tracy Arms". He heard Fentiman's voice and looked out through the window. He saw two ladies alight from the car that had stopped and then a tall, broad-shouldered man advance from the interior of the "Tracy Arms" to meet them. The chauffeur, who wore plus-fours, Anthony noticed, followed behind them with several articles of luggage. Anthony heard Fentiman's voice again calling to the tall man, who was on his way to greet the two new-comers. "Mr. Mulrenan." Anthony saw the tall man turn at the sound of Fentiman's voice and half turn back towards the "Tracy Arms". Fentiman went out and joined the party. Eventually, after a brief conversation, they made their way into the "Tracy Arms", the presumed chauffeur leading, with Fentiman and the man addressed as Mulrenan escorting the two ladies in a bunched group behind. So this was Mulrenan, the journalist! Which meant that already in one afternoon he had run across two of the three men given by Major Marriner as forming the late Forsyth's circle of acquaintances as distinct from that of intimacy. Mulrenan and the Vicar of St. Veronica's, the Reverend Charles A. Sellon. But Hatherley was speaking to him. His voice seemed to come from a distance.

"I'm going up to have a wash and change before dinner. Also I've got an idea. Not a bad one either. It'll keep for the moment, but I'll pass it on to you later. Is that O.K.?"

Anthony nodded his understanding.

"Right-o! I'll wait until you come down again."

Hatherley took a number of short, sharp steps across the room and disappeared. Anthony heard his footsteps going up the staircase. As he did so the door of the lounge opened and there came in, escorted by the man whom he had heard as Mulrenan, the two ladies who had recently alighted from the car and entered the hotel.

"I suggested three 'gin-and-Its'," said Mulrenan, "and as quickly as old Tom can serve us. I consider that they are definitely indicated."

Anthony took one of the easy chairs by the fire and, at the same time, careful stock of his three companions. Mulrenan had the easy, sophisticated assurance of the man of the world. But his laugh struck Anthony as insincere. One of the women who companioned him was undoubtedly attractive—fair, blue-eyed, and graceful. There was something about her companion, however, that was, to say the least of it, distinctly unusual. Mulrenan walked across and pressed the bell. An elderly woman with grey hair answered the summons. Mulrenan gave the order. Then Anthony realized what it was that was abnormal about the second woman. She was most decidedly deaf. Her companion, the fair, blue-eyed girl, leant right over to her and said very loudly:

"Cyril's ordering you a 'gin-and-It'. Or would you rather have a 'gin-and-French'? He wants to know."

The woman addressed moved her mouth in a most peculiar way. It suggested a smirk.

"Which would I rather? I'd rather have both, of course, like the first Bishop of Bath and Wells. Good gracious, is Cyril asleep?" She chuckled almost hoarsely as she made this remark. "Trust a Scotch padre to know what's good for him. I've known a few in my time and they all have."

The blue-eyed girl turned rather hopelessly towards Mulrenan and spoke in a low voice.

"It's no good. You see how she is. She's been like that nearly all the way down from town, and tonight she'll get worse."

Mulrenan replied to her in an equally low tone. His back was to Anthony so that Mr. Bathurst did not hear what he said. The elderly woman brought in the three drinks. Mulrenan handed one to each of his two companions.

"All the best," he said lightly, as he raised his own and toyed with the cherry, "and happy days for all of us."

The fair girl acknowledged Mulrenan's toast over the rim of her glass, but her companion disregarded it. Instead she craned her neck forward and said in the same strident voice that she had used before:

"I left a box of perfectly marvellous soap in that hotel at Salisbury. It's a damned nuisance. I could scream with annoyance."

At the remark Mulrenan and the fair girl exchanged significant glances. Suddenly the door of the lounge opened and a medium-sized man put his head around it.

"Mulrenan," he cried excitedly, "can you come into the bar? We want your advice. Oh, I'm sorry, old man; I didn't know that you were with anybody. A thousand pardons."

Mulrenan waved his acknowledgment. "That's all right, Skipwith. I can't come for the moment, but I'll see you in the bar after dinner this evening. Is the evening paper in yet, do you know?"

"Not yet," returned Skipwith. "I'm waiting for it myself, but the blasted bus from Hatchett has broken down or something. That's the third time this week. I'll let you know as soon as it comes in. Cheero." He withdrew his head and closed the door.

Here was more thought for Anthony. Skipwith now! One of Forsyth's "cronies", according to Major Marriner's information! A retired official from a similar sort of job to the one that Forsyth himself had formerly held. A younger man, too, than Mr. Bathurst had been led to anticipate. He decided that he might employ his time worse than by going into the bar of the "Tracy Arms" after dinner that evening. He would meet at least Skipwith and Mulrenan. And probably some others.

As he mused thus, the dinner-gong went. Two or three minutes later he drifted into the dining-room. He was pleased to find that he had been placed at a table by himself. On his immediate right was Hatherley, just behind him was seated Captain Falk Stromm, and at the table in front of him, to his surprise let it be said, were seated Mulrenan with his two lady-friends. The greater publicity of the dining-room made no difference, evidently, to the methods of the deaf woman. She addressed Mulrenan with her ordinary attack.

"If the food that I'm going to have here is appalling, Cyril, I shall be extremely annoyed with you and hold it for ever against you. I shall really, because if it hadn't been for you, and your worrying us, Heather and I would never have come down."

Mulrenan mollified her. "Don't you worry about your grub, Freda. If you never fare worse than you fare here. I'll promise you that you won't come to any harm."

Her voice rose in gusty laughter at Mulrenan's reply.

"Harm! I've come to enough already, God knows! That was why your letter alarmed me. Do tell me, are you sure that there's as much in it as you think there is? You must be careful what you do, Cyril, you know, for Heather's sake. I am very well aware that I owe her more than I can ever repay. Besides, how did you get into touch with the man in the first place? You mark my words. You'll wake up one morning and find a policeman in your bedroom, which will be much more unpleasant for you than it would be for me. I should say to him sternly, 'I'll give you twenty-four hours to get out.'" Again there came a gust of laughter.

Mr. Bathurst caught Hatherley's eye. The "Tracy Arms" at Upchalke was certainly going to prove well worth a visit.

Captain Stromm spoke across his table. Could any gentleman inform him what time the last post got in to Upchalke? Hatherley, of course, had such details at his finger-ends. He was of the type that always has. Stromm seemed genial and inclined to mix. He was on holiday, Mr. Bathurst remembered. Gradually, Hatherley, Stromm, and he found themselves discussing across their tables what Hatherley called "the revolt from Victorianism". Stromm, although attacked heatedly by Hatherley, always kept his dignity and his temper.

"I am Swedish," he said, "but I have always loved England. I will begin by making that admission. I have for many years now promised myself that one day I would come here for a holiday. At last my dream is realized. I have a friend who is the captain of the *Vaar*, a timber-carrying vessel. It happened to be putting into Chalke, and I took the chance he offered me to make the journey. And I shall always maintain, despite what our young friend here says, that your country's debt to its Queen Victoria—Victoria the Good, as some of you call her—well, it is immeasurable." His English was good, albeit with a strong trace of accent.

Hatherley grinned good-naturedly under Captain Stromm's opposition.

"I disagree entirely," he declared. "The Victoria that the present generation reads about never existed. She is a figment of fiction. She has been brought to life by two or three novelists who have allowed their imaginations to run riot. The result is that people nowadays are getting an absolutely erroneous impression of what Queen Victoria was like and what she stood for."

Captain Stromm bore the onslaught imperturbably.

"What you say, sir, is but a half-truth. You attach too much import-ance to it. Because of that, you are forced to wrong conclusions. That is inevitable."

Anthony said very little. He allowed Hatherley and Captain Stromm to play the principals. Every now and then he heard the voice of the girl called Heather as she spoke to Mulrenan, and once or twice he caught her glancing in his own direction. He himself was careful to betray no interest.

Dinner ran to its close. One by one the different people rose from the various tables and made their respective ways from the apartment. Anthony walked through the lounge and stood in the road outside the "Tracy Arms". It was a dark and windy night, but the stars were beginning to show in the sky. He looked at his wrist-watch. The time showed at twenty-two minutes past eight. The bar closed at half past ten—an interval of over two hours. He had plenty of time at his disposal. Turning at a slight sound, he found Hatherley at his side.

"I've an idea," whispered the latter. "I told you that I had. Walk down the road a little way with me, will you?"

Anthony consented.

"We can talk better here than in the hotel," went on the irrepress-ible Hatherley.

They walked about three hundred yards down the road until they came to one of the little rustic bridges that crossed the Chal at the side of the road. Hatherley offered Anthony a cigarette.

"From what I've managed to read in one of the local papers since I spoke to you last, this man who called himself Forsyth was at one time a local reporter down here. He was on the staff of a local rag known as the *Chalke Daily Gazette*."

"One minute," intervened Anthony Bathurst. "Where were you able to find a paper to tell you this? A good deal of time has elapsed—"

Hatherley came in quickly. "There happen to be several old local papers in my bedroom. Been left there. I picked up one of them whilst I was changing for dinner."

Anthony nodded. "I see. Well, what's your real point about it?"

"Just this. The local Press knew him well, didn't they? Amongst other things, I read that two or three of his old colleagues of the *Chalke Daily Gazette* went to his funeral. Well, what's the odds against them having a photo of him of some kind down at the *Gazette* offices? There's a chance of it, surely?"

He blew a ring of smoke with an air of triumph. Mr. Bathurst was silent.

"Well, what do you say?" demanded Hatherley again. "Don't you think it's a good idea?"

"It's possible, certainly," conceded Mr. Bathurst.

"Well, Mr. Lotherington," declared Hatherley, "I shan't lose anything by it, shall I?"

"No," returned Anthony. "You might try it, and it may come off. When will you go, first thing in the morning?"

"I think I might, don't you?"

Anthony nodded. "Don't forget that I shall be interested to hear how you get on."

"I shall let you know, of course. Well, that's that. Shall we walk back now?"

Anthony Bathurst and the elegant young man from the County Borough of Easthampton walked back from the bridge to the lighted comfort of the "Tracy Arms".

"Shall we have one?" queried Hatherley, with a quick tilt of the head.

"I think we might," said Mr. Bathurst. "Possibly two. I think well go in the bar and watch the locals at their devotions before the shrine of Bacchus. I should prefer that to sitting in the lounge. What do you say, Hatherley?"

"Suits me."

"Also, I think it would be wise on our part," continued Anthony, "if we avoided any mention of the Forsyth murder. In other words, I think it will be diplomatic if we do a spot of listening rather than of talking. Are you on?"

Hatherley nodded. "I agree."

They came to the front door of the "Tracy Arms". As they entered, a hurricane of deep-throated laughter met their ears and they heard a voice roar:

"So what did I do? I dropped his coffin down the hole and the blasted thing fell sideways, which would never do for a well-behaved cor-r-pse. So I jumped down the hole and jumped on the coffin too—until it lay reasonably flat. And that's how we buried Ar-rchie Bar-r-clay of Greenock, with a snowstorm accompaniment."

There came another roar from the assembled company. There always did when Andrew McCracken told stories. Anthony Bathurst and Hatherley pushed open the door of the bar and entered.

"Good evening, gentlemen," said Mr. Bathurst.

A chorus of "good evenings" greeted him.

Chapter V
QUERY ROBERT FORSYTH?

Andrew McCracken was on his feet. A dark, swarthy-skinned giant of a man. His sweeping breadth of shoulder and his lion-like head would have distinguished him in any company At Anthony's entrance he put his glass of whisky to his lips and drained it. There was something magnificent even about the manner of his doing this. He looked at Anthony, completely ignored Hatherley, and then proceeded to point the story that he had just told.

"And do ye know the saddest part of all about Ar-r-chie Bar-r-clay's dying? Why, that he never knew how well the wor-rld got on without him."

Another shout of laughter greeted this last sally. As it subsided, Anthony and Hatherley made their way to the bar. The majority of the company showed tendencies to rapid companionship. Fentiman greeted them.

"Good evening again to you, gentlemen. I'm pleased to be seein' you in here, I am. Right pleased. What can I get you, gentlemen?"

Anthony looked towards Hatherley.

"Ale," said the latter.

"Two tankards of beer," Anthony ordered.

Fentiman smiled at the order.

"Man's beer, sir, or boy's beer?"

Anthony grinned in retaliation.

"What's the difference between the two?"

Fentiman's smile this time was a smile of superior knowledge.

"Well, there's a difference in the strength and there's a difference in the price—that's what there is to it."

"Oh, in that case, man's," returned Mr. Bathurst, "and hang the expense."

Fentiman drew the beer. Anthony and Hatherley found seats near the bar. Anthony saw that Skipwith, Burns, and McCracken were now seated together in one group, although McCracken's recently finished story had been told to the entire company. When Andrew performed, he evidently performed for the benefit of the house generally. Anthony Bathurst felt a strange thrill of interest. Here, all together, at his side, almost, were the three men whom Major Marriner had depicted as Forsyth's chosen "intimates". They had known more, perhaps, of the conditions of Forsyth's last two years than any other person living. Burns, the retired motor engineer, like Skipwith, wore glasses. Anthony placed him as between fifty-five and sixty. He was sitting, and therefore Anthony was obliged to guess at some of his measurements. He could see, though, without the shadow of a doubt, that Burns was a tall, powerful, unusually long-armed man who must stand well over six feet in height. His face was ruddy and he looked the picture of health. Anthony looked significantly at Hatherley and the latter—understanding—commenced a commonplace conversation. Skipwith was the man who was talking in the other group. The mention of a name arrested Anthony's attention immediately.

"Well, Andrew McCracken can tell his lies about Scottish funerals and how he deals with refractory coffins, but he can't tell a better yarn than old Bob Forsyth could! Every time I stand in this bar I can see old Bob here with us, with his tankard in his hand. And, I tell you, it sort of grips me about the heart when I think of—"

Skipwith's words sent the bar into silence. Captain Stromm, who was sitting in the corner underneath the competition dart-board, looked up questioningly. Anthony saw that Stromm had not understood Skipwith's allusion to Forsyth at all. McCracken answered Skipwith.

"Ay, Randolph, I feel in the same shape myself. His passing's made a rare difference to all of us." He turned to Fentiman. "I'm a God-fearin' man, Tom, originally intended for the meenistry—so give me another whisky, quick!"

There came a half-hearted laugh at McCracken's rough jest. He grinned expansively as Fentiman served him with his whisky.

"Ay, you can laugh, all of you! And I'll be tellin' you this. You'll be so surprised that you'll start treatin' me when I've finished. About fourteen years ago I conducted a mission at a place called Glentarran with another young fellow named Wullie Struthers. We got to the kirk on a Setterday night and we put eighteen bottles of beer in the vestry just like for safety's sake, and slept there all that night! At least, we did the sleepin' part of it in between times! When the Sabbath morning came—and a rare fine mor-rn it was, as I well remember—we tossed up a coin to deter-r-mine which of us should do the preachin'. I lost. I had to preach the ser-r-mon, that means. I opened the Blessed Bible and the first words I read were—'For these are not drunken as ye suppose seeing it is but the third hour of the day.' Ay, and I preached a rattlin' fine sermon on it, too, although I says it that shouldn't."

He paused and there came another roar of laughter, in which even Anthony Bathurst himself joined. McCracken added an afterthought.

"And all the time I was preaching, do you know I couldn't help thinkin' what a little Simon Peter-r knew about the game after all."

He drained his whisky-glass. Then Burns made his first contribution to the conversation.

"Yes, Andrew. We all know that you're a damned clever chap, who likes himself just a little bit too much, and the best of good company, but nothing of what you've said yet has been at all constructive. That is to say, from the standpoint of putting a rope around the neck of Bob Forsyth's murderer. From what I can see of it, the police are just as far off a solution as they were the night that his body was found. And I don't think I'm far out in that."

Anthony Bathurst, listening hard as he chatted with Hatherley, thought that he could detect a note in Burns's voice that was not by any means too pleasant. Especially when you considered that the remark was addressed to one of his bosom cronies—McCracken. The latter, however, was imperturbable and accepted the challenge, albeit quietly and with much dignity.

"I've done just as much as you have, Mister-r Leonard Burns, in the way of what you call constructive criticism! So that there's no call for any damned satire from you. At the same time, if that's your attitude and your general disposition, I'll not be stayin' in your company this night. I promised my wife I'd stay in this week—one night. This is goin' to be it. Good night! 'Night, Randolph! 'Night, gentlemen!"

McCracken smiled broadly, turned on his heel, left the bar, nodded as he spoke his several salutations, and strode magnificently towards the door.

Captain Stromm half-rose from his seat by the dart-board as McCracken reached the door. It looked to Anthony as though he had a half-intention of reasoning with McCracken. The idea, however, if indeed it had been such, seemed to fade, and Captain Stromm resumed his seat in the corner beneath the dart-board of the "Tracy Arms".

Significant looks were exchanged by Burns and Skipwith. Burns laughed. Skipwith frowned.

"Oh," said Burns testily, "what's the use of looking like that? When Andrew talks 'big', I've no patience with him and I have to tell him so. And why not, in the name of conscience? He's had that basinful coming to him for some time now, and now it's there, believe me, it won't do friend Andrew any harm. He'll fall on my neck tomorrow."

"Still—" began Skipwith.

"Still what?" demanded Burns with a show of truculence.

"Well, I think it would have been better—certainly more discreet, with things as they are—if you hadn't said what you did. That's how it appears to me at least."

"Oh, shucks!" returned Burns impatiently. "You always did meet trouble half-way. Forget it! Andrew'll be as right as rain in the morning. He'll have forgotten all about tonight. Bet you drinks all round I'm right."

Anthony was talking to Hatherley all the time that this was proceeding, but he could hear all that was passing between Burns and Skipwith. He looked up to see Captain Stromm bending down to him.

"I am a stranger, I know, and not therefore used to English ways, but surely there is something . . . what you would call . . . peculiar . . . about this place tonight? All that talk between those men just now. I sense a shadow of some kind that rests upon the house. Is there anything that I do not understand? That I might be told about and thus have the knowledge?"

He put the questions with an eagerness that was almost childish. Anthony decided to play for safety—temporary safety at least. The last thing that he desired to discuss openly in this bar of the "Tracy Arms" was the Forsyth murder case.

"Forget it, Captain Stromm," he said quietly.

Stromm looked even more puzzled. Anthony went on to amplify his remark.

"Not here and not now, Captain," he said in an even lower tone. "You understand? It would not be discreet. Some other time and place, perhaps. Then I shall be happy to serve you."

He saw that Burns and Skipwith had become interested in Stromm's conversation with him. He therefore raised his voice deliberately.

"What will you drink with me, Captain Stromm? Give it a name."

Stromm bowed and took a seat between Anthony and Hatherley, who moved apart for him.

"I will drink a glass of Hollands, please, with just a touch of water."

"De Kuyper?" asked Anthony.

Stromm shook his head. "Preferably," he replied slowly, "Bols."

Anthony ordered in accordance with the Swede's request. Stromm took the glass and held it to his nose.

"I think I understand already a little better. Your health, Mr.—"

"Lotherington," replied Anthony.

"Mr. Lotherington, then," gravely announced Captain Stromm.

Skipwith rose from his chair and came over to them.

"Good evening, gentlemen," he said cordially.

Anthony saw at once that he was a little drunk. Skipwith addressed himself chiefly to Falk Stromm.

"You will excuse me, my dear sir, I know, but are you from the *Vaar*, the timber ship that's lying in Chalke harbour? I assure you, sir, that I am not asking out of idle curiosity."

Stromm smiled. He had now realized what Anthony had a minute or so previously.

"In a way I am," he replied. "That is to say, the *Vaar* brought me here. But only, as you would put it, as a passenger. There is a difference. Actually I am a retired officer of the Swedish Navy, who has come to England for a little holiday."

"Pleased and proud to meet you," cried Skipwith, thrusting out his hand. "Allow me to welcome you on behalf of the company of the 'Tracy Arms'. We'll have a drink together, you and your friends"—his unsteady wave of the hand embraced both Anthony and Hatherley—"with me and my friend, Mr. Burns. Mr. Len Burns when he's on his hind-legs and all brimmin' over with bloody dignity and blasted *nob-nob-noblesse oblige*. Ha-ha! Hey—Tom! Come and fill all these glasses up again and don't waste time, you old blighter."

Fentiman leant over the bar and collected the necessary glasses. Burns wisely ignored Skipwith's taunt. Skipwith fastened on to Stromm again.

"You know, Admiral, you remind me of someone I've seen before. That uniform and pointed beard."

Stromm smiled good-naturedly at him.

"I don't think, sir, that we can ever have met before."

Skipwith waved his fingers in front of him.

"I know. I've got it. Old Van Tromp in a picture. 'I've a broom at the mast,' said he, 'and a broom is the sign for me.' Don't you know the jolly old song?" Skipwith began to sing. Loudly and noisily, but not altogether unmusically.

Stromm still smiled at him.

"You seem a merry company, sir, at the 'Tracy Arms', if I may be allowed to say so."

Skipwith became suddenly almost comically solemn.

"We were, perhaps three weeks ago, but all is different now. You may not know it, sir, but bloody murder has been done in Upchalke. And a dear old friend of ours at that. Bob Forsyth by name. And the police are still looking for the dirty scoundrel that murdered him." He drank what his glass held at one draught. "For all we know," he cried again, glaring around him, "his murderer may be sitting in this very bar now."

Burns rose angrily. "Sit down, Randolph, for goodness' sake! Don't make such a damned fool of yourself."

Skipwith turned to him. "Rest easy, Leonard. Don't steal my thun-thunder. That's right." He pointed across the room. "One of these days when we're all sitting here, all good boys amic-amicable together, all early to school, all merry and bright, with homework all finished off nicely, that door down there will open and the police will come in and arrest somebody for the murder of old Bob Forsyth . . . and Eugene Aram will walk between with gy-gyves upon his wrists. But we're not sure yet who's goin' to be Eu-Eugene Aram, see?"

His unsteady finger still pointed across the room to the door. The company was silent. Then a strange thing happened. Before Skipwith could start again, the door at which he still pointed began to open slowly. Every eye in the room watched it . . . to see Mulrenan enter. Here, with sharp abruptness, came anti-climax. He was greeted with a burst of laughter, in which all joined with the exception of Randolph Skipwith. Mulrenan's lip curled. At the same time he showed not the slightest sign of embarrassment.

"Thanks—a million," he drawled. "Glad to see that you find things so darned amusing, Skipwith."

He strode to the bar, without looking to either side of him.

"Whisky-and-soda, Tom, please."

Then Anthony noticed that he leant over the bar to Fentiman and spoke something in an undertone. Fentiman looked far from pleased at what Mulrenan had told him.

"All right," he said rather grudgingly, Anthony thought. "I'll send them up as soon as I can."

Mulrenan nodded at Fentiman's reply, gulped his whisky, and walked out. Skipwith watched him all the way.

"Now *that*," he said owlishly, "was damned funny and singularly sensational."

He tottered. Burns rose with firm intention, caught him by the arm, and pulled him down. Skipwith sagged into a seat.

Anthony looked significantly at Hatherley. The latter took his cue, rose, and made for the door. Anthony said good night to Captain Stromm and followed him. Hatherley made for the front door and the road. Anthony joined him. They stood in the dark a few yards from the main entrance.

"For a country pub," said Hatherley, "not so slow, after all."

"Hatherley," returned Mr. Bathurst, "take my advice. Get your point *re* Forsyth's identity cleared up as soon as you possibly can. I don't like the look of things at all."

Something in his tone made Hatherley feel uncomfortable.

"I say—" he said. "How do you mean? I've gone all cold."

"Well—just that I think things are pretty bad, that's all. The atmosphere in this place is significant. Anyhow, don't worry over what I've just said. Do as I advise. Let's settle this identity question of yours first of all. You've got me interested, you see. Remember this, Hatherley, that we—you and I—may be the only people who suspect even that Forsyth of Upchalke was not the Forsyth who worked for your show up at Easthampton. Which fact alone should—other things being equal—give us an advantage."

"By Jove," said Hatherley, "you're right there! I can see that."

There was considerable noise from the main entrance to the "Tracy Arms". Anthony looked at his watch.

"Half past ten, Hatherley," he announced. "Closing-time, or, if you prefer it, 'chucking out'. The service is over."

Hatherley nodded. A man came running hard down the road. Anthony and Hatherley watched him.

"Somebody in a devil of a hurry," remarked Mr. Bathurst.

The runner tore on past them. His face was white and strained. He was a stranger to them. Little knots of people came out from the house, gathered in a bunch for a few minutes by the front door, and then dispersed. Anthony saw Mulrenan come out. He was walking in the opposite direction, accompanied by his two lady-friends.

"Mulrenan," said Anthony, as though he were giving expression to a simple thought. "Mulrenan of the somewhat dramatic entrance this evening. I'm told that he's a journalist, although I don't know what interest he represents. Any idea, Hatherley?"

Hatherley shook his head. "No—none."

"I'll tell you what," continued Anthony, "you've whetted my interest in this Forsyth case. If you've no objection, I'll come with you to the newspaper office when you go up there in the morning. Do you mind?"

"No," said Hatherley, rather slowly for him, "I don't mind. As long as we don't show our hands too clearly."

"We won't do that. We'll play for safety. That's on, then, is it?" Hatherley agreed.

The road was now clear. The cars that had been drawn up outside the "Tracy Arms" and the various people who had come in them had all departed. Anthony and Hatherley strolled slowly back to the main door. Anthony wished his companion good night and made his way upstairs to his bedroom. Once inside, he was careful to take in the main points of the room and to lock his door. His mysterious telephone message of the night before was still on his immediate horizon. On several occasions during the evening he had considered it. On the whole, he thought, as he took stock of the day and the day's happenings, he could claim, and that justifiably, to have made a certain amount of progress. Skipwith, Burns, McCracken. Hatherley, Mulrenan, Captain Stromm, the two unusual ladies. . . . Mr. Bathurst paused in the act of unknotting his tie. He stood—silent for a time . . . and motionless. An idea had come to him. If Hatherley's suspicions concerning the Forsyth identity could be *proved*—proved beyond question—Mr. Bathurst could see at once that there were at least three people in Upchalke whom he must interview . . . and that without delay. He opened his bedroom window and looked out into the darkness.

Chapter VI
THEN WHERE IS FORSYTH?

The sun was shining when Anthony Bathurst walked into Chalke with the industrious Hatherley. They chose the path by the Chal rather than the way of the main road from Hatchett.

"I know where the offices of the famous Daily Gazette are," said Hatherley. "I noticed them as I came through the town yesterday. They're on the left-hand side of the hill going down to the sea, just past Repton Straight. Between the post-office and the museum. Know where I mean?"

"Yes. Good! I think that perhaps I shall be able to help you with regard to the smooth running of our inquiry. I know a man who's pretty high up in the newspaper world. I usually carry one of his cards—it may oil the machinery."

Anthony's remark was an example of intended diplomacy. Hatherley turned to him and looked surprised. The statement was a definite challenge, it must be remembered, to his undoubted superiority complex.

"All right," he conceded rather grudgingly. "Very likely we shan't want it. I'll make the position clear enough when we go in. I flatter myself I can do that."

Half an hour's brisk walking brought them into Chalke, and Hatherley stopped outside a dark, sombre-looking building that showed a plate bearing the words "*Chalke Daily Gazette*. Proprietors, Winslow and Whitty."

"Come on," said Hatherley, "let's take the bull by the horns."

He strode in, and Anthony followed him. An untidy youth met them at no great distance from the doorway.

"The editor, please," remarked Hatherley. "Take him my card, will you, please?"

The youth looked unimpressed, but was sufficiently obedient to disappear with Hatherley's pasteboard credentials. The latter and Anthony waited in the dark passage until the youth should reappear. When he eventually did, he seemed even more unimpressed with the two visitors than he had been at the outset.

"This way, please," he uttered ungraciously.

Anthony smiled as he and Hatherley were shown into what was evidently the private room of the editor of the *Chalke Daily Gazette*. An elderly, red-faced man whose countenance was much creased and seamed, and whose hair was extremely unruly, stared across the room at them.

"Yes," he demanded brusquely, "what can I do for you?"

Anthony was content to let Hatherley open the battery. Hatherley explained himself and the purpose behind his call at the offices of the *Chalke Daily Gazette*. The editor heard him out patiently. Then he as good as ordered him out.

"I don't know of any photograph that we have of Forsyth, and if we did have one, I can assure you that I shouldn't show it to you. You seem to forget that Forsyth has been murdered and there is an investigation still going on by the police. Any action I took, I should take through them, and through no other channel."

Hatherley essayed argument. The editor stuck his heels in the ground and flatly refused the issue.

"They're my last words. So I'll wish you and your friend here a very good morning."

Hatherley stepped back, crestfallen. Or as near to being crest-fallen as Wilfred Hatherley, of the audit staff of the County Borough of Easthampton, could ever be. Then Mr. Bathurst took a hand. He smiled upon the editor.

"Pardon me, sir. I fully appreciate the position in which you find yourself and understand it thoroughly, but if this would assist in any way . . ."

Mr. Bathurst extended a card towards the Gazette editor. The man took it and read it and immediately his whole manner and attitude changed. Mr. Bathurst unobtrusively placed a finger on his lip. The editor noticed the gesture and acted accordingly. Hatherley was the victim of complete and utter amazement.

"This, of course," said the editor of the Gazette, "makes an enor-mous difference. Anything that I can possibly do, I will. Why didn't you show me this in the first place? I should have understood."

Anthony replaced the card in his wallet.

"A photograph of Forsyth, the dead man—that's what we'd like to look at. Can you possibly dig one up from somewhere?"

The editor put his head in his hands.

"Let me think . . ." he said manfully.

Anthony and Hatherley accepted the position and allowed him the privilege of thought. He sat there for some time, his head buried in his hands. At length he looked up.

"I *believe* I've got such a thing," he said slowly.

"You awaken my hopes," said Mr. Bathurst complacently.

"Hold on a minute," rejoined the editor of the Gazette. "Don't let's go too fast! I *think* that I can put you on to something. Now let me see. When was it?" He subsided again into deep thought. "I'm thinking of a photograph that was taken up at the 'Tracy Arms'—about last January twelve-month it would have been. It was taken on the occasion of the annual dinner of the Upchalke Skittles Club. Two or three of my chaps went up to it and Forsyth was then in what you might call a dual capacity. He represented the *Gazette* as a reporter and he also happened to be a member of the Skittles Club as well. There was a flashlight taken just as the dinner was finishing. I'm almost certain that we printed a copy of it in our next edition. Now that would be, unless my memory's playing me tricks, in our copy for the week-end dated January the 23rd. The dinner was somewhere about the seventeenth. I'll test that for you on the spot."

"Thank you very much," interposed Mr. Bathurst cordially. "It is extremely kind of you."

Hatherley, discomfited at his personal failure, had long since been reduced to silence. The editor knocked on a handbell. The youth of their previous acquaintance came in and shuffled up to the editor's desk. He also sniffed—successfully.

"Bring me a copy from the files of the *Gazette*, dated January the 23rd last year, Dobbs, will you? Be as quick as you can."

The youth, full by now of morbid interest, disappeared with relative alacrity and a succession of sniffs. Anthony, Hatherley, and the genius that presided over the *Gazette* sat there in silence. Eventually a whistle was heard outside the door. The youth Dobbs entered again, bearing his sheaf with him. True to his sniff, he placed a newspaper on the table in front of his chief.

"*Gazette* for Jan. 23rd, last year," he piped excitedly.

"Just a minute before you go, Dobbs. Let me make certain that this is the right one."

The editor picked up the newspaper that his henchboy had brought and glanced through it.

"All right, Dobbs, you can go."

With a look of intense disappointment and a supporting sniff, Dobbs made his exit.

"Got it?" asked Anthony laconically. "The one you want?"

The *editor* of the Gazette nodded.

"Yes, it's all right. Come over here, gentlemen, and have a look for yourselves."

Anthony Bathurst and Hatherley rose and ranged themselves on either side of him. The editor folded the paper and pointed to a group-photograph right in the middle of one of the pages of the newspaper.

"That's the reproduction I've been chasing," he said, tapping it with his forefinger. "There you are, you can read it for yourselves—'Annual Dinner of the Upchalke Skittles Club held at the "Tracy Arms", Upchalke, on Thursday evening last.'"

Anthony nodded and read the description under the photograph almost mechanically. Now it was up to companion Hatherley to do his stuff. Hatherley, with a gleam in his eye, bent over the paper excitedly.

"Do you mind pointing out Forsyth?" he asked of the editor.

The editor pointed to a man on the left-hand side of the group.

"There's Bob Forsyth," he said gruffly. "Sitting over there—that's the poor devil with such a terrible end the other day. He's smiling here, too. Good job we don't know what's coming to us. Perhaps it's the wisest of all Providence's dispensations that we don't know what waits for us round the corner."

Anthony carefully watched Hatherley's expression as he received the item of news for which he had been seeking, and then went and looked for himself.

"He's a cooler card than I thought he was," surmised Anthony. "He's giving nothing away."

"I see," remarked Hatherley eventually, with a slow nod of the head. "I just wanted to get a rough idea of what the man was like, as I had an idea I knew him."

"Satisfied?" asked the editor of the *Gazette*.

"Oh, quite, thank you," returned Hatherley.

"Only too pleased to have been able to assist you, gentlemen. Is there anything more that I can do for you?"

Anthony told him that they were more than satisfied and that the editor of the Gazette had surpassed himself for courtesy and efficient service. They then withdrew from the editorial presence and found themselves in the street again.

"Well," said Anthony quietly, "what's the verdict?"

Hatherley could scarcely speak for excitement.

"It's not Forsyth! Of course it isn't. I knew I was right. That thin-faced, hollow-cheeked man is no more Bob Forsyth, the ex-rate collector of Easthampton, than I am the king of the Cannibal Islands. I say, Lotherington, what's it all mean? Have you any idea?"

Anthony hesitated before replying.

"As I see things, your discovery raises more than one problem, Hatherley. Not only who is this murdered man, why was he murdered, and who murdered him, but also *where is the real Forsyth* of your own acquaintance?"

Hatherley nodded. "Yes, I can see all that."

They walked along in silence for some moments. Anthony was deep in thought.

"Question is," declared Hatherley, "what do we do now? That's what's worrying me. What's our next step? Is there any idea stirring in the old grey matter?"

Anthony digressed. "I noticed, Hatherley, in that photograph at which you and I have just looked, several familiar faces. I wonder if you also spotted them? Did you? I was able to pick out without the slightest difficulty many of our friends of the 'Tracy Arms'. Extremely interesting, I consider that. There were Burns, Skipwith, McCracken, Mulrenan, and, of course, dear old Fentiman, the genial host of the establishment himself. Forsyth—the pseudo-Forsyth, that is—was actually seated between Burns and Skipwith. Did you notice that? I find the entire problem most attractive. I wouldn't have missed it for worlds."

Hatherley turned and regarded him curiously.

"I say, your pal in the newspaper world must be a big shot! His name certainly worked the oracle for us with that editor bloke. Some influence, I'll say! You fairly took the wind out of my sails. Talk about 'open sesame'."

Anthony smiled. "I told you I thought I could oil the machinery, didn't I? You see, I happen to know what these journalists are. Very clannish. I've had a fair amount of experience of them, and it hasn't been lost on me."

"You haven't told me yet what our next move is going to be."

"That's a question easier asked than answered, I'm afraid. But I'll tell you what—I can't see myself doing very much painting during the next few days."

Hatherley grinned at what he evidently considered his companion's discomfiture.

"Bit of a poser that, isn't it, Lotherington?"

Anthony came to him again with a question.

"Forsyth! The real, authentic Forsyth, I mean—can you tell me anything about his antecedents? Any idea what his people were?"

"Oh yes, I can do that. His father was a corn-chandler. I believe he had a business in the East End of London somewhere. And his grandfather—that would be his father's father—was, I think, something to do with the sea. I fancy I can remember old Bob talking about it once or twice."

Hatherley stopped abruptly. Anthony, however, anxious for information, pressed him for further particulars.

"Can you recollect any details of the family? It might help us a lot if you could."

Hatherley thought for some time before shaking his head.

"No—I'm sorry. I can't—any more. But I can tell you this about the Forsyth family. I don't think that Bob Forsyth had any relations giving. If he had, I can tell you for certain that I never heard him talk of any of them."

"*That* direction's a dead end, then," remarked Anthony. "That's a pity."

"I say"—Hatherley swung round on to him—"was *Forsyth* intended to die, do you think? Or was it this other man? That's what's worrying me."

"How do you mean, exactly?"

"Why, just this. Did they intend to get Forsyth or the other chap?"

"Well, I should say, from what I've already seen of the case, that the trouble, if we may call it that, is centred round Forsyth. And I'll give you a reason why I think so, if you would care to hear it."

"I should. Because I've been looking for one myself and haven't been able to find it."

"It's just this, Hatherley. It paid the dead man to be Forsyth. It was all to his advantage. The dead man found it profitable to impersonate him, didn't he?"

"Not in the long run—whichever way you look at it."

"Not in the long run, certainly, I agree. But the end as it came to him was in all probability something he hadn't bargained for. It wasn't in his original contract. He never foresaw it and I'm fairly certain that he didn't fear it. Unless . . ." Anthony paused.

"Unless what?" questioned Hatherley.

"Well, it's only just a bare idea—unless he moved from Lanning two years ago because he wanted to run away from something. It seems to me that that *may* be a possibility which we ought to consider."

Anthony halted and looked down into the placid water of the Chal.

"I still don't know what we do next," remarked Hatherley. "Seems to me we're up against what is almost a stalemate. The case is more entangled than ever."

Anthony Bathurst shook his head. "Not at all. I disagree with you entirely. We're already learning parts about it that must help us towards an eventual elucidation. It is much easier to disentangle the strands of truth than it is to separate falsehood. We know now—you and I, that is—that the dead man isn't Forsyth. Next step, then, is, who *is* he? When we know *that*, we shall be yet another step nearer solution. And there's this, too, Hatherley. What you have learned this morning raises still another most interesting point."

"Which one is that?" queried Hatherley.

"The identity of Mrs. Winifred Forsyth, the widow of the dead man's nephew! Don't you see that? And not only the identity of the lady, but the general part that she has played in the whole business. Is she a real Forsyth who had never before met her 'uncle' and therefore was unable to identify him, or is she a pseudo too?"

"The latter—undoubtedly," replied Hatherley, "I'm positive. The more I think of it, I become *more* positive that the Forsyth whom I knew had no brother or sister, and therefore could have had no nephew. You can bank on that, Mr. Lotherington—take it from me."

"Yes, I think you're probably right. So that it means this—the true position must be established as quickly as possible. I've made up my mind, Hatherley. I shall go to the police."

"Yes, I think you're right. As I see things, there's nothing else that we can do—sensibly."

"The man in charge of the case is the Chief Constable of Remenham. I read that in the paper before I came down here—that's how I know."

They passed through the little wicket gate that led to the last stage of their journey back to Upchalke.

"Now what was the chap's name?" finessed Anthony. "I saw it somewhere, I feel sure. It will come to me if I give it time enough . . . Manning, Marryat . . . no, neither of those. I've got it . . . Marr . . . Marriner! Major Marriner. That's the man I'll try to get into touch with somehow. It shouldn't be difficult, either, if I play my cards properly."

Hatherley assented.

"In the meantime, Hatherley, as well, I suggest that you communicate with your people up at the Easthampton end of the tangle and acquaint them with the news of what you have discovered down here. To clinch matters, get them to send down a photograph of the real Forsyth. There must be one, I should say, knocking about somewhere. He worked for your authority many years, I understand."

Hatherley nodded.

"Tell them all the news in confidence," went on Anthony. "Ask them not to broadcast it, for the sake of giving the police a chance. Get the idea?"

"Yes I'll be guarded in what I say and I'll tell them to proceed on the same lines."

"Good," said Anthony. "And now our next step, Hatherley, is Major Marriner."

"The sooner the better," returned Hatherley with unusual gravity.

"I agree with you," replied Mr. Bathurst.

Chapter VII
BOMBSHELL FOR MAJOR MARRINER

When Anthony Bathurst and Hatherley were shown into the presence of the Chief Constable of Remenham, Major Eustace Brase Marriner, Hatherley was destined for yet another surprise. Major Marriner rose at once and greeted his companion with outstretched hand.

"Oh, how are you?" he said. "I got your letter, of course, Mr.—er—"

"Lotherington," replied Anthony, with steady composure. "That's the name."

"Oh yes, I remember now. Well, sit down, Mr. Lotherington, and Mr.—er—oh yes, Hatherley—make yourselves comfortable, do!"

Anthony and Hatherley took the two chairs that Major Marriner's eyes indicated. The Chief Constable went on.

"You wish to see me, I understand, with regard to the Forsyth murder."

"Yes, we have most important information for you concerning it." The reply was from Anthony.

Major Marriner looked across at them with some surprise. "Indeed? May I inquire the nature of it?"

"It is this. We are absolutely convinced that the man murdered in the bungalow at Upchalke and known as Robert Forsyth, and ex-rate-collector, was not Robert Forsyth at all."

Marriner seemed puzzled at Anthony's statement.

"How do you mean? I don't know that I—"

"Let me put it to you like this." Anthony deliberately chose his words. "I agree that anybody may answer to a name. That one name is as good as another. That a rose by any other name, and so on. But in this particular instance the name of 'Robert Forsyth' belonged to a person that was really identifiable. He was an ex-officer of the Easthampton County Borough Council. That same Easthampton County Borough Council paid him, every month, a superannuation allowance, in respect of contributory and non-contributory service under the 1922 act. Now here comes the flaw. The dead man in the bungalow at Upchalke, who had clothed himself with that Robert Forsyth's identity and who took Robert Forsyth's money, *was not this Robert Forsyth at all*! As I said to you a few moments ago."

Major Marriner received this piece of news in silence.

He gave expression to no sign of incredulity.

"How do you know all this?" he demanded at length.

Anthony Bathurst then brought Hatherley into the picture. "Tell the Chief Constable what you have already told me, Mr. Hatherley."

Hatherley was delighted to receive so quickly such a golden opportunity. Sensibly he started at the right place—the beginning. He felt flattered that Major Marriner listened to him with rapt attention.

Hatherley came in time to the visit of himself and Anthony to the offices of the *Chalke Daily Gazette*. As he listened to this, Marriner looked up intently, his eyes bright and hard with curiosity. Eventually Hatherley came to the conclusion of his story.

"Well, the editor got to work and found this particular photograph and showed it to us, to Mr. Lotherington and myself. He pointed out the man in the group whom they all knew down here as Robert Forsyth. Well, I can tell you this, sir. Directly I saw it, I knew without any possible doubt that the man who was pointed out to us in that photograph was nothing like the Bob Forsyth who used to be a colleague of mine! Nothing like him at all! Not a single feature. You understand me, don't you? Take the teeth question alone. Your murdered man down here had a tooth loosened by a blow from the murderer. *I* know for certain, however, that the real Bob Forsyth had worn false teeth for years. Top *and* bottom dentures. I've worked alongside him and know that all right."

In the telling of his story, Hatherley had half risen from his seat. Now he resumed it again. Major Marriner drummed with his fingertips on the desk in front of him.

"Who knows about this?" he inquired curtly. "Anybody other than you?"

"At the moment," replied Hatherley rather tartly, "we three only. But I feel that I ought to tell you this. I have written to my chief, the Borough Treasurer of Easthampton, Mr. Sharpe-Lodge, F.I.M.T.A., a discreetly guarded letter setting out most of the facts as I have just detailed them to you. I don't think that anybody could have been more discreet over what was actually said than I have been in the letter. I am awaiting his reply."

The Chief Constable of Remenham received this item of information without comment. Anthony Bathurst watched his face carefully. He saw him draw a piece of paper towards him and rapidly make certain notes on it.

"Will you let me have your address, please, Mr. Hatherley?"

Hatherley looked surprised. "My address here, do you mean?"

"Yes, if you please."

"I am staying at the 'Tracy Arms', Upchalke, with Mr. Lotherington, here. But only for the next couple of days or so."

Major Marriner made suitable notes. "The 'Tracy Arms', eh? Right in the thick of things there, aren't you? Forsyth—or, rather, the man we thought was Forsyth—used that house habitually. You'll let me know when you leave there, won't you?"

Hatherley gave the required assurance.

"I won't detain you, then," continued Major Marriner.

Hatherley rose to make his departure. Anthony prepared to follow him. But the Chief Constable intervened.

"If Mr. Hatherley will wait outside for a little while, I should like a few words with you, Mr.—er—Lotherington. Do you mind? Do you mind, Mr. Hatherley? Thank you."

Hatherley turned and made his exit. Anthony remained in the presence of Major Marriner. The door closed on Wilfred Hatherley.

"Well," said Major Marriner, coming down to Anthony, "and what do you make of it now, Bathurst?"

"Confusion worse confounded, sir. Pelion upon Ossa."

Marriner grimaced. "Is this fellow who was here with you reliable, do you think?"

"I think so. Although I must admit that I met him quite by chance just outside the dead man's bungalow."

"Have you checked up on him at all?"

"Yes, through the Yard. He doesn't know it, but I've already put a special inquiry through to Sir Austin Kemble. The Easthampton end will be tested thoroughly. This, too, will either disprove or confirm his story about the Forsyth identity."

"Oh, good! So you're still lying low, eh, as you hinted!"

"Yes, I'm a 'chiel in the midst of 'em—taking notes'. But this false-identity business has rather put the lid on things. Look here, I want you to do something for me—to arrange something, if you will."

Marriner smiled. "Say the word—and it's yours, Bathurst."

"Well, it's this. I want to look over the Forsyth bungalow as soon as you can arrange it for me. I'd like Dr. Thorold to be there at the time—that was the name of the police doctor, wasn't it, who examined the body?—and also the dead man's niece by marriage, Mrs. Winifred Forsyth. Can you manage all that for me?"

"Certainly. I shall simply see that it's done, Bathurst. I'll issue the necessary orders. That's all there is to it."

"Thanks awfully. One more point. Reticence—complete reticence, that is, on the part of everybody—towards the before-mentioned Mrs. W.F. regarding what we think we have discovered concerning the identity of her murdered uncle. Get me?"

The Chief Constable nodded. "I agree. If you hadn't suggested it, I was going to."

"Good. Will you let me know what day and what time I'm to be at the bungalow?"

"I'll let you know now, Bathurst. I'll fix it on the spot. Make it for eleven o'clock tomorrow morning. I'll see the doctor and I'll get into touch with the lady."

"Will you be there yourself, Major Marriner?"

"You bet I shall," replied the Chief Constable grimly. "I'm rather curious as to what's going to happen; whether you'll run across anything that my chaps have overlooked. Somehow I don't think that you will."

"If I do, don't be too hard on them, sir. Remember that I have an advantage over them in this respect. For one thing, I'm on to the false-identity business, whereas they weren't—it's bound to make a difference, if only for the reason that it's given me an entirely different angle from which to look at things."

"Yes, I suppose you're right," conceded Major Marriner, "and it's decent of you to point it out."

Anthony smiled and shook hands with him.

"Eleven ack-emma, then," he said quietly; "full-dress uniform, and all the troops assembled. Good-bye, sir, and many thanks for your help."

Hatherley met him outside with some impatience—impatience that friend Hatherley made no effort to conceal.

"What did he want with you that was so beastly private? Haven't you told him who I am?"

Anthony fenced with him. "Well, it was like this—more or less. He had your credentials to a certain extent, but he said he hadn't mine. You hold an official position, as one might say, but a private artist such as I am—almost entirely unknown and with no particular name or reputation—well, he may be called upon at any time to justify himself. But I satisfied him all right, don't you worry."

Hatherley heard him out and frowned at him.

"I like their style. Anybody might think we wanted something out of them, instead of rallying round to give 'em a hand and drag 'em out of a mess. Still, that's the police all over."

Anthony was amused at his bitterness. "Ah, well," he said, "they have their job to do like the rest of us, and very often under the worst possible conditions. So that it behoves us to be as charitable as we can and make allowances for them." He changed the subject. "Seen any of the 'Tracy Arms' crowd since breakfast?"

Hatherley assented gloomily. "Most of 'em, if the truth be told. Mulrenan with his two lady-friends took the car down into Chalke a few moments in front of us. Skipwith and Burns went off to Burnthouse Hill for a round of golf. Whom else did I see now? McCracken was off up to Admiral Mayhew's place. He was trying to get Captain Stromm to accompany him when I left, but I don't think the gallant Swede was having any."

"Hatherley," said Anthony, "you're a perfect treasure. I don't know what I should have done without you."

CHAPTER VIII
IN THE BUNGALOW

NEXT morning at breakfast Hatherley came round to the table and placed a letter in front of Anthony Bathurst. Anthony saw that it was signed "Fredk. G. Sharpe-Lodge, Treasurer and Accountant to the County Borough of Easthampton". Mr. Bathurst read it with undisguised interest. Taken in conjunction with the communication that he had himself received from Sir Austin Kemble, the Commissioner of Police, it was undoubtedly important. The Borough Treasurer of Easthampton expressed himself as utterly astounded at the terms of Hatherley's letter to him. Many details followed concerning the system on which the Superannuation Fund accounts of the County Borough of Easthampton were kept, with special reference to the signing of Life Certificates for superannuitants by persons possessing the requisite credentials. Anthony at once thought certain things.

"Credentials," he said to himself—"credentials rather than definite knowledge. Exactly."

Mr. Sharpe-Lodge, Fellow of the Institute of Municipal Treasurers and Accountants, although not by the direct route, concluded by remarking that he would endeavour to join Hatherley at Upchalke and submitted a physical chart of the real Forsyth "in the hope that it may prove helpful to the authorities". The details of this chart were as follows.

Age 73. Height, 5 feet 10½ inches. Hair white. Was originally fair—inclined to ginger. Weight, 14 stones 10 pounds. Eyes light blue. Complexion ruddy. Abnormally long arms. Also—this is interesting—had a tiny wart on the left-hand side of his nose. Wore glasses. Had false teeth—both at top and bottom. In addition to all these features, had a scar on the point of the chin. This scar was the legacy that Forsyth carried from a bad cut that he once sustained at a barber's shop when he was being shaved.

Anthony made a mental note of the various points as he read them and constructed a fairly satisfactory picture of the man. He handed the letter back to Hatherley, who returned to his own table.

On this particular morning, the breakfast-room of the "Tracy Arms" was quieter than usual. Mulrenan's table was, up to the moment, unoccupied. In addition, neither Tom Fentiman nor his wife had put in an appearance. The service so far had been in the hands of a woman hired from the village. But Captain Falk Stromm, in full enjoyment of his holiday sat at his table—a commanding figure even in repose. Anthony looked at his watch. Half past nine. He had ample time in which to get to the bungalow, "The Antlers". The bungalow of the dead Forsyth, where the carved ebony stag had been broken and its owner murdered. Mulrenan then entered the breakfast-room. Behind him came the two ladies, whom Anthony, from what he had heard, mentally called Freda and Heather, and then, rather surprisingly, further in the rear came the man whom Anthony had taken to be the chauffeur. They took their seats and almost immediately Anthony detected "atmosphere". The man that he regarded as the chauffeur sat there moody and sullen, and Anthony heard him say:

"You have no cause to blame me. I acted under orders. I had no option in the matter. But I give you my word, I'm not doing it again for a fortune. *Any* fortune! One that's there to be seen or one that's in the air. No, thank you! I feel that I must make my position in the matter clear to everybody."

The white-faced, worn-looking Freda laughed contemptuously as she crumbled bread on the cloth.

"So now you know, Cyril, exactly how we stand—or, rather, how the estimable Wagstaff stands. One might almost imagine that *he* employed *us*."

Mulrenan replied to her in an undertone. His mouth had a cynical twist to it. He looked across at the blue-eyed girl, Heather, and gave his shoulders just the suspicion of a shrug.

Anthony's eyes caught hers as she half turned away. In them, as she looked at him, there lurked, he was certain, a mute appeal. Freda continued her words of censure:

"I thought castles were in the air, not fortunes. But Wagstaff evidently thinks differently. What do you say, Cyril?"

Mulrenan again replied in low tones, but Anthony overheard the word "fortune" again. He glanced again towards the girl, Heather, and the thought flashed through his mind again that this might be the girl that had telephoned him to his flat and warned him off the case. For once in a way Mr. Bathurst was in a quandary as to what was best for him to do. She never seemed to be alone. Every time that he had seen her since he had been at the "Tracy Arms", Mulrenan and Freda had been in close attendance upon her. However, it might be that a suitable opportunity would come to him later. He decided that he would be the acme of discretion and watch points before committing himself in any way as far as the lady Heather was concerned.

Captain Stromm came over and stood by his table.

"Would you like to accept my . . . what you call . . . hospitality . . . for part of the day? The captain of the *Vaar*, that is the name of the boat which brought me over, has asked me to dine with him in his cabin before he returns to Sweden in the boat. I am permitted to bring a friend, he has told me. I have thought of you. There is nobody else here whom I would care to take. May I have the honour? This evening . . . yes?"

"It is very kind of you, Captain Stromm. I could accept for this evening with pleasure. Would that do? Earlier than that, I'm afraid, is impossible."

Stromm beamed at Anthony's acceptance.

"This evening . . . that is splendid. I am delighted! I will let Captain Vass know that I am coming and that I am also bringing you. He also will be delighted, I am sure." He clicked his heels gallantly. "I will meet you here, then, early in the evening, and we will go up to the boat together."

Anthony assented. Captain Stromm moved away and Anthony noticed that Freda's eyes were fixed on him as he made his exit through the door. Anthony looked at his watch again. He would have to finesse the position as regards Hatherley. For reasons of his own, he did *not* desire Hatherley to follow him to the bungalow. Direct methods would probably prove to be the best, he considered. He went over to the table where Hatherley was on the point of finishing his breakfast.

"I'll see you at lunch, Hatherley," he said, "in all probability. I've a spot of work waiting for me that I simply must do this morning. I dare not put it off for another day. Since I've been here I've become very much like a confirmed idler."

"Righto," said Hatherley. "As it happens, I've a spot of work in front of me too. So that we're more or less in the same boat. We meet here at lunch, then. That's agreed."

Anthony reached the bungalow almost on the stroke of eleven o'clock. He made his way there by a circuitous route, crossing three fields and climbing five stiles in the process, but he had the satisfaction of knowing that he had certainly not been followed. When he reached "The Antlers", Major Marriner was already there, waiting in the garden at the rear of the bungalow.

"Hallo, Bathurst," he opened, "you're in time for developments and no mistake! What do you think has happened now?"

"I won't guess," returned Anthony, "it's a pernicious habit in anybody. Tell me, please."

"There are two most surprising developments. The first is that this place has been thoroughly ransacked since I was last here. I discovered it yesterday evening. The whole shoot of it has been turned completely inside out."

"Good," said Anthony. "I don't know that it grieves me to hear you say that. But go on—what's Item of News number two?"

Major Marriner stared at him critically. "Mrs. Forsyth—that is to say, the lady who came home to find her uncle murdered—has disappeared. Since the murder she had been staying in the district with a friend. The police, I may say, were fully aware of it. She had told them in the first place—when she first went there. Well, I got into touch last night with the people with whom she had been staying, with the object of bringing her over here this morning to see you, and I'm told politely that she's cleared out! Walked out one evening last week, ostensibly to do some shopping, and hasn't been seen since! That's the story that's been put up to me. What do you make of that, Bathurst?"

"It doesn't please me at all, Major Marriner. Still, what's done can't be undone, and I dare say you'll be able to put your hands on her again without very much difficulty. Who are the people with whom she stayed?"

"A Mrs. Anderson of Carlton Street."

"Good. Is Dr. Thorold here?"

Major Marriner looked at his watch. "Not yet, but I expect him any minute now."

"Good again," returned Anthony.

"We'll go in from the front, if you don't mind," continued the Chief Constable. "I have the key of the front. Or, rather, one of the keys. Mrs. Forsyth has the other."

"What about the back?" inquired Anthony mildly.

"That has been kept locked ever since the murder. The key of the back door, of course, is still missing."

Major Marriner opened the front door and he and Anthony Bathurst entered the bungalow. Each room showed signs of considerable confusion. In the front room papers and documents were scattered everywhere. In other rooms vases and pots of all kinds had been overturned and left in the same position.

"This gives you some idea of what's occurred," remarked the Chief Constable, after they had been round the rooms, pointing to the disturbances.

"H'm," said Anthony, "somebody wants something pretty badly, that's very evident—something that he thinks is here. Something more, too, than a fraudulent superannuation allowance."

"Yes, but did he find what he wanted?" queried Major Marriner. "That's an important point."

"Difficult to say. Still, if he comes again, we shall know that he didn't."

"He may not."

"True. But there you are—there's always the chance. We shall have to watch the point."

"This is the room," said the Major, opening a door, "where the man who called himself Forsyth was murdered."

Anthony saw that it was an ordinary living-room, quite small as regards size.

"That's where he was sitting, Bathurst—in that chair there. His head rested on the table. The chair and the table were almost in the positions that you see them now."

Anthony measured distances with his eyes. "I see," he said quietly. "And blood was almost everywhere, I believe?"

"Yes," replied the Chief Constable, "all over the place, as might well be expected, considering the nature of the wound that the man had sustained."

Anthony walked slowly round the room, deep in thought. A voice outside suddenly caught their attention.

"Here's Dr. Thorold," said Major Marriner. "A trifle late, I'm afraid, but here nevertheless."

Major Marriner went to the front door of the bungalow to admit the police doctor. Dr. Thorold was a clean-shaven, fair, jovial man with a high-pitched, light voice. His hands showed distinct signs of nervousness. Major Marriner introduced him to Anthony Bathurst. Dr. Thorold smiled genially as they shook hands.

"Reconstruction of the crime, eh? That the idea?"

"Something like that," replied Anthony "although rather late, I fear. You don't mind if I ask you a few questions, Doctor?"

"Only too happy to answer them, my dear boy. That's what I'm here for. What's the first one?"

"When you were called to the dead man, Doctor, I understand that he was sitting in that chair?" Anthony pointed to the arm-chair.

Thorold nodded. "That's right."

"His head and arms were on that table. Yes?"

"Yes. Don't I remember it! When I lifted his head, his face looked terrible. It had a look on it of indescribable horror. I have seen hundreds of dead men in my time, but I never before saw anything like Forsyth."

"Really?" said Anthony. "Now tell me this, Doctor. Where exactly was the ebony stag?"

"Down there," answered Dr. Thorold, pointing to a spot on the floor. "Just about there. On the table," he continued, "were the tongs. Just there." The doctor indicated a position on the table towards the window.

"The what?" queried Anthony with surprise.

"The tongs," replied Dr. Thorold. "They had, I think, been taken by the murderer to smash the stag. At least, that was the impression I formed. He broke the stag into smithereens and then in his haste threw the tongs on to the table."

"Do you mind, Dr. Thorold," said Anthony, "showing me again the place on the table where you say the tongs lay?"

"Certainly. There." The doctor laid his hand on the table.

"H'm. Decidedly interesting. Another question, Doctor. There are two casement-windows over there. Can you remember if either was open?"

"I can. That one there was open, just as it is now."

Dr. Thorold looked across the room and pointed to the window on the right-hand side. Mr. Bathurst heard the doctor's answer and rubbed his hands. Major Marriner and Dr. Thorold saw a gleam come into his grey eyes.

"Thank you, Doctor, that's admirable. But somehow I don't think that the tongs were taken to break the ebony stag. No. You see, tongs aren't solid as a weapon of force. They're not held easily; they're inclined to bend. There's a metal flabbiness, shall we say, about a pair of tongs? Still, I'm tremendously obliged to you for the information that you've given me."

Dr. Thorold smiled at Anthony and nodded. He seemed even more genial than ever. Major Marriner sat in the dead man's arm-chair and said nothing.

"This man that we knew as Forsyth, Doctor—had you met him at all in the course of any of your duties before you were called here on the day of the murder?"

Dr. Thorold shook his head. "Never. I wasn't even aware of the man's existence when I received the call to come along here."

"You examined the body, of course, Doctor. How old would you say the dead man was?"

Dr. Thorold wrinkled his brow. "H'm. Age. Well, from what I can remember of him, early sixties, I should say. But, of course, you must understand that when I saw him he was dead and I wasn't worrying particularly about how old the man was." Dr. Thorold spoked with decided emphasis.

Anthony expressed his understanding. "Yes, I follow that—naturally. Early sixties, you'd say, eh? Well, I don't know that I want to find any fault with that. There was nothing peculiar—or shall we say unusual—about the body, I presume, Doctor?"

Dr. Thorold's face showed unmistakable signs of surprise. Anthony followed up his question.

"I'll explain myself. We have a new problem to solve, Doctor. Something has recently arisen which raises the matter of the man's identity. That's the real point behind my questions. Anything that may help us to discover who the man was must be tremendously valuable. Anything—no matter how trivial or unimportant it may seem."

Dr. Thorold nodded once or twice as Anthony Bathurst was speaking.

"I see, Mr. Bathurst. I must confess that I wondered what it was that really lay behind your questions. Well, I don't know that I have anything to tell you that will help you at all. No—nothing." He shook his head thoughtfully.

Anthony, who had been watching his face very closely, now suddenly asked with pointed emphasis:

"No marks or scars of any kind? Nothing physical worthy of mentioning?"

Dr. Thorold shook his head again. "No-o. As far as I know, the body was quite clean, not marked in any way at all . . . in fact, quite normal and . . . er . . . ordinary. Had there been anything of the nature that you suggest, I should most certainly have—" Dr. Thorold paused abruptly.

Anthony Bathurst intervened impetuously: "Yes, Doctor? You have thought of something?"

Dr. Thorold smiled at his eagerness. Major Marriner rose from the arm-chair by the table and came across to the two men.

"My dear doctor, you've made me as curious as Bathurst himself. I almost dread to hear what you are going to tell us."

The doctor's smile broadened. "My point is far from being dreadful, I assure you. In a way, it's rather remarkable that I should have recalled it. But you see it happened to be almost the last thing that I noticed about the dead man before I left. Don't be annoyed with me when I tell you what it was. His left sock was on inside out. There you are, Bathurst—if that piece of information's any use to you, you're welcome to it. But I'm very much afraid that it won't be."

Major Marriner smiled as broadly as Dr. Thorold had a few moments previously.

"Talking about curiosities," he said quietly. "I've just remembered something else that may interest friend Bathurst here. But when I came here early yesterday evening in connection with your visit today, Bathurst, the tongs were on the table again. In the place that you showed us just now, Doctor. I put them back in their usual place. Now what the deuce do you make of that?"

"Just a minute, please," intervened Anthony eagerly, "let me get all this straight. It's tremendously important. You, Dr. Thorold, say the dead man's left sock was worn inside out, and you, Major Marriner, say that when you came in here yesterday evening the tongs were again lying on that table. Is that so?"

Dr. Thorold and the Chief Constable nodded together.

"Where did you say you put them?"

"Back in the hearth there, where they are now."

"That's a little unfortunate, don't you think?"

"What are you thinking of? Fingerprints?"

"I must candidly admit that I was."

"They were tried for fingerprints in the first instance, without any success at all. There wasn't as much as a fingermark on them anywhere. If the murderer took care before, he certainly would do so again. That's how I reasoned. Remember that he's comparatively calm when he arrives on the second occasion. If he remembered such a thing in the emotion that must have been his just after the murder, he certainly wouldn't forget at a time when he had so much less on his mind. You won't get away from that, Bathurst. How can you?"

Major Marriner spoke with an easy confidence.

"I don't know that it *was* the murderer who handled the tongs on the second occasion. Aren't you inclined to take a great deal for granted?"

"Who else could it have been?"

"A number of people. Don't you agree? To name one—let me suggest the lady whom we know up to the moment as Mrs. Winifred Forsyth." Anthony continued. "She may have had an acute attack of nostalgia, you know, and given way to it. There are, I imagine, many more unlikely happenings. You said that she still has a key to one of the doors." He paused with dramatic suddenness. "Let me have a look at those tongs, Major Marriner, will you? If you've handled them, it won't matter much if I do, will it?"

Major Marriner bent down and picked up a pair of tongs from the hearth. He handed them to Anthony Bathurst.

"Frail things," commented the latter, "with which to smash anything to smithereens. Hardly an instrument that one would deliberately select, surely?"

"There is just this, though. It might be the nearest to hand," countered Major Marriner.

"Exactly," corroborated Dr. Thorold. "That's how it appears to me. It did in the first place."

Anthony looked carefully round the room. "Perhaps, you're right," he conceded after a moment's consideration. Then, turning to the Chief Constable, he said: "The broken ebony stag, Major Marriner. You promised me that I could have a look at it. Did you happen to remember to bring the pieces down with you?"

"I did, Bathurst. I've had them with me for some time to show you. I have them in my pocket here."

The Major took a large envelope from his coat pocket and shook the contents from it on to the table. Anthony saw at once that the carved object had been given an extremely heavy blow. All the various parts of it were in tiny wooden fragments, with the exception of the antlers—as far as he could see, that is, from an examination such as this. He judged the figure of the stag to have stood about two and a half inches in height and to have been just about the same size in length. When it had been made, it had evidently been screwed to an ebony base, as the screws were still showing in a part of the little wooden platform that had been comparatively undamaged.

"It would indeed be a mighty man," he remarked, "who could break this ebony stag as it has been before with a blow from that pair of tongs."

"It not only would be," returned the Chief Constable dryly, "it *was*. Aren't you overlooking a most important point? Don't we know that by the death-blow that Forsyth received? If you'd like further information about it, have a word with Dr. Thorold here. He will emphasize matters for you."

"It was absolutely terrific," urged the doctor as Marriner turned to him, "and God alone knows what the weapon was that the murderer used. Nothing that I've ever seen could have produced the great tearing wound that Forsyth had in his chest. I'll call him Forsyth. That name's as good as any other to me."

"Tell me more, Dr. Thorold. What *was* the wound like?" asked Anthony quietly.

"A great torn, gaping hole," replied Dr. Thorold gravely and carefully choosing his words.

"A spear?" suggested Anthony.

"No, I don't think so. Too big."

"A horn?"

The doctor looked up curiously. "How do you mean—what sort of a horn?"

"A unicorn?" Anthony seemed perfectly serious as he put the question.

"There ain't no sich animal," quoted the doctor, "and you know it, Bathurst."

"I wonder," returned Anthony. "But Hamlet, Prince of Denmark, if you remember, once warned a certain Horatio concerning the possibilities contained in heaven and earth that were omitted from their philosophy. Tell me, Doctor, could the wound have been made by the antlers of an angry stag? The possibility intrigues me." He was still smiling.

Major Marriner and the doctor swung round and stared at him in amazement.

"Are you serious, Bathurst?" expostulated the Chief Constable.

Anthony shrugged his shoulders. "Perhaps. Perhaps not. Who knows? I don't like to eliminate anything."

He stooped down and replaced the tongs on the hearth. As he straightened himself after stooping, his eyes caught the open casement-window. He thought of the outhouse in the garden into which he had gone on the first occasion that he had visited the bungalow. The other two men saw a strange look come over his breath, "Of course!" Then he left the room where they were and walked to the back door of the bungalow, to return again to the others within a moment or so.

"Did you look carefully through the dead man's papers?" he asked Major Marriner.

"I did," replied the Chief Constable. "I can give you my word that nothing was found of any value. Bills, receipts, and normal correspondence. If I'm any judge, you'll probably find most of 'em on the floor in the front room."

"I'll go and look round," remarked Mr. Bathurst. "Perhaps you two gentlemen would care to accompany me."

Chapter IX
THE MARRIAGE CERTIFICATE

"If you come with me," he added, "you may not be wasting your time. It's possible that the search may be interesting."

Major Marriner and Dr. Thorold followed him up the passage into the front room. As has been already stated, papers, old letters, and documents were scattered in confusion and profusion over the carpeted floor. Anthony lay full length on the carpet.

"I could never see any sense," he said, "in being uncomfortable when comfort is near to one's hand—or feet! Never stand when yon may sit. Never sit when you may lie."

Major Marriner and Dr. Thorold sat on chairs and watched him. He picked up paper after paper from the floor and examined it carefully. Those that he looked at and discarded he arranged methodically in a heap.

"Bills," he said. "Just as you said, Major Marriner—bills and receipts. Some to do with this place and some which date back to the time he lived at Lanning. Hardly anything else of any account whatever. I take it that they have all come from out of there." He jerked his head towards an old-fashioned oblong flat-topped writing-desk with a lid and brass locks.

"I imagine so," said Major Marriner dryly. "The dead man doesn't seem to have had any other hiding-place. At any rate, we haven't found one."

Anthony Bathurst nodded and went on sorting out the scattered papers. One by one he went through them, shaking his head from time to time as though he were in doubt about something. Suddenly Major Marriner heard him murmur something almost under his breath. The Major bent forward and saw that Mr. Bathurst was holding a marriage certificate.

"Well, gentlemen, what do you make of this?" he asked quietly.

As he spoke, he rose from the floor and the two others crowded round him to see what it was he had unearthed. Anthony pointed to the items in the various columns with the tip of his finger.

"A marriage solemnized between Horace Samuel Forsyth, Carpenter, and Winifred Nina Swan, Nurse. Dated December the 25th, five years ago. Observe that the bridegroom was fifty-eight. The bride was twenty-nine. At St Peter's, East Hanningfield, Essex. Bridegroom's father—George Forsyth, Plasterer." Anthony turned and looked at each of his companions in turn. "Well, gentlemen?" he repeated. "What do you make of this—a marriage between a carpenter and a nurse?"

"What you are looking at," said the Chief Constable, "is Mrs. Forsyth's marriage certificate. That's obvious. Look—there you are— Winifred Nina Swan."

"Do you know," said Anthony, smiling. "I shouldn't be surprised if you're right."

Major Marriner went on, heedless of Mr. Bathurst's gentle irony.

"We knew that she was the wife of Forsyth's nephew. This Horace Samuel Forsyth that she married, according to this certificate, must have been Forsyth's nephew. It seems to me that it proves that she *is* genuine."

"I wonder," remarked Anthony, rubbing the ridge of his jaw with the points of his fingers. "I wonder. According to this certificate, he would be sixty-three now. About the same age, according to the good doctor here, as the dead man. Take twenty-one as the average span of a generation, that would make his father about eighty-four."

Major Marriner nodded. "That's quite all right. The real Forsyth was supposed to be seventy-three. Horace Samuel's father was doubtless his eldest brother. Probably the eldest one of the family. Eleven years between the two brothers."

Anthony's eyes held a far-away look. "And yet, Major Marriner, our informant, Mr. Wilfred Hatherley, whom I brought to see you and to whom you will readily admit we already owe much valuable information, is insistent that the genuine Forsyth article had no relations whatever."

"As far as he knew," retorted the Chief Constable, "to the best of his knowledge—and when you've said that you've said everything."

Anthony shook his head. "I don't know that you can dispose of the point quite as easily as that, Major Marriner."

The Major gestured good-humouredly. "The real Forsyth probably wasn't proud of his relations. Nobody ever is. You'll find I'm right, Bathurst, don't you worry."

"You may be. But it's only fair to say that I feel much less certain about it than you do. Let me ask you a question—do you mind?"

"Go on. Ask away."

Anthony held up the marriage certificate of Horace Samuel and Winifred Nina. Dr. Thorold and the Chief Constable gazed at him interestedly.

"Did anything else strike you here, Major Marriner?"

"Yes, of course it did."

"And it was?"

"Why, the maiden name of the bride, of course. Winifred Nina Swan. I gave you information regarding that name of Swan when I first called upon you. It was given to me by Mrs. Forsyth as that of a constant visitor to the dead man's bungalow. A Mrs. Swan. Once a month she used to come. This marriage certificate makes it all the more clear. It's as plain as a pike-staff. Mrs. Swan, Mrs. Margaret Swan, was Forsyth's nephew's mother-in-law." Major Marriner concluded his statement on a note of triumph.

"Once a month therefore was probably enough," contributed the doctor with a chuckle.

"And yet," rejoined Mr. Bathurst gravely, "according to what you told me in the first place, this Mrs. Margaret Swan was a middle-aged woman whom the dead man had known for years."

"That's what Mrs. Forsyth told me," interposed Major Marriner.

"In other words, then," countered Anthony, "that description that I have just given you was Mrs. Forsyth's description of a lady who was no less than her own mother. Yes?"

There came a silence.

"Somehow, gentlemen, Mrs. Winifred Nina doesn't please me."

Major Marriner's face showed annoyance.

"The address of the Swans," proceeded Mr. Bathurst, "five years ago, in the terms of this certificate, was Number 22 Pemberton Street, Chelmsford. So that it should not be difficult to trace the family if we want to. The father of the bride is shown here as Charles Tindall Swan, a dairyman, full, probably, of the milk of human kindness."

He paused and waited for the Chief Constable's comments.

"Bathurst," he said at length, "I am beginning to think more on the lines on which you are thinking. I, too, am beginning to wonder." He paced the room with quick, decisive steps.

"I anticipated from sheer optimism that I should partly convince you," returned Anthony lightly. He stooped to pick up the pile of papers through which he had sorted. He placed them on the top of the flat-lidded writing-desk. "If we only knew what they're after! If we only had a clue of the flimsiest nature! But here we are with—" He swung round to the Chief Constable and spoke almost passionately. "It's all wrong, you know, sir! The dead man was not Robert Forsyth. Not on your life! I'll go the whole hog on that. And if we accept that as true,

Mrs. Forsyth, as we know her, was not his nephew's wife. She couldn't have been. Horace Samuel Forsyth was not Robert Forsyth's—" For the second time in quick succession he stopped abruptly.

Major Marriner and the doctor waited for him to speak.

"Well?" said the former eventually.

"Gentlemen," he said quietly, "can't you see now why Mrs. Forsyth disappeared? She knew that matters might become too warm for her if she stayed. She has taken fright, of course."

"Just a minute," said the Chief Constable. "Where are we? Say what you like—attempt to prove what you like—but that certificate conclusively shows that there *is* a Mrs. Winifred Forsyth who was *née* Swan. Is the woman who lived here she or not? You say that the man who died here was not Forsyth. Admitted that to be true, who, then, was the woman that lived with him? Was she also playing the part of a Forsyth? The whole thing seems to me very much as you yourself said—confusion worse confounded. If not, you are certainly finding difficulties where there weren't any, and in that case why meet trouble half-way?"

"Perhaps," returned Anthony, "but we don't know yet, and therefore it isn't any earthly use to keep on conjecturing. Let me try to attack from another angle. What puzzles me chiefly is this. Let us look at it. If the murderer was seeking something that he imagined was hidden somewhere here, why did he break up that little carved stag? I think that he must have *known* something which caused him to think that the stag might be, or even *was*, a likely place of concealment. That's point number one. Secondly, it seems to me that the broken stag *proves* something else, and proves it conclusively. I wonder if you are following me, gentlemen."

Anthony Bathurst paused and waited for possible replies. Marriner made no comment.

"Yes, I think I get your drift," said Dr. Thorold. "You mean that the object that is being sought by the murderer must be a very small one. Am I right?"

Anthony smiled. "Congratulations, Doctor. Take a hundred per cent. You have seen my meaning at once." He handed his cigarette case to his two companions. "Question," he said quietly: "*has* the murderer been successful in his search? How can we answer that?"

"We don't know. We can't tell. The only way by which we shall find out will be to see whether he comes again or not. And I'm presuming that he's already called twice." Major Marriner expressed himself emphatically.

Dr. Thorold looked up suddenly. "I say," he said, "did either of you fellows hear a step?"

"Where?"

"Outside the bungalow. And not far away at that. I'll swear I did—a moment or so ago."

"We will investigate. Come along," announced Anthony.

The three men went to the front door of the bungalow. There was nobody, however, in sight.

"Must have been mistaken, I suppose," muttered Dr. Thorold. "But I'd have sworn . . ."

Anthony led the way round to the back.

"There's a shed or small outhouse of sorts round at the back here," he said. "I made its acquaintance on the occasion of my first visit. It wouldn't be a bad idea to have a glance in there. It seems to me that it would be a comparatively easy matter for anybody to slip in there unobserved if a quick hiding-place were wanted. What do you think?"

Dr. Thorold and the Chief Constable followed Anthony round to the back of the bungalow. Anthony pushed open the door of the shed. But it was empty of any person. To his eye, it looked to be exactly as he had last seen it. There was the same miscellaneous collection of boxes, deck-chairs, and gardening implements.

"Our friend was evidently not a teetotaller," remarked Dr. Thorold, painting to the box on which were stacked the empty bottles. "I'm thinking it a pity that I didn't number him amongst my social acquaintances."

"Looks like it, certainly," returned Mr. Bathurst. He stood there for a few moments, looking at the various articles which the shed housed. "Gentlemen," he said rather sternly, "if you possessed something which had a purely extrinsic value and which somebody else wanted very badly, even to the limit of murder, you might attempt to throw dust into evil faces by hiding that something in a most unlikely place. It's conceivable, I think."

"It's possible, I suppose," conceded the Chief Constable, "putting it in the way that you have. Do you intend to search this tool-shed?"

Anthony made no reply. The Major persisted in his point.

"Do you mean to make an intensive, systematic search?"

"Well, it won't take long, will it? Even as it is, I have a hunch."

"In what direction?" demanded the doctor with undoubted eagerness.

"Towards those bottles," replied Anthony. "Who would look for anything valuable under a stack of empty beer- and spirit-bottles, eh, Major Marriner? Eh, Dr. Thorold?"

Anthony strode quickly towards the large box in which the bottles had been heaped. He carefully took them out one by one. Pints, quarts, and empty spirit-bottles. His enthusiasm must have been infectious, for the others watched him steadily. Gradually he worked his way down to the bottom of the heaped-up pile. Suddenly they saw his grey eyes flash. Mr. Bathurst carefully put his hand into a corner of the box and took out a small object. Major Marriner, standing where he was, was unable to see clearly. As Anthony Bathurst's hand closed over the object, the Chief Constable was still unaware as to what the object really was. He and Dr. Thorold crowded round Anthony to examine his find.

"An ebony stag, gentlemen," said the last-named, "a carved ebony stag, and I believe that ebony stags possess more than an ordinary interest for us. Especially as this one appears to be made of real ebony."

Chapter X
THE STAG'S MESSAGE

"Well I'm blessed!" declared Dr. Thorold.

"How many of these damned things are there?" demanded the Chief Constable.

"I fancy, sir," returned Anthony in answer to him, "that this one will be found to complete the collection."

"Why? I don't see how you can assert that. What grounds have you for saying that?"

"I think that this one will prove to be the authentic article. The broken one of the night of the murder was probably a fake. It was planted in the house, I would suggest, to deceive the murderer."

"Authentic?" queried Major Marriner, apparently puzzled by the word. "How do you mean—authentic?"

"Perhaps I shall be able to demonstrate my point to you." Anthony turned over the carved stag in his hand. "What I mean by my description of 'authentic' is this. I mean that this one that I hold here is, in all probability, the stag that was the desired object. The other—the one that was smashed, presumably by the murderer—was the substitute. If you prefer the word, the dummy, the fake. Now let us turn our attention to the one that we have here. I'm optimistic enough to think that it may bring us results." Anthony held the carved ebony figure in front of the two men. "I wonder what is the concealed value of this little object, gentlemen, that a man or men are prepared to go to such lengths to handle it."

"The workmanship is good," said Dr. Thorold. "Look at the antlers alone to see that. Beautifully carved." He pointed to the stag's antlers.

"The name of this bungalow is 'The Antlers'," said Mr. Bathurst softly. "I wonder."

"Strange," said the Chief Constable.

"Damned coincidence," said Dr. Thorold.

"I don't think so," returned Anthony with a shake of the head. "To me, much more like malice aforethought and design definite."

The doctor held out his hand to take the stag from him. Anthony Bathurst handed it to him. Dr. Thorold put his finger against the top point of the right antler.

"This fellow is what is known as a 'twelve-pointer'," he declared. "Here, see what I mean?"

As his finger pressed the point of the antler there came a faint click, and to the three men's utter astonishment a tiny ball of rolled-up, yellowish paper shot into the palm of Dr. Thorold's hand. Dr. Thorold gave a sharp cry of surprise as he saw the paper. The eyes of the Chief Constable showed his amazement. Anthony himself was overjoyed.

"We progress. I was right. This is going to help a lot," he cried.

The doctor handed the tiny pilule of paper to Major Marriner.

"Here you are, sir," he said. "This is your pigeon, not mine. You had better decipher it, whatever it is."

The Chief Constable carefully unscrewed the paper pellet and smoothed it out. As he did so, Anthony bent down and looked over his shoulder with eager curiosity. He saw some lines—eight in number—most carefully written. The letters were exceedingly tiny, but beautifully described. Calligraphy indeed! Anthony read the words that he saw there to the others:

> "When Death with Icy Wings did stalk,
> For twice two hundred human souls,
> I drew the Serpents from their Holes,
> To meet a Waterloo at Chalke.
> Try then the Sails that never fly,
> My Royal Burden Straight to find,
> For One shall Live if One shall Die,
> If Out of Sight,—*not* Out of Mind."

"Seems gibberish to me," said Major Marriner curtly.

"I agree," said Thorold.

"Gibberish it may be, perhaps," rejoined Mr. Bathurst, "but gibberish, nevertheless, with a wealth of hidden meaning. You can bet your life on that."

"Which we must find," declared the doctor.

"Which we must find," reiterated Anthony gravely, with a movement of the head. He repeated the eight lines aloud. "The presence of the 'Chalke' proves, gentlemen, that we are on the right track. That's obvious. But as to what the other lines mean—I'm afraid that our brains will have to be well racked indeed before a solution comes to us." He wrinkled his brow. "I wonder why he wrote—"

"Wrote what?" demanded the Chief Constable.

"'A' Waterloo—instead of 'my' Waterloo. Especially when you consider that the pronoun in the first person was employed in the immediately preceding line."

Neither the Chief Constable nor the doctor replied. It is doubtful whether either of them followed Anthony's line of reasoning. Dr. Thorold offered criticism again—of the lines this time.

"I never knew," he remarked dryly, "that anything stalked on wings. That's a new one on me. I always thought that you stalked on feet."

Anthony smiled. "I suggest," he said, "that death on this occasion 'stalked'—for the main reason that the word 'stalk' rhymes with the highly important word 'Chalke'. In fact, I don't think that there's the slightest doubt about it."

"Can you make anything of the verse, Bathurst?" asked Major Marriner.

"Nothing beyond general impressions at the moment, sir," responded Anthony. "For instance, the first two lines would seem to suggest a disaster of some kind. An accident which involved the death of four hundred people. But when it happened, or where—that's another matter. The next line, the third, concerning the serpent, I must candidly confess, leaves me stone cold. I haven't the slightest idea to what it refers. The same with the fourth. 'To meet a Waterloo at Chalke' might well mean anything. 'Try then the Sails that never fly', I take it, is a direction as to where something, presumably valuable, is buried. In that relation, consider the phrase 'My Royal Burden'. The rest, I'm afraid, signifies nothing to me. Or even less than nothing. I shall have to get right down to it later on, in the hope that in time I may be lucky enough to hit on a solution. Patience, gentlemen, and shuffle the cards. You know the idea."

Dr. Thorold, although listening intently, continued to study the small piece of paper.

"More than one?"

"I fear so. How old is this message, would you say?"

Thorold considered the question.

"Very doubtful, isn't it?"

"You have the colour of the paper and the style of the handwriting to assist you. Each may help you a little."

Dr. Thorold turned over the scrap of paper.

"Hello," he cried, "there's something else on this side."

"Letters," said Anthony, looking over his shoulder. He read them out aloud: "Z/J/AHEI."

"The murderer's monomark. About as intelligible as the rest of it," declared the Chief Constable with sarcasm. "Of all the unlikely letters, you have plenty there."

"And yet not one of them repeated," added Anthony Bathurst, "which fact doesn't make things any easier."

"What do the strokes in between represent?" queried Dr. Thorold.

Anthony shook his head. "That's something else that will require to be looked at, Doctor. Leave the contemplation of it for a moment and let us come back to the question that I asked you a moment or so ago. How old is that message?"

"No idea," returned Dr. Thorold. "None whatever."

"What about you, sir?" asked Anthony of the Chief Constable.

"If I ventured an opinion, it would be but a guess," replied Major Marriner. "What is your own opinion? That's more important."

Anthony looked hard at the little square of paper. "I should put the date," he said, "at somewhere about fifty years ago—perhaps at even a trifle more than that."

"On what do you base that opinion?" asked Marriner.

"Principally on the handwriting, sir. Or, rather, I should say on the style of the handwriting. Going a little further—on the way, let me say, in which the various capital letters have been formed. I have, I sometimes think unfortunately, three aunts and two uncles—I was once one worse off—and they all write like that. Look at the curls on the 'M' and the 'W'." His finger tapped the little piece of paper. "I may be wrong, of course, but I don't think you'll find that I'm very far out in my time estimate."

Dr. Thorold nodded his acquiescence.

"Yes, I know what you mean, Bathurst. I know many people myself who write very much in this style. It was probably taught at the time you mention by most of the writing-teachers."

The Chief Constable also expressed his agreement.

"Yes, I know what you mean, too. I also number amongst my acquaintances several people who write in much the same way. They would be roughly contemporary, I should say, with the people you have mentioned."

Anthony turned to him with a more practical issue.

"How many of your own men have you still working on the case, sir?"

"Three," answered Major Marriner.

"Any headway?"

"None at all." Chief Constable shook his head. "They run up against dead ends and blank walls every time and every way they go," he added.

"Pity," declared Anthony Bathurst.

"Occasionally they manage to pick up valuable information which, if they can't use it to advantage themselves, proves valuable in other hands when passed on. What's your own line of campaign now?" asked Marriner.

"Lines, sir, more than line. The lines of the stag. For one thing, I have to dig the meaning out of this message. For another, there is Mrs. Forsyth, *née* Winifred Nina Swan. I am also attracted by *(a)* the town of Lanning, *(b)* by the Rev. C.A. Sellon, Vicar of St. Veronica's, and *(c)* by various habitués of the 'Tracy Arms'. At the same time, though, this latest find gives me the greatest hope of all." He held out the message from the antlers of the stag.

The Chief Constable led the way out of the outhouse.

"If you want me again, Bathurst, during the next few days, give me a tinkle. And if you run across anything at all important that you think I ought to know, please let me know at once. Well, I'll be getting along now. Coming, Doctor?"

He and Dr. Thorold shook hands with Anthony outside the front door of the bungalow and left him to his meditations. Mr. Bathurst felt that the sooner he could get right down to a close study of the written message, the better. Slowly he made his way back to the "Tracy Arms". He was sorry now that he had promised to dine with Captain Stromm on the *Vaar* that evening. He felt that he could employ the time better, especially since this latest development.

When he reached the hotel, McCracken and Burns were standing in the entrance. The former greeted him boisterously. Mr. Bathurst smiled congenially and went straight to his room.

Chapter XI
SUPPLIANT LADY

LATE that afternoon Mr. Bathurst sat in a chair in his bedroom and examined the paper that had come, at Dr, Thorold's persuasion, from the antlers of the ebony stag. He had always been a disciple of order and method, and on that account he concentrated on the first line—"When Death with Icy Wings did stalk". A tragedy of some kind, undoubtedly, the happening of which belonged to history. He had already come to the conclusion that whereas "stalk" was a word which had been used for rhyming reasons, as he had previously stated, and was therefore unimportant, the word "Icy" was probably the key-word of the line. The death that had come as a result of this tragedy had come under conditions of cold—of extreme cold. The people who had perished had not died in a fire, for instance! Unless . . . Mr. Bathurst began to wonder. Unless the writer of the message had been a merchant of metaphors and was regarding death as always grim and chill and of the grave, no matter what route it came a-travelling. This might well prove to be an awkward complication. But, on the whole, as he thought over the problem, he was inclined to consider that his first supposition was the correct one—that this tragedy at which the verse hinted had occurred in the circumstance of extreme cold. He would start with those premises. Mr. Bathurst made an appropriate note to that effect on a pad of writing-paper that he had placed at his elbow. He had just finished making the note when, to his surprise, he heard a faint tap on his door. The surprise evaporated and Mr. Bathurst frowned.

The last thing that he desired at this moment was an interruption of any kind. He made no sound. On the other hand, he waited to see if the tap would be repeated, hoping that if he gave no response the caller would accept the position and decide on departure. But in this he was disappointed. After the lapse of a few seconds he heard the tap again. Mr. Bathurst's frown grew more intense. He carefully replaced the paper within his wallet and pushed aside the writing-pad before walking to the door to answer the caller, whoever it might turn out to be.

Mr. Bathurst opened the door, and to his utter amazement a girl stood on the threshold. It was the girl whom Anthony already knew as Heather. Her eyes held both anxiety and entreaty.

"I am terribly sorry to trouble you, but may I come in for just a few moments? I am almost desperate. I want your help badly. I have watched you—you look kind, and I feel that I can trust you. You see, a girl always knows." She rattled these sentences at such a pace that she finished up almost breathless.

For a split second Anthony was in doubt what to do. Then—as was his usual habit—he took a chance.

"Please come in," he said.

The girl obeyed, needing no second bidding. She slipped through the door with delicate grace. Her deep-blue eyes and corn-coloured hair made her infinitely attractive.

"Sit down," said Anthony to her quietly.

Without any apparent selection, she took the chair that be had vacated in order to answer her knock. Anthony disdained the other chair and stood opposite to her.

"Now, what is it that you want of me?" he asked her.

"Your name is Anthony Bathurst, is it not?" she asked him tremulously.

"It is. How did you know?" He spoke evenly, but her statement gave him a shock of surprise. Not for a moment had he expected her to undermine his incognito so summarily and strangely. He made no attempt to defend it or deny her statement.

"I have seen your photograph many times and recognized you at once, I have a friend who's a film-star. She was photographed the same afternoon as you at one of the West End studios—Helena Thesselmar. She told me all about it at the time. It was partly through knowing who you were that I plucked up courage enough to come up here to your room and speak to you. Believe me, I should have never approached a man whom I regarded as a complete stranger."

Anthony now assumed the defensive. "Would you please tell me this—who else knows of my identity besides you?"

She shook her head. The gesture seemed the epitome of innocence.

"Do you mean because of me and my knowledge—anybody whom I have told?"

He smiled at her gravely. "That was the meaning I intended to convey."

She realized what he meant. "Oh, nobody—through me. Not a soul, I assure you. I haven't breathed a word to anybody. I wouldn't dream of doing so."

Somehow Anthony felt that she was speaking the truth. If she were not, then, indeed, she was a consummate actress.

"I am glad of that," he said quietly. "Not that it matters a great deal, but I am here for a few days' rest and would prefer, if possible, to be let alone."

"I am sorry, then, that I have troubled you. But I have been getting you wrong. I have been imagining all the time that you were spending your time here on account of the bungalow murder. What else would one think? You will forgive me?" She spoke with eager impetuosity.

Anthony evaded the direct issue. He smiled at her.

"In the circumstances, perhaps a legitimate and understandable mistake on your part. We will agree to forget it. But all this, I take it, has nothing to do with the reason of your coming here to see me now?"

"Of course not. I hardly know where to begin." She twisted a handkerchief in her hands as she spoke to him.

Anthony said nothing. He awaited her pleasure. She chose her words carefully.

"You have seen me and my party in the dining-room—I know that. The lady who is with me is my employer. Perhaps that statement is a surprise to you?" She waited for his reply.

"It is. I had not considered that possibility."

She nodded, as though confirming her opinion. "I thought that perhaps you hadn't looked at us in that light. The lady's name is Freda Glen. You may remember her as an actress. I am her companion." She paused. "First of all, I ought to tell you that she suffers extremely bad health."

Anthony interrupted her. "Is that strictly true? I don't think that you've told me your name yet."

"I am sorry. My name is Barton—Heather Barton."

"Is your statement, Miss Barton, concerning Miss Glen's health strictly true? Would it not be more accurate to say that much of Miss Glen's ill health has been, and is, brought upon her by herself?"

"You mean—?"

"I mean that unless I am greatly mistaken, this lady who is your employer is in the habit of taking dangerous drugs. Am I right, Miss Barton?"

Her eyes wandered wildly round the room. Then she nodded her head slowly and spoke almost in a whisper.

"Yes, that is true; you are quite right. But how did you know? It is partly about that that I have come to see you."

"It was a fairly long shot on my part. I formed that opinion from the lady's general appearance and from her habitual manner."

"The trouble is drink, unhappily, as well as drugs. She has recently spent six months in a private nursing-home. When she came out, she was certainly better—for a time. But the last few weeks have been terrible. She is almost as bad again as ever. When Mr. Mulrenan—"

Anthony Bathurst interposed deliberately, "Who is Mulrenan—I mean, in relation to Miss Glen, or even to you?"

"Mr. Mulrenan is an old friend of Miss Glen's. She used to be on the stage, as I told you just now. He knew her in those early days of hers. I ought to tell you as well that Miss Glen is an exceedingly wealthy lady."

"Indeed?" Anthony raised his eyebrows.

"Yes. When she was on the stage, her aunt died. She had suffered bad health for years. This old lady was very rich and Freda was her only relation in the world. She left Freda the whole of her fortune— over forty thousand pounds and a house in Lancaster Gate. Freda left the stage immediately the legacy came to her. She still—Freda, I mean—keeps up the establishment, but of recent times we haven't spent a great deal of time in town. For one thing, Freda doesn't care for it, and, for another, her health is better in the country. A week ago Mr. Mulrenan wrote a letter to Freda and invited her to come and stay down here. I wasn't attracted by the offer at all. I advised her not to come, but she is dreadfully obstinate. I should have known better. You see, it's like this. Any suggestion that you make to her, or any piece of advice that you give to her, seems to make her only the more determined to do the opposite. That's always the case. So, of course, the inevitable happened and we accepted Mr. Mulrenan's invitation and came down here to Upchalke."

"And what was behind Mr. Mulrenan's invitation?"

She looked at him with startled eyes. "That is what I am coming to. I am afraid of him. I think"—she looked round the room apprehensively as she spoke and lowered her voice—"I think that he is trying to get Freda out of the way in order to get hold of her money. Indeed, I am sure of it."

"But how can he do that?"

"I know that it seems utterly absurd, but he has a tremendous influence over her. He dominates her completely. He keeps on making her drink and I am almost sure that he is supplying her with more and more cocaine. I think that he is trying to get her more and more stupefied until one day or night, without her knowing what she is doing, he will induce her to make a will in his favour. He has also a plan to make her invest a lot of money. Promises a tenfold return, but I'm certain it's a fake."

"This 'will' business to which you have made reference is a very difficult matter to prove, Miss Barton, if I may say so."

"I know. Only too well."

Her eyes met his. He saw how moved she was.

"That is what makes me all the more frightened."

"Who is the other man staying here with you?" inquired Anthony.

"That's Wagstaff, the chauffeur. He has been Miss Glen's chauffeur ever since she left the stage. I think that he can be trusted. In his queer way he's very attached to Freda—but even he seems swayed by whatever Mr. Mulrenan says or does."

Anthony thought hard. "I see. What do you want me to do?" he asked her.

"Anything that will help me. I fear that every day I delay the position becomes more critical, Mr. Mulrenan may achieve one of his objects at any time, it seems to me."

"I'll you what to do," said Anthony hopefully. "Get into touch at once with Miss Glen's medical adviser and also her solicitor—I've no doubt that you know them both—explain the position as you see it to both of them. If you want any more help in making the case clear to them, let me know and I'll come in as your support willingly."

She looked at him. Her lips were parted.

"I know her doctor, of course, and I'll try to find out who her solicitors are. Thank you. I'll do as you suggest."

She rose from her chair, preparatory to departure.

"Thank you again, Mr. Bathurst. You have been most kind."

"Don't worry over that, Miss Barton. Any help that I am able to give you will be given, I assure you, most willingly. Don't hesitate to call on me again should you so desire. But watch Mulrenan as closely as you can."

As he looked at her now, he was impressed more than ever as to the extent of the girl's worry and anxiety. She looked dazed. Her eyes wandered round the room again as they had when she had first entered. She stood irresolutely by the door, as though in a quandary which way to turn. Her hand stopped on the handle of the door.

"Mr. Bathurst," she said, "there is one more thing that I must ask you before I go. You will not mention to anybody that I have come to you like this for help, will you? Promise me, please. I ask you this because it is important."

Anthony Bathurst went quickly to her side.

"Rely on me, Miss Barton. This visit shall remain entirely between you and me."

"Thank you," she said again. "If it were known . . . to certain people . . . that I had been to see you like this . . . the consequences to me might be very unfortunate. You understand me? I don't think that Mr. Mulrenan would be altogether pleasant if he found out that any of his plans were thwarted, and I am not a very brave person. I am afraid of what he might do."

"Don't think about that, and don't worry about anything. He shall never know from me, Miss Barton."

She flashed a look of gratitude from out of her blue eyes and slipped through the door.

Anthony closed it quickly behind her. He went back to the chair in which he had been sitting when Heather Barton's entry had interrupted him. "Strange business that!" he thought as he seated himself. "To a woman alone in the world and comparatively unprotected, the possession of money is far from an unmixed blessing. There's usually some damned scoundrel on the look-out for bites. Drink and drugs and an unprincipled scoundrel at the woman's side make a particularly pernicious combination. Ah, well . . . let's hope that the intervention of accredited people will be in time to spoil Mr. Mulrenan's little game, whatever it may be!"

Mr. Bathurst took his wallet from his pocket and turned his attention again to the message from the antlers of the ebony stag. He carefully re-read the note that he had already made with reference to Line Number One and recollected his thoughts. It will be remembered that the second line ran, "For twice two hundred human souls". That is to say death for four hundred people. This was a comparatively simple matter. This reference was intended undoubtedly to a tragedy or disaster of some magnitude involving the fate of four hundred people, just as he had outlined to the Chief Constable and Dr. Thorold. So far, so good. Now for Line Number Three. "I drew the Serpents from their Holes". Utterly unintelligible! Mr. Bathurst shook his head. Who or what draws serpents from holes . . . beyond, possibly, a snake-charmer? He determined as a second resort to take the line in conjunction with the line that immediately followed it. "To meet a Waterloo at Chalke." Equally unintelligible! Mr. Bathurst's mind cast here and there in a variety of directions. He tested this allusion and that significance. To no avail. His brain remained sterile. And he had made no headway whatever when his wrist-watch told him that the time had come for him to dress for dinner with the skipper of the *Vaar*, Captain Vass. He slipped the papers that he had been studying into a drawer. His wallet he locked up with them. It was too bulky to be carried comfortably in the pocket of a dinner-jacket.

CHAPTER XII
MR. BATHURST DINES ON BOARD

ANTHONY Bathurst waited for Captain Stromm in the vestibule of the "Tracy Arms". The gallant captain was a trifle late and he apologized to Anthony profusely.

"I have been out walking this afternoon," he explained, "and I went farther than was my intention. The result was that I tired myself somewhat. The scenery over by Bride Bay . . . it is truly delightful."

Anthony conventionally assented.

"I have ordered a car for us," went on Captain Stromm. "It will take us down to the harbour in what you English call—no time. It should be here."

As he spoke, the car arrived. On the way to the harbour, Stromm talked of his appreciation of England and English customs. Anthony, in no mood for argument, accepted his conclusions cheerfully. They reached the corner of the harbour, where the traffic was forced to stop. Stromm paid the driver and joined Anthony on the path.

"I've arranged for him to pick us up at 11.45," he said.

Suddenly Anthony noticed Hatherley, standing on the cobbled path leading to the end of the harbour, with a camera in his hand. Hatherley turned and waved to him.

"Getting a few snaps," he cried, "before I go home. Mustn't miss *all* the beauties of nature. Cheero!"

Anthony waved back, and then accompanied Stromm along the top of Chalke Harbour past the ancient customs-office and toll-re-ceipt-house until they reached the *Vaar*. She was a trim little craft and, emptied of her cargo, rode saucily on the top of the water.

"She goes back to Narvik the day after tomorrow," said Captain Stromm. "That is why Vass wanted me to dine on board either tonight or tomorrow evening."

Pleased with what he could see of the boat, Anthony followed Stromm aboard. He noticed that the *Vaar* was well kept and clean. All traces of the débris of the cargo-unloading of the previous days had already been cleared away. Captain Stromm beckoned to him and led the way down the companion to tap on the door of what was obviously the captain's cabin. A short, stout, florid-faced man with the vestiges of a fair moustache answered the knock.

"Ah," he said, "it is you, Captain Stromm! I was expecting you. And this is your friend that you have brought with you? I am honoured. Come in, sir. Welcome to the *Vaar*."

"This is Mr. Lotherington," returned Stromm, "and this is Captain Vass, master of the *Vaar*. Although I have only known him at all intimately for a few days, I already feel that Captain Vass is an old friend, and when he asked me to dine with him before he returns to my native country I felt that I could not refuse."

Anthony entered the cabin and shook hands with Vass. The man's face and manner at once appealed to him.

"It is not my habit to take passengers," said Vass, "but on this little voyage it is somewhat remarkable that I have had two. Captain Stromm here, and a young doctor from Narvik who is taking a few days' holiday from the rigours of his profession. This is his idea of a holiday, if you please! Did you ever believe? It is certainly not mine. He has helped the crew to unload the timber every day that they have been at work. He wears gloves—his hands are so soft but he works well. He is no—what you say?—Ciss-ee. Indeed, he is far from that. But he calls it, you understand, Mr. Lotherington, a holiday. The absurd humour of some people. Ha, ha!"

Vass's voice merged into a rumble of heavy laughter. His English was excellent.

"He has gone on shore tonight. I expect that he will find a girl. He is young, and therefore foolish. Ah, well, who am I to blame him? But sit down, Mr. Lotherington, and you, Captain Stromm. Dinner will not be very many minutes. I have whipped it up so that I should not disappoint you. Are you better, Captain Stromm?"

Stromm nodded. "Oh yes, well—quite well now."

Vass turned to Anthony. "He was unlucky on the voyage here. A bad cold kept him in his bunk."

Vass went to the door of his cabin and called for the steward. Anthony heard him give orders, to the man who came, in a sharp tone. The skipper returned to his two guests, rubbing his hands.

"Dinner will be served within five minutes, gentlemen. In fact, the steward tells me that he is almost ready now."

Captain Stromm murmured a commonplace. Anthony put a question.

"How often do you find your way to Chalke, Captain Vass?"

"About once every two months, Mr. Lotherington. At other times I go to one of your other English ports—Marstone. One voyage I go there—the next I come here. Unless, of course, I am commissioned specially and the profit is good. The last time I was here in Chalke was just after what you call your August Bank Holiday. Crowds assembled here on the harbour to watch my crew at their work of unloading.

I felt as though I were one of the big summer attractions that I see everywhere advertised."

A knock on the cabin door heralded the steward and dinner. As the courses followed one another, Anthony realized that their host was indeed "doing very well". An excellent turtle soup, a lobster salad, and a beautifully tender duck were accompanied by three different wines, the quality of which in each case could not be questioned. In addition, Vass, for his station, proved to be a well-informed man, and, with Stromm in opposition to him upon most counts, the conversation speedily became of distinct interest, and time passed on rapid wing. When the meal came to the finish, Vass offered to show Anthony over the boat.

"Do you know what I'm going to do? I am going to make Captain Stromm wish that he were returning with me," he declared jocularly, "instead of staying in your country for another month to enjoy his long-delayed visit."

Stromm laughed at Vass's pride in his vessel.

"There are other boats, Captain Vass, which will be pleased to take me back home when the time comes for me to return. I shall find one, never fear," he replied.

Vass shook his head jovially. "There is only one *Vaar*, so that your statement does not 'hold the water', as you English say. But come, Mr. Lotherington, let me show you over my grand little boat. I can tell you that I am very proud of her. I have every modern convenience and even carry a wireless-operator—in case, you know."

Anthony followed him up the companion.

"I am just a little bit of a tease. I like to chaff him," he said, in explanatory reference to Stromm; "but he is a good fellow."

"Do you often carry passengers?" inquired Anthony.

"Very seldom. Just sometimes, when an occasion comes along. But Captain Stromm, you see, he lives in Narvik. I believe that he has lived there many years. He was very flattering to me when he came on board at Narvik to see me. Told me how often he had admired the *Vaar*, and had always intended to sail in her when the time came for his holiday in England. Passengers?" Captain Vass paused, shook his head emphatically, and then continued his speech almost immediately. "Passengers, you say? That to me is a remark full of interest.

For from memory I think that I have carried eight on all my voyages during the last two years. We will test it. It is interesting. For let me tell you, Mr. Lotherington, that if I am proud of my boat, I am also proud of my memory."

They stood on the *Vaar's* deck. Vass called aft:

"Volla, come here, will you?"

The steward who had brought in the dinner came running up. Vass gave him an order in Swedish. The steward nodded his understanding, touched his forehead, and clambered quickly down the companion. Within two minutes he was back on deck with them, carrying a brown-covered book almost of ledger size and shape. Vass took it from him and opened it.

"My passenger-list," he remarked proudly. "Here you are, Mr. Lotherington; here we have a complete list of the passengers that I have carried since I took over the command of the boat. That's six years ago—over six years. It was six years on the 22nd of July last. Here are the names of the passengers during those six years and three months."

Anthony saw that Captain Vass was engaged in counting the names.

"Eight!" he cried, with a note of triumph. "I said eight and, by Saint Christopher, I was right! I can well remember each and every one of them who has sailed with me. From the first one that I carried, down to our good friend Captain Stromm here, who came to me and asked me to bring him a week ago." Vass held the book in front of Anthony Bathurst. "Look for yourself, Mr. Lotherington, and see that I am playing the game and not cheating you. You can read the names."

Anthony, secretly amused at Vass's eagerness to prove his point and vindicate his power of memory, took the *Vaar's* passenger-list from its skipper's hand. He at once saw that it was true that Vass had been accurate in his statement. Anthony glanced almost idly at the list of names. From Rolf Larsen, the first name in order, to Dr. Erik Hölm of Ranna and Captain Falk Stromm of 14, Heertje, Narvik, Sweden, who had embarked on the ship on October 22nd, and whose was the last name on the list. Then something caught Anthony Bathurst's eye and arrested his attention. The fifth name in Captain Vass's passenger-list was McCracken. More than that—it was no less than Andrew McCracken. Vass seemed to understand what it was that had riveted Anthony's attention.

"You have seen Mr. McCracken's name there, yes?"

Anthony nodded. "Is it the Mr. McCracken whom I have met at Upchalke? I might describe him as a fairly frequent visitor to the 'Tracy Arms'."

Vass nodded eagerly. "Yes, of course. None other than he. And a charming man, too. And a man with a wealth of anecdote. A truly wonderful companion."

"What, then, has brought him on the *Vaar*?" inquired Anthony innocently.

Vass spread out his hands with a suggestion of resignation. He puffed out his cheeks in mock heroics and his eyes bulged with good-natured humour.

"A holiday, Mr. Lotherington. No more and no less. Mr. McCracken had seen me and my ship here in the harbour more than once and, like Captain Stromm at Narvik, had fallen in love with my craft. I took him to Sweden a year ago and brought him back. Very much the same as I am doing now with Dr. Hölm, except that the good McCracken did no work. Oh no! He only drank beer, which meant that he had no time for work. It is a grand holiday, let me tell you, on the *Vaar* if the weather remembers to be on good behaviour. It might even make a man of an old woman."

Anthony, deep in thought, returned the passenger-list to Captain Vass. The latter called again to the steward, Volla, and gave instructions for the book to be replaced. The companionable Vass linked his arm in Mr. Bathurst's, and as they turned they were joined by Captain Stromm. At Vass's request, the three men made a short tour of the ship. Vass was always keen and enthusiastic to point out the many excellences of the vessel which he was so obviously proud to command.

In due time they returned to Vass's cabin. He winked knowingly at his guests, bent down, opened the door of a small cabinet, and produced a stone bottle of Hollands gin.

"I am not a Dutchman," he said, almost with an air of apology, "but I must confess that I am more than partial to this spirit of theirs. What you call the old 'Squareface'. You gentlemen will do me the honour to join me, I have no doubt. You will find cigars on the table there. Better than that—first-class cigars!"

Vass poured out the spirits and handed the glasses to his two companions. Anthony chose his cigar and lit up.

"Your health, Captain Vass, and good fortune to the *Vaar*. A trim little craft if ever there were one, with a skipper who is more than worthy of her. What say you, Captain Stromm?"

Stromm's genial face bore testimony to his agreement.

"I echo your opinions, Mr. Lotherington. When I selected the *Vaar* for my long-delayed visit to your country, it was the result of no haphazard or idle choice. I did so deliberately. I had watched her closely many a time as she lay in the harbour in my home town. And, believe it or not, I flatter myself that I know a good thing when I see one."

His eyes twinkled and Vass's face was wreathed in delight at Stromm's praise of his ship. The three men sat. Vass poured out more of his favourite cordial. The conversation grew more boister-ous. It was half past eleven when Anthony and Stromm started on their return journey.

Chapter XIII
CAPTAIN STROMM'S RIGHT ARM

Captain Vass insisted upon accompanying his two guests about half-way down the cobbled-stone harbour-way. There he stopped, looked at his watch, shook hands fervently, saluted smartly, and bade them good night. A few seconds after Anthony and Stromm had left him, they turned and saw him waving to them. Nobody could have waved with more enthusiasm.

"A good fellow, I think, that," said Stromm. "Nobody could possibly have made a man more comfortable on a voyage than he did me; especially as I wasn't feeling any too fit, as you say." He, like Vass, looked at his watch. "Just on a quarter to twelve, Lothering-ton. We are in good time. Our taxi friend should be showing on the corner there is a minute or so."

They walked on and reached the end of Chalke Harbour, where it suddenly turned, lost its own identity, and seemed to become part of the cliff road. It was a very dark night now and the moon was hidden behind heavy banks of clouds. But the wind had freshened into gusty squalls, and Anthony, noticing this, remarked to Stromm that the rain would come as soon as the wind dropped. Stromm nodded. He—an old campaigner—was peering ahead for the lights of his anticipated taxi-cab.

"Our man's late," he said.

"That's the worst of these fellows that you hire for jobs of this kind. They never seem able to keep their time. Take too much on, that's what it is as a rule, and as a consequence can't keep faith with all their customers. I wonder how long we shall be kept kicking our heels here."

As he spoke, Anthony's ear caught another sound from the distance.

"What is it?" said Stromm, noticing the expression on Mr. Bathurst's face.

"Somebody running, I fancy. Running fast too. Two people, I think. And, if I'm not mistaken, they're coming in this direction."

Stromm's face twisted into bewilderment. "Strange! People running. In a place like Chalke. At this time of night. Wonder what's doing."

The water lapped strongly against the sides of the harbour, but the running footsteps came nearer and nearer, and suddenly two dark forms showed and then broke out of the darkness. Anthony saw that they were two men. As this realization came to him, another, born of intuition, almost immediately succeeded it. This second apprehension was accompanied by a sharp stab of fear. Anthony felt—knew, rather—that danger was close at hand. These men meant mischief to him and his companion. As he stood fast in his tracks, he was perilously close to the sea-wall, with Captain Stromm on his left, as they faced these two running men. He called sharply to his companion, and his shout of warning, as it happened, was not a second too soon.

The two men charged straight at them, and Anthony saw that their faces were covered with masks cut from black cloth. Stromm pushed a useful-looking left into the teeth of the man who had made for him and brought him up sharply, while Anthony adroitly side-stepped his assailant, and as he slipped by him, brought his right beautifully into the point of the man's jaw. The man staggered, but did not fall. He recovered his balance almost immediately. Then Anthony's heart was chilled and his spirits sank to zero point. For, to his utter dismay, he saw that each of the men had drawn a business-like revolver. A shot rang out from each almost simultaneously. Anthony felt something whistle unpleasantly close to his cheek, and saw Stromm throw himself like a huge, shaggy-haired dog on the man who had fired at him. The man lurched unsteadily at the impact and then fell with Stromm on top of him.

Meanwhile Mr. Bathurst's antagonist had raised his revolver to fire a second shot. Anthony knew that he was taking steady aim and had never before felt so helpless. Clutching at a straw, as it were, with a desperate effort he flung himself to one side, to see, with a thrill of excitement, Stromm's outstretched hand catch the man by the heel and jerk him with a crash to the ground. The shot that he had fired flew harmlessly wide just as the hoot of a car sounded close at hand. Before Anthony could raise himself from the ground in order to help the now prostrate Stromm, the two men who had burst from the blue picked themselves up from the ground and took to their heels and ran in the opposite direction to that from which they had come and from which, too, the car was coming.

Anthony and Captain Stromm, deciding discretion the better part of valour, ran towards the approaching car.

"You're late," panted Stromm to the driver, "almost too late. While we've been waiting for you we've been nearly murdered. Quick, man! That way! As hard as you can go."

The driver opened his mouth in what was undoubtedly incredulous amusement. "M-m-murdered?" he gasped. "I don't understand you. I really—"

"Never mind that," shouted Stromm, as he and Anthony jumped in. "After the scoundrels, as I told you. That way! Quick!"

The man, pulverized into obedience by Stromm's personality, drove hard in the direction that Stromm had indicated.

"Little chance of catching them now," said Anthony. "There are literally hundreds of places where they could hide. Call it the needle and the haystack and you won't be far out."

Stromm assented gloomily.

The car went on at a good pace for some appreciable distance. When Stromm gave the driver the order to stop they had seen or passed nobody. The lights of the *Vaar* twinkled across the harbour.

"Turn around," said Stromm, "and drive us back to the 'Tracy Arms' at Upchalke. Somebody's going to pay for this in the morning." His face was hard and grim.

Anthony spoke to him quietly. "Although I am a little late in the matter, Captain Stromm, please accept my very best thanks for all that you did just now. I should have been in an extremely awkward position without your assistance. In fact, now I look back at the incident in cold blood, I am not altogether sure that I should have been alive to tell the tale."

Stromm grunted unintelligibly. Anthony could see, as he sat in the car at the man's side, that his spoken gratitude had embarrassed Stromm. Anthony continued in much the same strain.

"When I come to look back on everything, I have little doubt, Captain Stromm, that that little spot of bother from which we have just escaped, was intended for me. Primarily, at least, that is. In other words, you happened to be unfortunate this evening with regard to the company that you were keeping at the time."

Stromm shook his head. "Oh, forget that, my good friend. I did only that which any man in my place would have done. But I am sorely puzzled. I cannot think who knew for certain that you were down in the quarter of the town with me."

Anthony nodded. "I have been thinking much in the same way and along the same lines for some little time now. An extremely interesting point."

There was a silence. The taxi-cab was slowly climbing the hill to Upchalke. Stromm broke the silence just as they reached the summit of the hill. He turned to Anthony and looked him directly in the face.

"What's the name of that friend of yours? Hatherley, isn't it?"

"Call him an acquaintance rather than a friend," replied Mr. Bathurst. "It would be nearer the truth. But Hatherley certainly is his name. May I inquire why you ask?"

Stromm spoke slowly and carefully rubbed his cheek as he did so.

"I am inclined to think that he knew you were dining with me this evening. I think that he overheard my invitation to you. Nobody in the room was near as he was. And what is more, he was down there at the harbour when we drove down to Vass in the early part of the evening. You saw him there as well as I. I don't like it. The longer I look at it, still less do I like it. I'd like to know what it was that he was really there for."

"He was taking photographs, our Mr. Hatherley," returned Anthony lightly. "Didn't you notice his camera when he stopped and waved to me?"

Stromm grunted again. It was obvious that he was far from satisfied by Mr. Bathurst's answer.

"As far as I can remember, your friend—I beg your pardon, I should have said your acquaintance—Mr. Hatherley, was the only person who knew of your engagement with me for Captain Vass, and that causes me to become suspicious. Have those facts that I have mentioned occurred to you, Mr. Lotherington, may I ask?"

Anthony shook his head. Stromm's eyes held interrogation.

"What I have said is true, is it not?"

"Not altogether."

"How . . . not altogether? Where is it that I am wrong? Explain, please."

"Why, in this way, Captain Stromm—you assert that Hatherley was the only person who knew of my visit with you this evening to Captain Vass. That is a statement that may be true and yet it may not be. There is nothing like certainty about it." Anthony paused.

"How exactly do you mean?" inquired Stromm.

"Why, in this way. Hatherley is the only man whom we know to have known where we were going. How about the people *unknown* to us who were aware of our intended visit? Therein lies the real point of my argument, Captain Stromm, and there's a substantial difference."

Stromm nodded his head slowly. "Yes, I see what you mean. I hadn't thought of that. All the same, you can't get away from the fact—we *know* that Hatherley knew and we also know that he was actually down there when we arrived. All the rest of which you speak is conjecture. Ours is real information."

"Granted, Captain Stromm. And we'll tuck it away in our brains and remember it, we'll hope, to our advantage. It may be more than useful to us at a later date. Beyond that, I'm afraid, we can't go—with safety, that is. And here we are at our destination, I fancy." Anthony peered through the window of the car. "Yes, here's our perfect pub, our haven of rest. Before we get out, what are we doing about tonight's performance. 'Phoning the police from here? Is that the card we play?"

"I certainly think that we should. Who knows but that you may be attacked a second time . . . when perhaps I shall not be with you?" Directly he had spoken, Stromm's heavy face broke into a genial smile. "Forgive me, Mr. Lotherington. Of course I should not have reminded you of that. It was in the worst possible taste."

Anthony got out of the car with Stromm behind him. Anthony smiled too.

"Why not? I consider that you were entitled to. Who better?"

Stromm put his hand in his pocket and paid the driver. The man touched his cap, backed the vehicle for turning, and drove off again into the darkness. Stromm strode forward and rang the bell of the inn. Immediately a roar of laughter resounded from the back of the house. Fentiman grinned as he heard the noise.

"The missus and I are entertaining a few friends. Mr. Mulrenan, Mr. McCracken, and Mr. Skipwith are in there. It's Mr. McCracken's birthday and he's pushed the boat out. Would you two gentlemen care to join us?"

Captain Stromm shook his head with firm determination. Fentiman spoke to them again.

"You two gentlemen would be very welcome, I assure you—to all of us," he urged.

"You will excuse us," said Anthony. "Your invitation is most charming, but I am tired and I know that Captain Stromm is too. Another time, perhaps, we should be very pleased."

When he heard Anthony's reply, a curious look came over Fentiman's face. It seemed to hold something rather more than ordinary disappointment. But, whatever it may have been, he passed it off well.

"I understand, gentlemen. Of course, your dinner party has tired you. But Mr. Skipwith, particularly, will be disappointed. He was most anxious for you both to join us."

"Then convey our regrets to him, will you, please?" countered Stromm. "Tell him that I will argue with him another time."

Fentiman fell back smiling, and Anthony and the gallant captain made their way up the main staircase. The landing reached, Mr. Bathurst turned to his companion and spoke in a low voice.

"I will 'phone the police in the morning, Captain Stromm. And when I do, I shall not 'phone from the interior of the 'Tracy Arms'. Somehow I don't think that it would be advisable. I don't think that it would be advisable. I don't know that it's what I'd call a healthy place. Good night."

"I understand, Mr. Lotherington. I think that you have come to a wise decision. After all, if we 'phone now we can do no real good. Good night to you."

Anthony responded suitably and entered his bedroom. He took off his dinner jacket and dress-vest and hung them in the wardrobe. Slowly, for he was more than usually tired, he proceeded to undress. As he did so, he thought of the succeeding events of the day. Progress! Possibly! On the whole yes! Undoubtedly—if he could but read the truth from the message of the ebony stag, he felt certain that he could solve the entire problem. It was abundantly clear, though, that heavy forces were now mustering against him. Tonight's attack. Was it directed against him as he was, as he appeared to be, or was it directed against his *real* identity—Anthony Bathurst? But who among the people here knew of that? As far as he himself could tell, Major Marriner alone. Oh . . . and Heather Barton.

Here was yet another problem demanding his keenest attention and the best of his powers. A strange case this. Those lines again. They ran through his brain. "When Death with Icy Wings did stalk". Mr. Bathurst kicked off his shoes. He would have another go at those lines now. Why not? Concentration should be moderately easy now. He found the key of his locked drawer. He had placed the paper from the bungalow underneath his wallet. Mr. Bathurst opened the drawer. The wallet was there. He moved it to one side. The paper was gone! There was no getting away from the fact. The drawer was comparatively empty of articles and the absence of the paper could be seen at once.

Mr. Bathurst sat on the side of his bed and cursed sweetly and scientifically. Chiefly he cursed himself and his own innocent simplicity. Matters, then, were considerably worse than he had thought. And the enemy was near at hand. In some respects, uncomfortably near. Mr. Bathurst took pen and paper and at once rewrote the lines of the stag's message. Thanks to his power of memory, he was no worse off in himself—even though the enemy had relatively bettered his position. Mr. Bathurst cursed again. In due course, he feel asleep.

Chapter XIV
SHOCK FOR MAJOR MARRINER

It is probable that Mr. Bathurst was more interested in the doings of his fellow man at breakfast on the following morning than on any previous morning so far during his stay at Upchalke. When he took his seat at the table, he noticed that Mulrenan had not yet put in an appearance or had either of his lady-friends.

Stromm walked by Anthony's table, and as he did so held out his hand and showed Anthony a scratch across his right wrist.

"A memento of last night," he said grimly, "and do you know, Lotherington, I never realized I had it until just before I got into bed."

"It looks pretty angry to me," remarked Anthony.

Stromm grinned. "And I feel it! The more I think of last night's outrage, the more my blood . . . boils . . . that is what you say, is it not?"

"Quite right, Captain. It proves to me also that I am even more in your debt than I had realized."

"You will oblige me by making no further reference to it . . . please . . . Mr. Lotherington. Let me know what the police say about things."

Stromm smiled and walked across to his table just as Wilfred Hatherley entered.

"'Morning, Captain Stromm! 'Morning, Mr. Lotherington!" It was clear to the most casual observer that Hatherley's normal exuberance was well to the fore this morning.

Stromm, Anthony noticed, deliberately featured the scratch on his wrist. Mr. Bathurst at once realized what was behind Stromm's action. But Hatherley from Easthampton either didn't see what Stromm was doing or purposely refrained from comment. Anthony noted the fact carefully.

The woman whom Fentiman employed to wait at breakfast came in, and Captain Stromm gave his orders to her. The woman came to the others in turn. Hatherley was talkative. More talkative than even ordinarily. His conversation was irrepressible.

"Well, what sort of a time did you have last night aboard the schooner *Hesperus*? I happened to see you go aboard. Did the old boy do you well? When I saw you, do you know, I'll confess that I envied you. Landlubber as I am and probably always will be, boats exercise an eternal fascination for me. Always have done since I was a tiny kid. I used to sail model yachts on ponds in parks and pleasure gardens. And when I saw you two fellows step on the deck last night I'd have given you a fiver to have been a member of your party. I would have done—straight! But no—I had to content my little self with taking photographs, worse luck."

A curious look flitted across the face of Captain Stromm. Anthony it must be admitted, was profoundly puzzled. Surely Hatherley's candour was not the projection of a guilty man? He waited therefore to let Stromm reply to Hatherley's statements.

"Captain Vass of the *Vaar* is not exactly a stranger to me. The invitation that I extended to Mr. Lotherington was not what you would call an everyday invitation. It did not altogether lie in my power that it should be extended to include all and sundry. You understand me, I hope, Mr. Hatherley, as I think I am understanding you?"

Hatherley nodded, not in the least perturbed.

"Oh, quite. And don't misunderstand me either. I've never been one to push my nose where it wouldn't be welcomed. Oh no. That's not Wilfred Hatherley—except, of course, professionally. As an auditor one must. I just like to be frank about things, that's all." Hatherley came over and stood by Anthony's table. Here he bent down and spoke in a lowered voice. "I'm going up to see my Chief this afternoon. Catching the 1.22. He wants to see me. It's about the Forsyth murder case, of course. And I'm almost certain—as certain as I can be at the moment—that I can fix things up with him so that he'll let me come back for a few more days. It'll be worth it too."

Anthony murmured perfunctory appreciation.

"I told you because I thought you'd like to know," added Hatherley.

"Thank you," returned Anthony, not to be outdone in courtesy.

Hatherley, his mission accomplished returned to his table. At this moment Mulrenan entered breakfast-room with Freda Glen and Heather Barton. Wagstaff, the chauffeur, was not there. Anthony noticed that Miss Barton kept her eyes resolutely averted from his direction. Mulrenan was talkative—like Hatherley, much more so than usual. Also, he seemed in extraordinarily high spirits, and then Anthony noticed another thing. Mulrenan's conversation was directed entirely towards Miss Glen. He ignored Heather Barton completely. Anthony fell to wondering with regard to the story that Heather Barton had brought to him on the previous day. Was Mulrenan in these high spirits because Freda Glen's will was gradually weakening and approaching breaking-point? Was Mulrenan appreciably nearer to his objective? At any rate, Anthony thought, he would know from Miss Barton, doubtless, if the situation as previously depicted by her became any more desperate. At the moment there were matters confronting him of more pressing importance.

Anthony, still watching Miss Barton unobtrusively, finished his breakfast. He spoke to Captain Stromm again before he left the apartment.

"All right," returned Stromm. "Let me know how you get on when you come back. I'll be in the lounge."

Anthony took care that he left the "Tracy Arms" quietly and unostentatiously. From what he could see of things, Fentiman didn't appear to be doing the usual jobs that ordinarily occupied him of mornings. There was no sign of him in the garage or in the garden behind the house.

A quarter of a mile down the road to Chalke Anthony entered a telephone kiosk. He had previously observed that the kiosk was there and had deliberately made for it. He was fortunate to get Major Marriner almost immediately. Marriner was curt and officious until he realized who it was at the other end. Then his manner changed at once.

"I'm sorry, Bathurst. These idiots didn't tell me it was you when they called me. Many apologies. Well, what's the best news you have this morning?"

Anthony countered. "First of all, sir, have you any news for me? Any developments in any direction, or any particular progress?"

"Very little, Bathurst, I'm sorry to say. I've had inquiries put through at the Lanning end, as you suggested—nothing doing so far. Also, up to the moment we haven't been able to trace Mrs. Forsyth. Not that that matters overmuch—we're bound to put our hands on her sooner or later. That's merely a matter of routine and time. Well, now you tell me—how are things with you? I don't suppose you're ringing me to ask me when the Harvest Festival is or the date of the next Flower Show. Come on, let's have it off your chest."

Anthony told the Chief Constable of the events of the previous evening. He thought, when he had finished, that his story must have impressed Marriner considerably. There was, for instance, an appreciable pause before he replied:

"But this is a most extraordinary thing that you're telling me, Bathurst. Beyond me, there's not a soul in the place that knows you're here—I can't get it at all."

A sudden idea struck Anthony and he listened carefully for Major Marriner's next remark.

"You were shot at, you say?"

"Most assuredly, believe me. The shot whistled past my cheek. A matter of inches—no more. Luckily I wasn't alone and my companion put in some decidedly useful work. I thought that I had better tell you about it. I even thought that you might care a lot to know."

"Well, to be perfectly candid, the whole business amazes me. All I can say is, there must have been some faulty staff work somewhere. But it beats me altogether."

"Well, it's perfectly true, sir, I assure you. Almost too true. And frankly, if the luck hadn't broken my way, I mightn't be here now to tell the tale. However, I'm not grousing at that—that's all in the game and neither here nor there. It's just a spot of useful information for you and there's no doubt that we must both watch our step. Well, that's the news. Cheerioski!"

But Major Marriner was evidently not done with yet.

"Hold hard. Just a minute, Bathurst—for your own sakes, if for nothing else. Your news definitely disturbs me. I shall have the matter looked into at once. These men may have been noticed as suspicious characters. In a way, I feel so responsible for you, you see. As a matter of fact, Sir Austin Kemble was on the 'phone yesterday. The old boy's getting a wee bit impatient, I fancy. He'll be calling you off if we're not careful. Perhaps I should say—if *I'm* not careful. I've no desire to hand up to Sir Austin the carcase of a dead Bathurst—not on your life."

Anthony smiled to himself as he heard the details of the Chief Constable's last statement. This particular point of view of Marriner's rather amused him.

"And how is the Commissioner these days?" he contented himself with asking.

"Oh, all right, I think. Bar the touch of impatience that I just mentioned. But tell me now, Bathurst, apart from your spot of bother near the harbour wall last night, have you anything else for me at the moment? For example, have you had any luck with the stag's message?"

"Not a lot," came Anthony's quick reply. This last question of Marriner's bordered upon the awkward. Anthony had no wish to tell him of the latest position—at least, yet awhile. News of the loss of the paper could be kept till later. To tell Marriner now, Anthony considered, would effect nothing at all.

Marriner's next question was direct and to the point.

"Made any advance towards a solution?"

"No. Afraid not. But, in justice to myself, I haven't really had a lot of time. Last night's affair not only took up my time when it happened, but since then has also rather filled the bill. But I shall be getting down to it again before very long—I can promise you that much—with strong hopes of success if nothing else."

"So that actually you may be said to be *in status quo*. Is that a fair statement?"

"Well, not altogether. Perhaps I have moved just a little. I am already toying with one or two theories. They may be a little fantastic, perhaps, but on the whole I don't dislike 'em."

Marriner's voice came back at him. "Don't like the sound of 'fantastic'. Still, you know your business better than I do, even though it happens to be mine as well. Come round and see me in a day or so. Good luck and good hunting."

Anthony Bathurst replaced the receiver and for a moment or so stood there in the kiosk thoughtfully. So Sir Austin Kemble had already entered upon a condition of impatience. Anthony waited outside the kiosk for a few moments. He thought that he would, in nautical terms, "scan the horizon," for possibilities. Nobody, however, was in sight. He had not been followed, then, from the "Tracy Arms". So far, so good. After a few moments' thought, Anthony decided to return to the inn. For one thing, he desired a word or two with Captain Stromm before the latter started upon his morning activities.

As he entered by the front entrance, he saw the burly form of Andrew McCracken but a few paces in front of him. It seemed that McCracken must have business in the "Tracy Arms". At all times he seemed able to come and go as he desired. Mr. Bathurst was the victim of a sudden impulse. He went straight up to McCracken and spoke to him.

"Good morning, Mr. McCracken! You will forgive me for troubling you so early in the day but, believe me, I have a good reason."

McCracken's native geniality did not desert him. He had always been a good "mixer" and good companionship to him was as the milk of his mother.

"I don't doubt that you have, sir. And if you give a name to your reason, I shall doubt you still less. Which proves that, though I'm Scotch, I might well have been Irish, and therefore better off in some ways, but decidedly worse in others."

"You pay my race an undoubted compliment, Mr. McCracken. Compared with a witty Scotsman, an alleged witty Irishman is as mere crackling leaves. But let me talk to you in the terms that I first mentioned. Do you know, I discovered yesterday for the first time that you and I had a mutual friend."

"Again I have no doubt of it. I should say that the good god Bacchus has been doubly fortunate."

Anthony smiled at McCracken's jovial rejoinder.

"Your reference is attractive, but unhappily the wrong one. The descent will be almost from the sublime to the ridiculous. In other words, from Bacchus himself to the homely Captain Vass of the *Vaar*. I regret the declension, but there it is. There is no help for it."

Anthony could have sworn that McCracken's face clouded a little. He puckered his forehead as though in an endeavour to remember.

"Captain Vass of the *Vaar*?" he repeated. "I don't know that I— Oh yes, I remember! I had a trip with the man about a year ago. Not a bad fellow either. He gave me a damned good time on his boat . . . Good grub and good liquor to wash it down. By Jove, how he worships that boat of his! When were you last aboard her?"

Anthony flashed his reply at him. "As recently as last night. I dined on board with Captain Vass. He was kind enough to extend me an invitation, I entirely agree with you in your generous assessment of his qualities. During our conversation at dinner, Captain Vass happened to mention your name—that's how I knew. I left Vass about half past eleven."

McCracken smiled and glanced ruefully at the dock in the hall by the main staircase.

"I see. Extremely interesting. But the time annoys me. It should be later—then I could join you in my favourite occupation. Observe that I refrain from saying 'ours'."

"We might drink a toast to Captain Vass . . . for want of any better employment."

"We not only might, Mr. Lotherington, we most certainly should."

"But as the time is not any later than it is . . ." Anthony paused.

McCracken finished the sentence for him. "We will reserve the pleasure until a future occasion."

McCracken turned sharply on his heel and left Anthony wondering. Mr. Bathurst watched him make his exit and then turned into the smoke-lounge in the hope of discovering Captain Stromm. His hope materialized. Captain Stromm was sitting in an armchair reading a Swedish newspaper. He put the paper down directly he saw Anthony enter.

"Well, what fortune did you have? Tell me, Mr. Lotherington—I am much interested."

"I did what I intended to do. I 'phoned to the police from a tele-phone call-box. That one up the road—just opposite to what I'm told is Skipwith's new house, He's moving in some time next month. As far as I can tell—and I kept my eyes skinned—nobody spotted me and nobody followed me out of here. That was just how I wanted it. I got through to a Major Marriner—I think they said he was a Major; something of a 'big shot', I should imagine, from his tone and general conversation."

Stromm nodded. "You told him of all that occurred to us last night, I take it?"

"Every bit. You bet I did. I wasn't missing anything out. Words and music one penny."

"What did he say when you told him? I suppose he wanted to know all about you who you were?"

Anthony nodded. "I gave him my name, of course, and told him that I was staying here on a holiday—at the 'Tracy Arms'. The police, I gather, will make inquiries in the matter. There'll be a local 'comb-out' to discover if there are any suspicious characters knocking about the neighbourhood. That was the description the gallant Major used."

Stromm growled as he heard the news. "We shan't get much satis-faction out of that, if you ask me. But tell me, Mr. Lotherington—I am a little, as you say, hazy—did you notice that there were any other boats in the harbour besides the *Vaar* of our good friend Vass?"

Anthony thought over Captain Stromm's question. He shook his head.

"No. I don't think there were any others. I can't remember seeing one. Why?"

"Well," Stromm replied, very slowly and carefully choosing his words, "this morning, now that I am more cool and collected, I have given last night's matter a great deal of thought and mental concen-tration. It was so altogether unusual that it made a deep impression on me. And it came to me that those men who were so unfriendly to us *might* have been off another ship. Some of the crew. That seems to me very probable. I find it difficult to explain to you—but one does not associate violence of the kind that we experienced last night with a sleepy, old-world place like Chalke is. It is—what is the word I want that you English use?—it is foreign to a place such as we know Chalke to be." Stromm concluded his carefully worded statement and looked at Anthony for his opinion.

"I have attempted to visualise the scene and I don't remember any other boat of any size being in the harbour," reiterated Mr. Bathurst.

"No," returned Stromm, "I don't think that I can either. But I wasn't sure. That was why I decided to ask you. So that it looks as though my theory won't hold enough water. All the same, I must confess that I am very puzzled. Have you an enemy or are we just in the way of a couple of armed thieves with designs on our money and valuables?"

"That is what we have to find out," replied Mr. Bathurst, "and for our peace of mind, the sooner we do that the better."

"I agree with you," returned Captain Stromm gravely. Then he smiled. "I had no idea that my long-desired holiday in your country would turn out to be so—so entertaining. Is that a correct word?"

Anthony smiled back at his companion. "It will do," he said, "as well as any other."

"Good," said Stromm with unconcealed satisfaction. "I am pleased to hear you say that. I like to think that my English is not—too bad."

Chapter XV
THE BOROUGH TREASURER OF EASTHAMPTON

IT WAS the irrepressible Hatherley who produced the Borough Treasurer of Easthampton for Anthony's edification. He did so with an air of triumph. The venue was the smoking-lounge of the "Tracy Arms". But Anthony found it difficult to understand why. Frederick Gulliver Sharpe-Lodge, at the age of fifty-five, was a tall, thin man with black hair that grew long and thick over his collar. Beyond the gift of a most unusual and shrewd personality, he appeared to have but little to commend him to men of even moderate culture and erudition. He had certainly not been cradled in the terminology of the schools, although it must be conceded that nobody who encountered him would have ever suspected otherwise.

"'Morning," he said with a sharp curtness that it pleased him to think was professional. "Pleased to meet you, Mr. Lotherington. Hatherley has told me a lot about you. I've been most interested. Yes."

He opened a gold cigarette-case with an almost boisterous click and proffered it to Anthony Bathurst with a curious, bird-like movement of the head. The latter saw with some surprise that one half only of the case held cigarettes. The other half, which showed at a right angle as a back as it were, was filled with an unusually large visiting-card. Anthony could see that the card bore the inscription, "Frederick Gulliver Sharp-Lodge, O.B.E., Borough Treasurer, Easthampton." As he held the case, his little finger protruded from behind it at an absurd angle, and Anthony noticed that he was wearing a ring containing a large diamond.

"Thank you," said Anthony. He waited for his companion to go on.

"Extraordinary case. Definitely extraordinary. Especially at this juncture. According to Hatherley here, my authority has been paying out to the wrong man for some time now. Can't altogether stomach that, you know. The time isn't opportune. Far from it. Must look into it. Lot of faith, you know, in my Internal Audit section. Highly efficient! Not convinced yet. By any means."

Anthony, somewhat taken aback, murmured a suitable reply. Sharpe-Lodge cocked a muddy eye at him and smiled as a jocular fish might smile.

"How about the murder itself, Mr. Lotherington. Plenty of clues there for the police, I suppose? As a rule in these cases, you can find clues in dozens—everywhere. One behind the other, like rabbits up a ladder."

Anthony rallied and collected himself. "I believe that the authorities have made but little progress, which points rather to a shortage of clues than to an embarrassment."

"Really? You surprise me. Should have thought my man Hatherley could have solved the problem for them by now." His eyes twinkled. He laughed immoderately. "A man that can solve the mystery of a secret Trust Fund and clear up the St. Angela's kidnapping case in less than a month shouldn't be beaten by a common-or-garden murder. Oh, dear, no, sir! Come, Hatherley, what have you to say for yourself? What about the reputation of Easthampton?"

Hatherley smiled at his chief's exuberance. He had mastered a habit which was expected of him.

"Afraid this is a bit beyond me, sir. Away from our usual line."

The treasurer of the County Borough of Easthampton heard his subordinate and assumed an air of heavy tragedy.

"I can't believe that there is any loophole in my system appertaining to the signing of the Life Certificate. Not for an instant! There can't be! At the same time, I must admit that I find the matter distinctly disturbing."

Anthony adroitly took a hand. "Perhaps you will allow me to venture an opinion, sir? Merely a lay opinion, of course. You must understand that I have already discussed the matter to some extent with your Mr. Hatherley. I'm afraid that there *is* a loophole in the direction of the Life Certificate, and this man who has been known here as Robert Forsyth found it."

"How do you know that, sir, for certain? And understand—I do *not* admit it. I admit nothing. You don't catch Sharpe-Lodge—oh no! I am not providing you, sir, with ammunition to stab me in my own back. I wasn't born yesterday! Not on your life, sir!" Sharpe-Lodge shook his head vigorously, paused for breath, and then proceeded again most emphatically. "What about the District Auditor, sir? Let me you this. The smartest man in the game audits my accounts, Mr. Lotherington. Not an elective auditor, mind you! Do you think that I could pull a fast one over him? I should have to burn many hours of midnight oil to do that, I assure you. Do you know, sir, that Flower— that's the name of the auditor I mentioned—has more suicides to his credit than any other auditor in the country? He misses nothing—he passes nothing. Not even a compliment. This year alone he's put his finger on no less than *eight* rogues holding positions of trust. What has been the result? Three shootings, two hangings, one drowning, one self-poisoned by the exhaust of his car, and the other, a rate-collector, absconded—vanished into thin air. I tell you, sir, that S.E. Flower, Esquire, has a record of which he can well feel proud. The ratepayers of this country have much to thank him for."

Anthony was at a loss to place this remarkable man. He decided to let Sharpe-Lodge, as possible, do all the talking. This decision was by no means difficult to carry out.

"What do you say to that, Hatherley—about Flower, I mean?" demanded Hatherley's chief.

"I know how right you are, sir," said the dutiful Hatherley.

"Of course you do. That's what I like about you, Hatherley. You live and learn. A good many people don't. That's the pity of it." He turned to Anthony. "Would the time be opportune, do you think, for me to have a word with the police? My opinion would carry a great deal of weight, I should imagine. It usually does in my own district, let me say."

"No doubt the police would welcome you," replied Anthony quietly.

"Good," returned Sharpe-Lodge. "I think you're right. Then I'll make it my business to see them and give them the benefit of my opinion and experience. I'll let you know what transpires, of course. If I am convinced that the two Forsyths are not one and the same—oh yes, I know what Hatherley thinks about it—I shall inform the police at once. And you afterwards, having regard to the fact, of course, of what you have already done." His smile exuded self-satisfaction.

Anthony put a question to him. "Did you know Forsyth, your old colleague, very well?"

Sharpe-Lodge regarded him quizzically. "Naturally. Seeing that I worked with him over a great many years. You get to know a man when the two of you are serving the common weal. Blood is thicker than water."

"No doubt. But I said 'very well'. I was referring more to whether you had a psychological understanding of him rather than a mere conventional knowledge. Could you tell, for example, what he would be likely to do when he encountered certain varying sets of circumstances? Did you ever happen to meet any of his family, Mr. Sharpe-Lodge?"

Sharpe-Lodge waved his hands and answered both questions at once.

"I don't know that I could. And no. I always understood that he had no relations."

"I see. Has Hatherley mentioned the matter of Forsyth's teeth to you?"

"Oh yes. He has written to me several times since he has been staying down here. The teeth have been prominent, if I may say so, in the correspondence. Good job Hatherley came, in a way. The matter of the teeth—yes, I am familiar with the position."

"And you agree with Hatherley?"

Sharpe-Lodge saw where Mr. Bathurst was leading him.

"Superficially—yes. That is mainly why I'm here now. But of course one never knows in what quarter of the wind the blood is curdling, and much water will flow up the Thames, believe me."

Anthony nodded. He was quite sure that he didn't, but was more than ordinarily confident when it came to an assessment of Mr. Frederick Gulliver Sharpe-Lodge. He turned and spoke to Hatherley again Now that it had fallen to his lot to meet Sharpe-Lodge, he felt that he liked Hatherley a little better.

"Mr. Hatherley, I seem to remember that you told me on the day that I first met you about your going down to Lanning to visit the genuine Forsyth. You did say that, didn't you?"

"Quite right, Mr. Lotherington. I popped down to Lanning to see Forsyth several times. It was an easy half-day run, you see, Victoria."

"When was the last time that you saw him?"

Hatherley carefully considered Anthony's question.

"About a month before he moved to Upchalke."

"You didn't correspond at all, I suppose?"

"No. Chiefly because Bob Forsyth hated letter-writing. I used to drop him a line each time, just before I went down to see him, telling him that I was coming and what train to expect me by. You know what I mean. He always used to come and meet me at Lanning station."

Anthony nodded. "I see. And you say you saw him about a month before he moved. Did he give you any idea on that last occasion that he had a move in his mind?"

Hatherley shook his head. "Not an inkling. He never even hinted at such a possibility. In fact, I was amazed when I discovered that he *had* moved. And even a little annoyed, perhaps, that he had been so secretive with regard to it. That feeling of annoyance and the fact that this new place was so far away compared with Lanning were the main reasons why I hadn't been to see him again. The Chief knows that to be true." Hatherley spoke emphatically.

The Borough Treasurer nodded mysteriously. "I can support Hatherley's statement. Definitely. when news of Forsyth's move reached my office, I can well remember his discussing the matter with me and intimating his surprise thereat. We agreed that it was, to say the least, unexpected."

"You were informed by letter, I presume?"

Sharpe-Lodge smiled—almost indulgently.

"Naturally. I have the letter here. In my room, at least. I brought it down with me—together with certain other papers and documentary evidence that I considered might prove highly useful."

Anthony, although not too certain of his ground, jumped in. "Would you care to show it to me? And any other papers that you say you have—with regard to Forsyth, I mean."

Sharpe-Lodge showed no boisterous inclination towards the concession. "Well," he demurred, "they're official documents, you know, and as such should be kept strictly private. Oh yes. If you persist, young man, in following this case up too closely, I fear that I may be compelled to speak to you in Latin."

Anthony stared at him in wonder. He had never met a man like this before.

"Vox," he suggested, *"et praeterea nihil?"*

"Er, exactly," replied F.G.S-L., "under the 1922 Act."

Anthony contrived to catch the eye of Wilfred Hatherley. Hatherley was intelligent. He understood at once what Anthony desired him to say.

"Mr. Lotherington has been very helpful to me, sir, while I have been staying down here. I must admit that. Both with the police authorities and with the newspaper people, his influence assisted me considerably. He and I have been, as it were, hunting in couples. A sort of 'double-harness' effort—if you know what I mean."

The muddy eyes of Sharpe-Lodge twinkled again.

"Two of you on to me, eh? I like that. Going to make me hold a candle to the mangle, are you? Is that the idea? Ah, well, I'll see what I can do. But it's a good job I wasn't born yesterday. Wait here a minute or two, gentlemen, and I'll bring back the secrets of the bedroom."

Sharpe-Lodge turned with the alacrity of a conjuror and disappeared.

"Wonderful man," remarked Hatherley, in tones of nervous adoration. "You'll never get the better of him."

"He probably hasn't any," replied Anthony laconically.

Hatherley looked puzzled at Mr. Bathurst's remark.

"You don't know him well—"

"Thank God!" said Anthony.

"He makes a big stir wherever he goes. I assure you that it is so."

"So does an electric drill."

"He gets to the bottom of things."

"He scarcely has to move."

"You're prejudiced. There's nothing two-faced about him."

"There can't be. Otherwise he'd have left that one at home."

Hatherley shrugged his shoulders. "He's fair. He can always see two sides to everything."

"Yes. His own—and the blasted nonsense the other bloke talks. I know his kind."

"You should hear him with his committees. They never corner him. His talk leaves them guessing. They take—"

"Minutes to waste hours, I'll be bound."

Anthony refused to be comforted. Hatherley was on the point of essaying further effort in defence of his chief when the door opened to admit Sharpe-Lodge again.

"Here you are!" he cried. "For once in a while I've allowed my better judgment to be over-ruled. But half a loaf is better than no bread, and blood must be thicker than water, as I said to Mr. Lotherington just now and also as I explained in my recent lecture to the Cadetta Society on the basic principles of the 'On Cost Suspense Account'. First of all, here's the letter from Forsyth giving notice of his change of address. Here you are. Look at it for yourself. Nothing here, I suggest, to excite comment."

He held the letter in front of Anthony Bathurst and Hatherley. Anthony read the letter. It was headed:

The Antlers,
Braemar Road,
Upchalke.
October 22nd, 1936.

Dear Sir,

I beg to inform you that my address from now on will be as above. Kindly forward all cheques to the new address.

Yours faithfully,
Robert Forsyth.

All was typed with the exception of the signature.

"H'm," remarked Anthony, "all the tomorrows shall be as today. All typewritten, you observe, bar the signed name. I feared as much."

Sharpe-Lodge blinked at him. Rather apprehensively Anthony thought.

"What s your point, then, with regard to that?"

"An obvious one, surely?" Anthony smiled.

"I should appreciate it if you would enlighten me." Sharpe-Lodge was curt.

"With pleasure. As I see things, this is the explanation. That whereas the pseudo-Forsyth had learned by October 22nd, 1936, to forge the genuine Forsyth's signature, he wasn't capable of imitating his handwriting well enough to write an entire letter that would pass unchallenged. Therefore it was necessary that the main body of the letter should be typed. Any criticisms here, gentlemen?"

Anthony smiled again as he threw out his challenge. Sharpe-Lodge questioned.

"But I don't understand. Why should the fraudulent Forsyth write the letter at all?"

"Why?"

"Yes—why? Why didn't the genuine Forsyth write it—that is, if he *had* moved from Lanning to Upchalke, as it states that he did?"

Anthony shook his head. "For the best of all reasons. He couldn't."

"Couldn't?"

"No. Couldn't."

"Why not?" Sharpe-Lodge looked bewildered at Anthony's reply.

"Because he was dead. Gathered to the Forsyth forefathers and sporting in the Valhalla of all true rating and valuation officers. He died at Lanning. The pseudo-Forsyth then moved to Upchalke . . . to die there eventually himself. A nasty death too."

The eyes of Hatherley goggled at Anthony's statement.

"Died at Lanning, you say?" The words were almost whispered.

"Forsyth died at Lanning."

"Old Bob Forsyth? What do you mean exactly by that, Mr. Lotherington? Tell me, please. Do you mean that he was . . . murdered down there, too?"

Anthony reflected. He knew that the eyes of his two companions had never left his face. Then he slowly shook his head again before he answered them.

"No. I don't think that the real Robert Forsyth, ex-rate-collector of Easthampton, was murdered. From the data that the case has so far given me, I incline to the idea that he died a natural death. I may be wrong, of course, but I don't *think* I am."

"Extraordinary," puffed the Easthampton Treasurer. "And equally, if I may say so, disconcerting. It means that these aren't worth the paper that they're written on." He fluttered at Anthony a number of papers.

"What are they?" asked Mr. Bathurst.

"These are the signed Life Certificates of Robert Forsyth for the last three years. Twelve of them in all. They're submitted to my department quarterly. I have the last four here that came from Lanning and all those that have been sent to me since from Upchalke. Here they are. You look at them."

Sharpe-Lodge handed the documents to Anthony. The four that had come from Lanning were signed by "Ralph Udal, M.D." Address: "Mahasu, Endicott Road, Lanning." The last was dated October 2nd.

"Ralph Udal, eh?" murmured Anthony. "Shades of Roister Doister! Dr. Udal! Now let's have a glance at these later ones. Which is the first in date order? Here we are—January 8th, 1937, signed by the Rev. Charles Ashmore Sellon, Clerk in Holy Orders." Anthony looked at Hatherley. "That's in keeping with what you've already told me, Hatherley. The spurious Forsyth, you see, sought comfort with Holy Mother Church. Forsaking medicine, he sought sanctuary—superannuation sanctuary—with the Vicar of Saint Veronica's."

"And got it," chirped Sharpe-Lodge.

"And got it," repeated Anthony. "I can't deny it."

Hatherley intervened with a pertinent question.

"This impersonation—because we can call it that—what was the main idea behind it? Just to get hold of the real Forsyth's superannuation payment? The four-pounds-a-week stunt?"

Anthony rubbed the ridge of his jaw. "No, I don't think so. It's possible that it may have been an added incentive, but I don't think it was anything more than that."

Sharpe-Lodge looked critical. "An added incentive? I don't know that I get you. You leave me groping in the dark. What other incentive was there?"

"That something which brought murder to him. I regret that at the moment I can't be more explicit. In a week from now . . . perhaps . . ." Anthony shrugged his shoulders.

Sharpe-Lodge paled and shook his black hair from his forehead. "Murder?" There were several adjustment accounts in the ledgers of the County Borough of Easthampton, a few of which were really necessary but none for murder.

"When do you intend to go to the police?" Anthony put the question to him casually.

Sharpe-Lodge consulted his watch with an air of gravity. "Within an hour from now. Why?"

"I was merely thinking, the sooner the better. That was all. Well . . . good luck and many thanks for your courtesy in the matter of those documents. No doubt I shall see you again before you go back home."

Anthony waved to the two Easthampton officials and immediately walked straight down the road to the telephone kiosk which he had used before. Again he communicated with Major Marriner. In a few words he outlined the facts that he had so recently obtained from the Easthampton Treasurer.

"He's coming to see me, you say?"

"He will be with you in less than an hour, and he has to be seen to be believed."

"All right. And you're determined to do what you say?"

"Yes, I leave for Lanning tomorrow morning. I may call on the Vicar of Saint Veronica's this evening if I have time. I shall try to, for several reasons. But that's by the by."

"What do you expect to pick up at Lanning particularly?"

Anthony smiled as he spoke into the mouthpiece.

"When I come back from Lanning, sir, I'll promise you this. That I'll give you the *name* of Forsyth's murderer . . . and I hope to give you with it the reason of his murder at the same time."

Anthony waited in patience for Major Marriner's reply.

"You seem remarkably confident, Bathurst."

"No, just building on a foundation of reason. Nothing more than that, I assure you."

"Just a minute. I've been thinking over what you just said. Two questions. Your words were 'the name of Forsyth's murderer'. What about an arrest? That's the first question."

"Don't know, sir. Don't know where he may be . . . *or what his name is now*. That's the real point. Still, no pessimism—we'll hope for the best. I think that we shall be able to turn the trick. Now tell me your second question."

"Why do you keep on talking about 'Forsyth's murderer' when everything points to the fact that the murdered man *wasn't* Forsyth?"

"Oh, but he was—without doubt."

Anthony waited for the inevitable response.

"He was?" The Major's tones were almost shrill with incredulity. "He was? What hare are you chasing now? Good God, Bathurst, it's been your contention all the time that the dead man was a fake, that he couldn't have been Forsyth. Now you've gone all the other way."

Anthony smiled sweetly into the telephone apparatus.

"On the contrary, sir, my point has been that he couldn't have been *Robert* Forsyth. No more than that! You see, he happened to be Horace Samuel Forsyth! 'A little less than kin and more than kind . . .' Don't you remember that we found his marriage certificate?"

Anthony replaced the receiver, chuckling to himself.

"I wonder what he's thinking of now . . . our eminent Chief Constable."

Mr. Bathurst was still smiling when he returned to the "Tracy Arms". All was quiet. Christopher Robin might have been saying his prayers.

<h1 style="text-align:center">Chapter XVI
DEATH IN THE KITCHEN</h1>

As he entered, Anthony became immediately conscious of an unusual atmosphere. The smoke-lounge was empty. There was no sign or sound of either Fentiman or his wife. True, it was at a time when the hotel was closed to the public, but even on these occasions it was customary for Fentiman and his wife to be either in or near to the bar. After some little time, Anthony heard a subdued murmur of voices coming from what he thought must be the kitchen. He stopped in the main hall for a moment or so and listened. Certain snatches of the conversation arrested his attention and caused him to furrow his brow in absolute perplexity. He decided to risk a charge of interference. The issue seemed to him to be far too big for him to neglect it. He made straight, therefore, for the kitchen door. His hand was almost upon the handle for opening when the door opened from the inside and Fentiman himself came out of the kitchen. The man's face was white and strained. The emotion on it was plain to see. He made as though to brush Anthony to one side. Anthony, however, deliberately prevented him.

"What's the trouble, Mr. Fentiman?" he inquired quietly. "Can I be of any assistance to you?"

Fentiman shook his head—almost violently.

"No. You aren't a doctor, are you? Let me get to the 'phone at once."

Anthony made way for him and let him go. He heard Fentiman ask for a number which he knew meant that the man was communicating with the police. When he was put through, Fentiman asked for Dr. Thorold. Anthony heard him distinctly and wondered what was the exact nature of the trouble. Fentiman continued to speak in such a tone that Anthony could not help hearing all that he said.

"Will Dr. Thorold please come at once to the 'Tracy Arms'? Yes, I have . . . that's been seen to. Constable Sharman is here already. Yes . . . there's been, I very much fear, another murder. Yes, actually in the 'Tracy Arms'. It's the landlord speaking. Very good, sir. I'll see to all that. And Dr. Thorold will be along as quickly as possible? Thank you very much. Very good, sir. That shall all be arranged."

Fentiman hung up the receiver and walked slowly back to where Mr. Bathurst was still standing. Fentiman passed his hand nervously across his brow. It was the action of a man wearied and worn.

"I don't know, sir," he said, "what's come over the place. I don't really. First Mr. Forsyth down at 'The Antlers' and now this. My place will be ruined. It's dreadful . . . the premises branded . . . and I a God-fearing man all my life."

"Tell me," said Anthony, with gentle persuasion, "what has actually happened? You forget that I'm in the dark. It's possible that I may be able to help you."

"Murder's been done. In there. On my premises. Less than half an hour ago at that. And I've always been a moral man too."

Fentiman pointed a trembling finger to the kitchen door. Anthony came to grips with him at once.

"Who's been murdered, Fentiman?"

"Mrs. Bryant. The poor woman that helps the missus with the cooking and the waiting when we've got more than the usual number of guests staying here You must have seen her, sir. A poor innocent woman who wouldn't willingly have hurt a sparrow. From time to time she's waited on the tables in the dining-room. More than once since you've been down here."

Fentiman's statement came to Anthony both as a shock and a shattering surprise. He had been much more prepared to hear many other names than the name that Fentiman had given to him.

"What a terrible thing! As you say, who could have wished *her* any harm, Fentiman? It seems utterly absurd to me."

"She's dead right enough, sir."

"How was she killed?"

Anthony was secretly hoping for a certain reply, although he hardly knew whether there was logic behind his hope.

"Strangled, sir. By a scarf round the throat. It seems to me, sir, that somebody must have crept up behind her and twisted the scarf round her throat. At least nobody seems to have heard her cry out at all, and several of us must have been pretty close to her."

Anthony thought hard over Fentiman's statement.

"Where was the body found?"

"By the kitchen sink, sir. Mrs. Fentiman—my wife—found her there. It's a good job she went in when she did, sir. The cold-water tap was running. Another few minutes and the kitchen might have been flooded."

"Have you any objection to my seeing the body, Fentiman? As a matter of fact, I've always had a sort of sneaking desire to be in on one of these murder investigations, and I shouldn't like to miss a chance now that one's come."

Fentiman seemed ill at ease. He rubbed his mouth with his finger.

"Well, sir, there's a constable in there now. You see, sir, he might object and make things bad for me. You mustn't touch anything, you know, sir . . . even if . . ." He spoke very doubtfully.

"Take me in, Fentiman," urged Anthony, "with you—when you go back there. Perhaps the constable won't mind very much."

Fentiman surrendered reluctantly. "All right, sir, I'll chance it. But you mustn't blame me if Sharman cuts up rough. He's not everybody's money by any manner of means. I've known him funny-tempered over much smaller matters than this. Come along with me, sir."

Fentiman led the way slowly back to the kitchen. Anthony followed him at a respectful distance. Fentiman knocked gently on the door. A voice said, "Who is it?"

"Constable Sharman, of course," thought Mr. Bathurst.

Fentiman replied, "It's me, Constable." He put his finger to his lips for Anthony to keep silent. Then he beckoned to Anthony to accompany him as Sharman cried, "Come in!" Anthony slipped quietly through the door behind Fentiman. A man in the uniform of a policeman was standing by the fireplace.

"Did you 'phone, Tom?" he asked.

"Yes, I 'phoned."

Then Sharman shifted his feet and saw Anthony. He frowned. Then he turned to Fentiman.

"Who's this, Tom?"

"This is a gentleman staying in the hotel. He asked me, if you'd mind—"

Constable Sharman summarily cut short the rather shamefaced Fentiman.

"You had no right for to bring him in here. And, what's more, you know it. I must ask you to withdraw, sir."

Anthony smiled courteously. "As a matter of fact, Constable, if you don't mind my mentioning it, I fancy that Major Marriner, your chief, is an old friend of mine. If that—"

"Can't help that, sir. Don't mean a thing, in the circumstances as they are here. Will you kindly leave the room?"

From the corner of his eye, Anthony could see the body of a woman lying by the sink at the far side of the room. So Fentiman's details in so far as that was concerned had been accurate.

"If you don't mind, sir," came the voice of Constable Sharman insistently.

As he spoke, Anthony heard voices in the hall of the "Tracy Arms". Major Marriner and Dr. Thorold, no doubt. Sharman evidently heard them too. He looked across the room at Anthony with some agitation.

"Now, sir . . . if you please . . ."

At that precise moment the Chief Constable and the doctor entered. Sharman's hand went to his helmet.

Major Marriner's quick eye took in the points of the situation at once. Anthony saw that Fentiman had brought up the rear and was standing immediately behind Dr. Thorold. Anthony looked meaningly at Major Marriner.

"Haven't we met before, sir . . . some years ago . . . surely?"

"Of course," returned the Chief Constable, advancing a few paces. "Lotherington, isn't it?" He turned to Constable Sharman. "It's all right, Constable. I'll see to this. I know this gentleman."

As he spoke to Sharman, Anthony caught the expression on Fentiman's face. Fentiman understood. He would have to remember that—it might make a difference later on, from more points of view than one.

"Here you are, Dr. Thorold," said Marriner. "Here's the body. What do you make of this?" He pointed to the dead woman on the floor.

Thorold at once went on his knees beside the body. "H'm . . . h'm!" Anthony watched him intently. "H'm! Almost 'Thuggee'," Anthony heard him say. Mr. Bathurst thought of what the words implied and the dreaded stranglers of India. Slowly Dr. Thorold regained his feet. "Strangled," he said curtly. "By this scarf." He held up a long, thin blue-and-white-coloured scarf. "It was pulled quite tight from behind her and then, I should say, sharply twisted. Who is the woman, Fentiman? Anybody I know?"

Fentiman, who had come farther in and was now standing with his back against the door, looked as white as a ghost as he took it upon himself to answer the question.

"Mrs. Bryant, sir. Lives in the village. She helps my wife in the kitchen here."

"Bryant?" repeated Dr. Thorold. "I know a man called Bryant. Isn't he the steam-roller driver for the Hatchett Council?"

Fentiman nodded corroboration. "That's right, sir. That's the man. This is his wife. I don't know what he'll do now, poor fellow."

Anthony looked at the Chief Constable with raised eyebrows. Marriner nodded as though in agreement with something. Anthony at once spoke to Fentiman.

"How long ago is it, Fentiman, since your wife found her here?"

"Not more than half an hour. sir."

"How long dead, Doctor?"

"Still warm, Lotherington."

"Good," thought Anthony; "he's remembered when he might be excused forgetting."

Thorold continued: "Not more than an hour, I should say. Have a look at her for yourself."

"Thank you, Doctor," Anthony nodded. "And when Mrs. Fentiman found her, I understand that one of the taps of the sink was still running. That's so, isn't it, Fentiman?"

"Yes, sir. That's quite true," replied Fentiman sturdily.

Anthony conferred with the Chief Constable. Quietly and shrewdly Fentiman eyed them. Anthony drew Marriner a short distance from the others.

"We shall have to speak to Mrs. Fentiman, I think," said Anthony, "don't you, sir? Nothing else for it, it seems to me. Don't suppose friend Fentiman will be over-pleased when he hears, but we can't help that."

Major Marriner nodded. "Yes," he returned sharply, "I entirely agree." He detached himself from Anthony and walked over to mine host of the "Tracy Arms". "I'm afraid that I shall have to have a few words with your wife, Fentiman. I'm compelled to ask her one or two questions. Will you please send for her?"

Fentiman regarded him gloomily. "Mrs. Fentiman isn't very well, sir. The shock of this affair—of her discovery—has been, as you may guess, very severe."

"Where is she now?"

"She's lying down upstairs, sir. She almost collapsed. One of the maids is with her."

"Well, that will be all right. Dr. Thorold's here, Fentiman. If she's poorly, the doctor will look after her and soon put her right. So go up to her, will you, Fentiman, and ask her to come down here to have a word with me?"

Fentiman hesitated, gave the impression that he was about to speak, and had then thought better of it, and shuffled rather than walked out of the door. They heard his footsteps as he ascended the stairs. Anthony walked to the sink. He looked into it and saw that it was unusually deep. He came back from the sink to Dr. Thorold.

"The running tap is important, Doctor. It proves, I think, that when Mrs. Fentiman found the body, Mrs. Bryant couldn't have been dead many minutes. It will depend, of course, upon what Mrs. Fentiman is able to tell us. When we've heard that, I'll prove to you what I mean."

Major Marriner looked at his watch. "He's taking his time, I must say—or, rather, she is."

"They both are," murmured Anthony Bathurst.

The Chief Constable went to the door and listened.

"Here they come," he said eventually. "Fentiman's bringing her downstairs. They don't seem too pleased, either, judging by the tone of Mrs. Fentiman's voice." Major Marriner came away from the door and waited for the two Fentimans. When they entered, Anthony could tell at once that the woman had undoubtedly suffered a severe shock. The suddenness of her discovery had doubtless accentuated it. She looked white, strained, and, in Mr. Bathurst's opinion, perilously close to fainting. Dr. Thorold went forward to her.

"Sit down here, Mrs. Fentiman." He placed a chair for her in such a position that the body of Mrs. Bryant was invisible to her.

Major Marriner nodded to Anthony. Anthony knew what the nod signified. Also he wondered what Fentiman would think. Still, things had now come to such a pass that there was no help for it. He must question Mrs. Fentiman. The Chief Constable obviously desired him to do so.

Mrs. Fentiman was a tall, thin-faced, sharp-nosed woman with dark-brown eyes and hair that once had, without doubt, been a light auburn. Horror still lurked in her eyes. Dr. Thorold took a bottle from his pocket and held it to her nostrils.

"Take a sniff at that," he said. "Go on. Right up."

Mrs. Fentiman obeyed him. Then she handed the little bottle back to Thorold with a smile of gratitude.

"Thank you, Dr. Thorold."

Anthony could see at once that Mrs. Fentiman was not a country-bred woman. Her accent effectively disposed of the latter idea.

"Mrs. Fentiman," he asked her quietly, "how long ago is it that you found Mrs. Bryant?"

Mrs. Fentiman looked across at the big grandfather clock that stood in the corner of the old-fashioned kitchen.

"Exactly three-quarter of an hour ago. As a matter of fact, I happened to notice what the time was when I came in."

"And Mrs. Bryant's body was just by the sink?"

"Yes. She was lying there—just as though she had fallen down as she peeled the potatoes."

"*Was* she actually peeling the potatoes? It isn't an irrelevant question, I assure you. I'm definitely interested."

Mrs. Fentiman nodded. "Yes. Actually scraping the potatoes for lunch today. The potatoes are getting old now and they take more time to get ready than they did a month or so ago."

"Thank you, Mrs. Fentiman. Now what about the taps? I understand that they were running when you came in."

Mrs. Fentiman shook her head. "Only one, sir. The cold-water tap. Mrs. Bryant had it running so that she could hold the potatoes under it."

"How high was the water in the sink when you came into the room, Mrs. Fentiman?"

The woman looked somewhat surprised at the question.

"No height at all, sir. Mrs. Bryant had the sink-hole open. As the tap ran, the water just ran away."

Anthony looked disappointed. Fentiman himself intervened.

"I was wrong, sir, about the place might have been flooded—what I said to you. I didn't think of it as it was, you see. About the sink-hole being open."

"If it hadn't been," put in Mrs. Fentiman, with chilling emphasis, "and the tap had run for a long time, it would have been all right. Because the waste-holes towards the top of the sink would have carried the water away. I can't think where your brains could have been, I'm sure."

Anthony turned to Major Marriner. "I can't establish what I wanted to, sir; Mr. Fentiman's statement rather misled me. I had hoped to prove almost exactly when Mrs. Bryant died. All that I *can* say is that the person who murdered her took full advantage of the conditions."

"How do you mean exactly?"

"Why, consider the household noises concurrent with Mrs. Bryant's duties. One—the running of the water from the tap into the sink, and two—the scraping of the potatoes. There is little doubt in my mind that Mrs. Bryant was taken utterly unawares. The killer crept up behind her, footsteps masked by the noise of the two activities that were going on, and strangled the unfortunate woman with that scarf."

Anthony pointed to the scarf that lay on the table. Constable Sharman coughed. The Chief Constable went to the table and picked up the scarf.

"What completely baffles me," he said, "is why anybody should want to take the life of this woman. Just a local working woman who, I shouldn't have thought, had a single enemy in the whole world."

"Possibly she hadn't, sir," contributed Anthony.

"You mean—"

"I mean that she may not have been killed for reasons of enmity. I would hazard the theory that she *knew* something. That particular piece of knowledge meant that she died."

Major Marriner nodded. He turned over in his hands the blue-and-white-coloured scarf.

"Whose scarf is this?" he asked. "Is it yours, Mrs. Fentiman?"

Mrs. Fentiman shook her head emphatically. "No, sir. It's not mine. I don't know that I've ever set eyes on it before."

Anthony waited to hear her out. For the moment he was undecided as to what course to take. Eventually he came to a decision.

"I rather fancy that I can tell you who owns that scarf. It belongs to a lady stopping here in the hotel."

Marriner turned on him. "What's her name?"

"She's a Miss Heather Barton, I believe. She's staying here with a companion—a Miss Glen."

"How do you know this is her scarf?"

"Perhaps I expressed myself somewhat carelessly. I've seen her wearing that—or another exactly like it."

Anthony scratched his cheek. Fentiman interposed with a remark. With an air, it seemed to Anthony, of a man clutching at a straw.

"Yes, sir. Mr. Lotherington is quite right. I've seen Miss Barton with a scarf like that."

"Wouldn't it be as well if you had a word with the young lady?" said Fentiman.

"I will—at once. If she's on the premises. Do you happen to know if she is?" Major Marriner looked inquiringly at Fentiman.

"I don't, sir, but I can find out for you."

The Chief Constable nodded. "Do so, will you?"

Fentiman made his exit from the room. The others waited patiently for him to return. When he did, he came back alone.

"I'm sorry, sir," he said apologetically, "but I'm informed that Miss Barton went out about an hour ago."

Anthony cut in. "May I ask who told you that?"

"Mr. Mulrenan, sir. I met him coming downstairs. He's gone into the lounge."

"What do we do now?" said Dr. Thorold.

"We'll wait for Miss Barton's return. Was anything said, Fentiman, as to how long she's likely to be out?"

"No, sir. Mr. Mulrenan had no idea, sir. I him the same ques- tion myself."

"Who is this Miss Barton? Know anything about her?"

"Merely a guest staying here. At Mr. Mulrenan's recommenda- tion. I know nothing about her beyond that."

"I see. Well, we must wait for her, that's all there is to it. Constable Sharman! Get on the 'phone to the station and make arrangements stout the body."

"Very good, sir."

The Chief Constable shook his head in a puzzled manner. "It beats me," he muttered—"it beats me completely."

CHAPTER XVII
MR. BATHURST AND ANALYSIS

ANTHONY Bathurst heard Major Marriner issue certain instructions to Constable Sharman. Then, seeing that Miss Barton's arrival might not materialize until some hours had elapsed, he returned to the privacy of his bedroom. Even though he had made no further headway with the message that had been taken from the antlers on the stag, he was determined to put certain data on paper and analyse them. On this occasion he turned the key in the lock and thus made himself secure from intrusion. Anthony "listed" the names of the people whom he had encountered round the "scene of the crime". He detailed the names in the order in which, as far as he could remember, he mad met the various people.

Anthony chuckled to himself as he thought of the customary theatre-programme phrase, "characters are named in the order of their first appearance on the stage". Fentiman, Hatherley, Mulrenan, Heather Barton, Freda Glen, Captain Stromm, Burns, McCracken, Skipwith. Mr. Bathurst paused. Then he carefully added other names. Mr. Bathurst never took any chances. Wagstaff the chauffeur, Captain Vass of the *Vaar*, F.G. Sharpe-Lodge, Mrs. Bryant (the murdered woman). Mr. Bathurst paused again. Then he commenced to prepare a second list. "People not yet seen but heard of." Mrs. Winifred Forsyth, Mrs. Margaret Swan, Dr. Innes, Rev. Charles Ashmore Sellon. Yes, they were the "noises off".

A third list. "People so far excluded from the two lists." Major Marriner, Dr. Thorold, Mrs. Fentiman. Anthony knew it for a certainty. So far, he felt that he had handled the case disgracefully. Bungled it badly at almost every turn. He had chased this hare and quested after that red herring instead of sitting down intelligently to the problem and letting loose a stream of cold logic upon it. Somewhere in that list of names was Forsyth's murderer. Yes, and more than that—Mrs. Bryant's murderer! Why hadn't Marriner produced

Mrs. Winifred Forsyth—the "niece" of the murdered man? Had she got clean away? Mr. Bathurst shook his head.

"Let me reconstruct. The real, genuine, pukka, original Forsyth died at Lanning. From that time onward I have no doubt that he has been impersonated. By whom?" Here again Anthony chuckled. "Very neat—that." Why had the impersonator been murdered? A secret, probably, of considerable value. "My Royal Burden Straight to find"—a line of the doggerel. Why had Mrs. Bryant been murdered? Because she *knew* something that she might use to the detriment of the murderer—even to his utter disaster. Anthony smiled. Many of his difficulties were slipping away. Why hadn't he analysed the case before? "I will eliminate those who are conclusively innocent either from conditions as to whereabouts, etcetera, or because of their antecedents." He spoke these words softly to himself and struck out the names of no fewer than nine people. "I am taking a chance, perhaps, with regard to one or two of these, but from what I've heard and been told, I imagine that I'm on comparatively safe ground." Excluding the name of Mrs. Bryant, there were still ten "possibles" left. Ten! Even now, far too many for him to survey the case with any equanimity.

Anthony Bathurst came to a definite decision. Come what may, he would go to Lanning in the morning. The cryptogram could go hang for the time being. Somewhere at Lanning lay the key to the mystery, and Anthony felt confident that he could wrest something from the place or the people that Marriner's men had so far failed to do.

He sat back in his chair and lit a cigarette. He often recalls how near he had been to missing the step that he was now contemplating—Mrs. Bryant. A working woman strangled by a scarf as she stood and worked by a kitchen sink.

He sat back in his chair and lit a cigarette. He often recalls how near he had been to missing the step that he was now contemplating—Mrs. Bryant. A working woman strangled by a scarf as she stood and worked by a kitchen sink. Whose husband drove the steam-roller for the Hatchett Urban District Council. He smiled. He wondered how F.G. Sharpe-Lodge would deal with the depreciation of steam-rollers. Mr. Bathurst had once inspected the inventory of a certain local authority wherein a steam-roller was priced at threepence! Where did the Bryants live? He would find that out from Fentiman at once.

Mr. Bathurst unlocked his bedroom door and went downstairs again. It was evident that Heather Barton had not yet returned. A few quick words with Fentiman, who was in the corridor near the bar-door, confirmed this idea.

"Oh," said Anthony casually, "could you tell me where Mrs. Bryant lived? I don't think that I've ever heard that."

"Yes, sir, certainly. Over at Tophill Cross. The third house on the left as you go down the hill on the other side of Tophill."

"Which way is that? When I leave here, in which direction do I go?"

"I'll come to the front door with you, sir, and show you, so that you can't make any mistake."

"Thank you, Fentiman. I shall be obliged."

Fentiman took Anthony to the front door of the "Tracy Arms". He then pointed straight across the road.

"Straight up there, sir, you go. Past Andrew McCracken's place, turn round by Copestake's, the butcher's, and then right the top of the hill. Go over the top and then the third house on the left."

"I see. Past McCracken's, you say?"

"Yes, sir. A rare one he was for chippin' poor Mrs. Bryant, as she walked down here to work, about the potatoes she used to peel. Her husband grew 'em and dug 'em, you see, sir, and then she used to come along here to scrape 'em."

Anthony listened with interest. "Yes, I see," he said quietly.

Fentiman wasn't sure as to Mr. Bathurst's reference. Anthony went on.

"Well, good-bye for the present. I'll go along to Tophill Cross now. Thank you."

Fentiman watched him cross the road and then, shaking his head, returned to his wife, who was seriously in need of him.

Anthony Bathurst followed the directions given him, strode out briskly up the hill, and found the little house that had been the home of the two Bryants. He wondered if he would be fortunate enough to find Bryant at home. There was a distinct chance, he thought. The man would obviously have been called from his duty and might possibly have returned again from the gruesome task which no doubt had been set him.

Anthony walked up to the little front door and knocked on it quietly. Listening carefully, he heard sounds of movement coming from inside the house. Anthony refrained from knocking again. He was justified. Steps came up the passage. The man, or whoever it was inside, had heard him and was on his way to the front door. More than once he seemed to stumble. Anthony waited. The door opened. Anthony saw a little, shy-eyed man standing in front of him.

"Mr. Bryant?" he asked.

"Yes, sir."

"My visit is unexpected, Mr. Bryant, I know, but I should very much like to have a little chat with you. May I have that—honour?"

The little man blinked at him pathetically. "Yus, sir. Of course, sir. Come in, sir."

Anthony followed him into the little passage.

"Come in here, sir, will you? It is—it was my best room."

Anthony saw the little man brush the tears from his eyes. Anthony gripped his hand.

"I'm so sorry! Courage! I have need of you."

"Need of me, sir? What can I do?"

"Help me to avenge her. It may not be a Christian virtue, but it's damned human for all that."

The little man sat down in a chair and made a big effort to steady himself. Anthony let him be. felt that the effort would be all to the man's benefit. He watched Bryant carefully. The man was close to the edge of things. Suddenly the tiny man—it was difficult to imagine that he drove a steam-roller—turned to Anthony with an impetuous question.

"Why did they kill her, sir? My poor girl! She was good . . . and kind . . ."

Anthony went to him and grasped him by the shoulder.

"We don't know-but we're going to try to find out. And that's where you're going to help."

The little man grasped the sides of the chair in which he was sitting.

"Yes, sir," he said, with a sort of pathetic helplessness.

Anthony took a chair and sat beside Bryant.

"Tell me, had your wife been recently—let me see, what shall I call it—had she been worried recently about anything?"

Bryant shook his head. "No, sir. Not that I know of, sir."

"If she *had* been, would she have confided in you—for certain?"

Bryant nodded in a numbed manner. "Yes, sir. Rose and me had no secrets from each other. Not in all our twenty-two years' married life."

"I see. Can you make any suggestion? Think, Bryant, think—*anything* that may help me?"

Bryant shook his head again. "No, sir, nothing at all. Nothing ever happens to us down here—well, you know what I mean . . . until now."

Bryant broke down. His grief hurt Anthony. He knew not what to do. All that he had succeeded in doing so far was the further upsetting of this sorrow-stricken man. He must pull himself together and wrest some sparkling fragment of truth from Bryant before it was too late. He turned sharply and swiftly to the man.

"What has she talked about lately? Tell me, Bryant, if you can. Think! Think! Think! What did she talk to you about this morning . . . last night?"

"Just the usual, sir. Nothing."

"Are you sure? Absolutely sure?"

Bryant passed his hand across his forehead. "I'm trying to think, sir. Trying hard. Let me be for a moment, sir. Don't think that I'm afraid. I served in the Light Infantry right from the early days of 1914 . . . was wounded twice . . . once badly . . . my poor girl nursed me. I've been through a rare lot. Last night . . . just before we was going to bed . . . she did mention something . . . not an ordinary thing . . . I know . . . it was about the lodger that we had who suddenly went away. Yes . . . that was it . . . I remember. She told me . . . that was yesterday . . . that she had been thinking of him all the day."

Anthony's heart throbbed thankfulness. To Bryant had come the light of inspiration. He would hold him in his hands and comfort him—and make him talk!

"Yes, Bryant, yes! Tell me all that you can remember. Who was this lodger? Tell me! When did he go—and why?"

But Bryant just stared at him. Anthony realized again how close the man was to the border-line. He must treat him with the greatest care—he saw that clearly. Anthony waited patiently for a sign from Bryant. At last it came.

"We sometimes take lodgers, sir. Boarders, if you like. It helps me a bit, you see, with the weekly budget. Being a childless couple, Rose and me, we had the room to spare in the house. A really nice and comfortable bed-sitting-room."

He stopped dead. Anthony made neither sign nor sound. He waited for Bryant to continue as patiently as he had before. The policy was successful. Bryant began again.

"We started about five years ago. Very often Tom Fentiman up at the 'Tracy' would send somebody along to us, knowing that everything here was clean and tidy, and Rose a good plain cook with nothing fancy. The lodger I spoke about just now was the last one we had . . . the last one that we shall ever have."

Anthony murmured a sympathetic response.

"He came about the middle of September—no, more like the end of September."

"Just a minute, old man," contributed Anthony. "Did you advertise the fact that you had a room to let?"

Bryant nodded. "Yes, sir. My old girl used to put a card in the front window."

Anthony nodded. "Thank you. Now go on again, please."

"This man was a very nice gentleman—I'll say that for him. Nobody could have behaved better or treated the missus and me any better than what he always did. A strong sturdy fellow by the name of Stone— Mr. Peter Stone. He paid us thirty shillings a week for what he had of us. He was quite satisfied, and we was too. Always made himself thoroughly at home, and never gave us no trouble. He stopped with us about a fortnight—on holiday he was. He reckoned to stay with us about a month—so he told us when he first came and fixed up to stay. Then one morning he said he was leaving. Just after breakfast he broke the news to Rose. I wasn't here. I was driving my roller over at Hatchett. Rose told me when I got back to tea in the evening. His reason was—so she told me—that his mother had been taken bad at her home and that he must go to her in case it was something very serious. That was the last we saw of him. He paid up. Paid Rose for what he owed us and just cleared out."

Bryant stopped, rose from his chair, walked to the little window of the room, and stared out.

"Bryant," said Anthony, "I *must* ask you some questions. What you have told me is most important. Will you promise me that you'll answer them to the very best of your ability?"

Bryant turned away from the window and took his seat in his chair again.

"Yes, sir. Of course. You know I will."

"Good. Where did he come from, this lodger of yours?"

"No idea, sir. Never had no occasion to ask him. He paid up regular when he owed us anything. I never worried about anything else—I had no need to."

"What was he like, then? Describe him. Tell me everything that you can remember about him."

Bryant passed his hand across his brows. Like Cassius, he was a-weary of the world.

"A hefty sort of man, sir. Strong, I should say. Not young—no. Between fifty and sixty, I should say, sir."

Bryant stopped. Anthony questioned him immediately.

"You say 'hefty'. Do you mean very tall?"

"No, not exceptionally so, sir. But I'd call him big, all the same."

"Was he fair or dark?"

"Dark, sir. Almost black."

"Educated man? As far as you could judge?"

"Yes, sir. Quite. Spoke well."

"H'm! Anything else you can remember about him?"

"No, sir, nothing. You see, I wasn't here with him very much—being out at work all day. Most of his talkin' was done to my missus when she wasn't working up at the 'Tracy'."

"Yes, I suppose that would be so. Now what else was I going to ask you? Let me see . . . it was on the tip of my tongue. Oh, I know, post—correspondence. Did he have any letters come here while he was staying with you?"

"Oh yes, sir. Of course he did."

"Addressed to Mr. Peter Stone, naturally?"

"Yes, sir. To that name as I said. Although I'm not much of a scholar, as no doubt you've guessed by now. They never learned me much at school. Not much more than the alphabet and a bit of simple reading—although I've improved a bit now. My missus, poor girl, used to take all his letters in to him whenever they came. She fussed him a bit, I suppose, in her quiet little way."

"Did he have many of these letters come during the time of his stay here?"

"A fair number, sir. Not every day. Say about three letters a week. That would have been about the average."

"What did he do with himself while he was here, mostly?"

"Well, sir, from what the missus used to tell me when I got home from work of a night, he'd be out best part of most days. Like the usual run of people when they're away on a holiday. But I don't think he talked much of his doings. Or of his goings and comings. Bit secretive like. I can't say as 'ow he had any special hobby."

"Did he smoke?"

"Yes, sir."

"Drink? Not a teetotaller, I mean?"

"He never had drink 'ere, sir. Not in the house, that is to say. But I'm pretty certain that he did take a drop when he fancied it."

"Did he ever ask any questions-about the village; about anybody in it; about anything that was local?"

Bryant paused to think. "Yes, sir. The first night he was here. About the 'boozers' in the district. How many there were and where were they exactly. I remember tellin' him. The 'Tracy', 'The New Inn', 'The Black Spaniel', and 'The Lion and Lizard'. He seemed very interested for me to give him some facts about all of 'em." Bryant nodded slowly, as though he were confirming what he himself had just said.

Anthony emulated Bryant's example. He thought hard.

"Was that when he first took the rooms? I mean, was that one of the first questions that he asked you?"

This time Bryant showed no hesitation whatever. He nodded quickly, immediately.

"Oh yes, sir, I'm quite sure of that."

"Did he ever tell you that he had been to any of these places? Mention that he had paid any of them a visit—specially?"

"No, sir. Not in so many words. But he did go into some of them. I know that. I know one or two people—mates o' mine—who saw him. In the 'Tracy' chiefly that would be."

"Tell me, Bryant, did he habitually use the 'Tracy'?"

"I should say, as a rule, sir. But I wouldn't care to commit myself further than that."

"I see, Bryant. I must thank you now for all that you have told me. For I don't know that you can tell me any more. Thank you very much."

Anthony rose. Bryant rose with him. As the latter moved away towards the door, Anthony noticed a peculiar expression cross his face. Anthony watched him carefully.

"What is it, Bryant? Thought of something that you think I ought to know?"

Bryant passed his hand wearily across his brow. His eyes still held their scared, far-away expression.

"Put me down for a scatterbrained fool," he said emotionally. "You've been askin' me about that feller's letters and suchlike, haven't you, sir?"

"I have that. Why, Bryant—particularly at the moment?"

"Why, sir? Because there's one on the mantelpiece in the kitchen now. Or there *should* be, unless Rose has seen to it the last day or so."

Anthony was a little puzzled. "How do you mean, Bryant? Surely it's some time since Mr. Peter Stone left you?"

Bryant nodded. He stood with his hand still on the handle of the door.

"Let me tell you, sir, in my own way. It will be better for both of us. How I forgot it, I don't know, except, I suppose, that the blow I've 'ad 'as shook me up a bit. But it was like this. About a day—not more than a couple—after Mr. Stone left us, a letter came for 'im. You know what I mean, sir—when me and Rose weren't quite certain in our minds as to whether 'e'd be comin' back to us or not. So we kept it on the mantelpiece, intendin' to give it back to old Uncle Alf Garrett, the postman, next time 'e give us a knock. Well, two or three days went by, and then one day the missus, when she was givin' the kitchen a bit of a clean, must 'ave knocked this 'ere letter down, for we couldn't lay hands on it. It was missin' for a couple of weeks or more, and then—lo and behold—a few days it turned up again. And where do you think, sir?"

The long speech temporarily exhausted Bryant's powers. He stopped for breath.

"I've no idea," contributed Mr. Bathurst. "Where?"

"Well, sir, it's very peculiar." For the first time during the interview Bryant seemed to be tinged with a form of excitement. "Very peculiar. Just like one of these queer things you read of in books. Last Christmas, sir, Rose bought a box of fancy biscuits over at Shepton. You know the sort of thing I mean, sir. Well, it was shaped like a coal-scuttle, and at the back of it was a square groove what took the little shovel. After we'd eaten all the biscuits, Rose said as 'ow we'd take the little shovel out and use the box on the mantelpiece as a tea-caddy. My poor old mother always used to do much the same with her Christmas biscuit-tins. Well, in some way that I can't explain, sir, Mr. Stone's letter 'ad got into this square groove at the back. I expect Rose 'ad been dustin' one day and, careless-like, 'ad flicked or knocked the letter in there in some way. At any rate, whatever it was she did, we found it in there." Bryant forgot, and smiled at Anthony for the first time. "And that's the whole story, sir. I'm very sorry I didn't tell you all about it before."

"That's most interesting, Bryant. What little things, to be sure, turn the course of big events. I'm inclined to think that what you have just told me will turn the scale, probably, with regard to—er—everything." He smiled back at Bryant. "Well, there's only one thing left to be done. Bring me the letter so that I may have a look at it."

Bryant blinked at him. "I shan't get into trouble, I hope, sir, if I do that. The police'll be bound to question me—about my missus—and I shouldn't like to get into their bad books at my time o' my life. I've never been there yet, sir, and as a servant of the Hatchett Council, it might turn out pretty awkward for me, and I never could stand Tom Smart, one of the coppers up at Chalke station. 'E's as big as bull beef as it is, and 'as always 'ad 'is knife in me over one or two private matters."

Anthony shook his head disclaimingly. "Trust me, Bryant. I'll give you my word of honour that I'll take all responsibility for everything. I know I'm a perfect stranger to you, but you trust me."

Bryant assessed him. "Very well, sir. I will. I'll go and get the letter, sir."

Anthony waited. Something told him that he was on the very verge of a most important discovery. He heard Bryant close what was doubtless the kitchen door. He heard his steps come slowly up the passage. He came to Mr. Bathurst with the letter in his hand. Anthony's eyes took it in greedily. The postmark was Lanning! First blood to Mr. Bathurst.

CHAPTER XVIII
THE VICAR OF ST. VERONICA'S

ANTHONY Lotherington Bathurst talked seriously with Major Marriner in the latter's private room at Chalke.

"Amazing," commented the Chief Constable more than once. At other times he muttered a word which sounded like "incredible".

Anthony concluded his recital on a note of triumph. He took something from his wallet and handed it carefully to Major Marriner.

"And there, sir, is the letter in question. Posted in Lanning, as you may see from the postmark, on October 3rd. That is to say, on the day of Forsyth's murder. Yes . . . I shall still continue to refer to him as Forsyth."

Marriner took the envelope from Anthony.

"Delivered on the 4th or 5th, you say?"

"Yes, that's so, according to Bryant."

"Addressed 'Mr. Peter Stone, c/o Mrs. Bryant, Rose Cottage, Tophill Cross'. And it's lain there, you say, ever since?" Marriner fingered the envelope with curious interest. "I'm going to open this, Bathurst, and explain to the Postmaster later. I anticipate that we shall find something interesting."

"I agree. That's why I brought it along to you."

Major Marriner looked at him curiously. "Before I open it, Bathurst, tell me—what do you expect to find?"

Anthony considered the question carefully. "Well, sir, you're asking me rather a lot, aren't you? It may be anything—or nothing. We'll hope that it's something, and something that we may be able to turn into an 'importance', as Monsieur Hanaud might well say. But, come what may, we know now that when Forsyth was murdered, Forsyth, who had come to Upchalke from Lanning, had living near him a man *who had also come from Lanning*! Open the letter, sir."

Marriner took a paper-knife from his table and carefully slit open the envelope. Anthony drew his chair nearer to see what the envelope contained. Marriner took out a single sheet of paper.

"Typewritten. No date. No address," he said bluntly.

"The first and second don't matter. As for the third—didn't expect any. Ergo—no disappointment. Go on, though. What does it say?"

Marriner read out the typed words.

"Dear Peter,

"All well this end. No inquiries that need cause you the slightest anxiety. Your letter was very welcome and it only proves how marvellously lucky we were to see the picture when we did. Had it been on the Thursday instead of the Wednesday—well, what about it then? And just became an afternoon turned out wet. He little thinks that you are on his track. 'Where ignorance is bliss', etc. As I said to you when you came to your quick decision and left here, I think it's a bad policy and quite mistaken tactics for me to write this, and send it on to where you are, but I am content to be guided by you because I realize that you probably know best.

"Fancy about the E.S.! Who would have thought it? But, as you say in your letter, he's proved himself a cunning devil in every way. I bet he still thinks that he's got away with it. Well, let him think so, and those that live longest will see the most. But, all the same, how nearly he did! The way you put McCracken in his place was splendid—really lovely! His type are always the same. Crumple up when challenged. I told you he would when you got to close quarters. Well, good-bye, Peter, and the best of luck. I shall not write again because I think it's dangerous, but shall expect to hear from you—do you hear? Please be careful!

"Your loving Throstle.

"P.S. I should love to see his face when you make your entrance! B D'A. E S M M T E."

Marriner looked at Anthony over the top of the letter. "Well, Bathurst, and what do you make of all that?"

Anthony extended his hand for the sheet of paper. The Chief Constable passed it over. Anthony re-read it before making any comment.

"Well, sir, there's this about it—it clinches the matter."

Marriner nodded. "I agree. The references—you mean—are decisive. McCracken, for example."

"I don't quite know what to make of that. I must give it a lot of thought. No, I referred rather to the reference 'E.S.'."

"'E.S.'?" Marriner furrowed his brows.

"Exactly, sir. Surely we shall find that the letters 'E.S.' stand for 'ebony stag'?"

Marriner whistled softly. "Of course—of course. And it occurs again too. 'E S M M T E.' What's that? 'Ebony stag . . . must mean . . . the end.' How's that, Bathurst?"

"Oh, jolly good show—but somehow I don't think so."

The Chief Constable frowned. "Oh, and why not? You can't prove that I'm—"

"Just a minute, sir. Let's look at it like this. Take it in connection with the context. The phrase occurs at the conclusion of the postscript. The letter proper has been signed 'Your loving Throstle'. It may be intended to mislead, but I deduce a lady. Now look at the two messages to which I'm referring. 'B D'A. E S M M T E.' Note carefully, sir. B, D, *apostrophe* A. That looks to me very much like *'beaucoup d'amour'*. That is to say, heaps of love—in fact, I'd take 'evens' about it."

"It's plausible, I agree. But you haven't explained the other—where you consider that I've gone wrong."

"I regard that as much the same. One of the ways that lovers use. Their methods are usually moderately simple. Shall we have a stab at it? Let me see. 'Heaps of love—ever so much more than ever.' How's that, sir? Still plausible?"

Marriner nodded rather grudgingly. "As you put it, I suppose it is. But it's pure guesswork, isn't it? Just as mine was?"

"In a way, perhaps, but there's the context, you see, sir. and that's what I'm going on."

The Chief Constable took it into his head to change the subject.

"What are they after, Bathurst? An old master? this reference to a picture rather suggests to me—"

"No, sir. I don't think so. Think of the rainy afternoon."

"Think of the—how do you mean?"

"Surely, sir."

The Chief Constable shook his head again. "I don't know that I'm able to—"

Anthony cut in. "My point is this, sir. The reference in the letter to the 'picture' is a reference to a film—or if you prefer the more usual word—to a 'flick'. On a rainy afternoon some time ago, friend Peter, accompanied by his loving Throstle, went to see a picture. It hadn't looked like rain in Cherry Blossom Lane when they first set out, but early appearances were deceptive—and rain it did. And something that this loving couple saw in the 'flick' programme that was presented to them induced one of them to commit murder. Truly a strange world, sir."

When Anthony finished, Marriner's face was hard and grim. "And a remarkable case," he added.

"But, thank God, almost over, sir."

"You think so?"

"I am extremely confident. The key to the mystery can be found somewhere in Lanning." Anthony pointed to the letter. "That's obvious. Now the question is, sir, shall I go to Lanning or would you rather send one of your own men?"

Marriner was a trifle hesitant. Eventually he spoke. Anthony noticed how quiet the man was.

"You had better go, Bathurst. I'll have another word or two with Sir Austin Kemble. I'm afraid that he's showing more signs of impatience. When do you intend to go?"

"Immediately, sir. I don't think that I can do better. Do you?"

"As you have put it to me—no. By the way, have you made any more progress with the mysterious message that we found in that carved stag? I'm curious about that."

"I've shelved it for the moment. After my visit to Lanning, though, I have high hopes of hitting upon the solution. It seems to me that it all depends on that."

"Right you are, then. You get off to Lanning as soon as you can and report back to me here directly you pick up anything."

As the Chief Constable finished speaking, there came a tap at the door. Marriner looked up in some surprise. Then he looked across the room at Anthony. The latter made no sign.

"Come in," said Major Marriner, raising his voice.

A uniformed constable entered.

"Yes?"

"You'll excuse me, sir, for the interruption but there's a clergyman wishes to see you, sir. It's the Reverend Sellon, the Vicar of Saint Veronica's. According to what he tells me, sir, he has something very important to report in connection with the Forsyth murder. Will you see him now, sir, or shall I ask him to wait?"

Anthony had risen from his chair during the time taken by the constable in the delivery of his message. Marriner turned and eyed him inquiringly.

"This is an extraordinary thing, coming at this psychological moment. But I suppose that my experience should have taught me to be prepared for almost anything."

Anthony nodded. "True. True every time. But I find myself wondering."

"What the reverend gentleman has to tell us?"

"Yes. I find myself asking the question—has he just discovered what we've been suspecting for some days?"

The Chief Constable spoke to the man who had just entered. "Show Mr. Sellon in, will you, Green? Tell him that I shall be pleased to see him in here at once."

"Very good, sir."

Marriner motioned Anthony back to the chair from which he had recently risen.

"We'll let the Vicar sit here," he said. "On the opposite side to you. Then we shall both be able to have a good look at him." Marriner placed another chair in the position that he desired.

The door opened. Constable Green announced:

"The Reverend Mr. Sellon, sir. Major Marriner, the Chief Constable."

Anthony was more than surprised to see the man who came in. The Vicar of St. Veronica's, as befitted an old Oxford Blue who had represented his 'varsity at Queen's Club for putting the weight, was a truly magnificent physique. Anthony Bathurst, at a quick assessment, estimated that he stood at least six feet four inches and turned the scale at somewhere round fifteen stone. His hair was jet black and his complexion sallow.

"You've chosen the wrong calling," commented Mr. Bathurst inwardly, as the tremendous form came towards him.

"Good morning, Vicar. Come in, do. I believe that we have met before at one or two social functions, though I can't remember exactly where. This is a friend of mine—a Mr. Lotherington. He knows the whole case of the . . . er . . . Forsyth murder. You can speak quite frankly before him. Lotherington—the Rev. Mr. Sellon, Vicar of St. Veronica's, Chalke."

The Vicar advanced another pace and shook hands with both Marriner and Anthony.

"How do you do? I'm delighted to meet you. Shall I sit here? Thank you, Major Marriner. Thank you."

The Vicar took the chair that Marriner had designed him to take. The Rev C.A. Sellon was in his stride almost immediately.

"Now what I wanted to see you about, Marriner, was this." The Vicar put his black soft hat over his left knee-cap. "Poor Forsyth, I knew him well. And his niece. Good people! Pleasure to know them. Charming people. Always ready to help in any direction that might be needed. Now, of course, I've read a good deal about the case in the papers and I know what the police have found—to a certain extent, that is." The vicar leant forward. "Tell me, Major Marriner, what was the weapon from which poor Forsyth met his end?"

Major Marriner leant back in his chair and shook his head.

"We don't know, Vicar. That is one of the points that has so far eluded us."

The Vicar nodded almost as though in corroboration of the Chief Constable's statement.

"Exactly. That is just what I have understood."

His eyes contracted as he spoke and Mr. Bathurst saw that the Vicar was a victim of acute myopia. Again he leant forward towards

Marriner, repeating the movement that he had made a moment or so ago.

"Have any theories been tested as to the weapon that the . . . er . . . murderer used? I understand from what I have read of the case that the fatal wound was an . . . er . . . extraordinarily terrible one. That is so, is it not?" The Vicar peered at Marriner.

"Yes, that is so, Vicar. In all my official career, I have never before encountered such a ghastly wound."

"Good—I mean, that's what I myself understood. Now tell me, gentlemen, could this dreadful wound have been committed by a . . . er . . . *harpoon?*"

Anthony caught his breath as Sellon asked his portentous question. The Vicar was right. He knew it! The Vicar put into words an idea that he found mentally considering for some time. He found himself wondering regarding the form that Marriner's answer would take.

"A harpoon?" The Chief Constable repeated the word after the Vicar.

"Yes, Major Marriner, a harpoon! And I assure you that I am not speaking idly. Believe me, I have a very definite reason for saying what I did. A harpoon! Well, what have you to say to me?"

Marriner drummed uneasily with his finger-tips upon his table. But he replied calmly.

"It's true that I *hadn't* considered the possibility of Forsyth having been killed by a harpoon, but now that you've put it to me . . . I must say I regard it as highly probable, from the nature of wound, and also according to one or two other things. Mr. Sellon, I believe that you've solved something that has had the police guessing."

Sellon blinked in appreciation. His left eye was partly screwed up in the effort. Marriner continued.

"What gave you the idea, Vicar? I'd be interested to hear."

The Vicar indulged in a wry smile. "I fear that I can accept no laurels. I wish I could. It is a human desire that we should shine in departments other than our own, but it is not so in this case. When I left Oxford—I was a Brasenose man, Major Marriner—I became a curate in South Africa. I brought back from there a most interesting collection of weapons. My vicar there presented me with several— knobkerries, spears, assegais of all kinds, and several harpoons. One of the churchwardens there had served on a whaler. The walls of my library at Chalke have been adorned—yes, I stick to the word—for several years now with those weapons."

Marriner stared at Sellon curiously. The Vicar was conscious of it.

"You are wondering where all this is leading. I will tell you without wasting any more time. Gentlemen, I noticed today when I entered my library one of my harpoons was missing."

Anthony rubbed his hands at the Rev.'s statement. Marriner intervened.

"Is it your contention then, Vicar, that Forsyth was murdered by this harpoon of yours?"

"Well, putting it like that . . . hardly my contention. I'm merely advancing the idea as a distinct possibility. Based on the undoubted fact that one of my harpoons has been taken from my library. I'm not arguing the point, as it were, through thick and thin."

The vicar spoke to Marriner, but looked towards Anthony Bathurst with an invitation for argumentative support. Major Marriner shook his head rather impatiently.

"But, my dear Vicar," he said with some curtness, "Forsyth has been a month. And you have missed a harpoon today. Now—I ask you!"

The Vicar of St. Veronica's joined immediate issue.

"The mere fact that I *missed* the harpoon today doesn't mean that it was *stolen* today, does it?" He peered again at the Chief Constable with a smile of something like bland satisfaction.

"Do you mean that the harpoon might have been missing for all that time and you haven't missed it?"

"Exactly. That's just what I *do* mean." The Vicar sat back again like a saint on earth who in concert has sung.

"Is it at all likely, Vicar?"

"Yes. And I'll tell you why. This harpoon was not hanging on a wall. It *had* been, but one of the clips which held it had started to perish and I had the harpoon down for safety's sake until I could get Milton—that's my gardener and odd-jobber—to make me a new clip for it. Now do you see what I'm getting at? When the harpoon was taken down—which was quite as long as a month ago—Mrs. Sellon stood it in a comer up against the wall out of the way of my children.

My boy Theodore is rather a young hooligan, I regret to say—" The Vicar broke off. His smile was eloquent.

"And you missed the harpoon for the first time today?"

"I missed it for the first time today!" The Vicar repeated Marriner's words with strong emphasis.

Marriner spoke to Anthony. "This puts a different complexion on it, Lotherington—what the Vicar has just told us."

"Oh, undoubtedly. I wonder if Mr. Sellon could tell us if he suspects anybody of having taken the weapon?"

The Vicar shrugged his tremendous shoulders. "Oh, dear, no! I am no 'suspecter of persons'! You mustn't expect me to do those things. Besides, I interview very many people in my library. Hardly a day passes without several people coming in there for a variety of purposes."

"So that any one of several people might have laid hands on the harpoon?" Anthony put the question almost guilelessly.

"Oh yes, quite!"

Anthony knew now that his chance had come.

"I've been wanting to ask you a certain question, sir, for some little time now. May I?"

"With pleasure. I only hope that I shall be able to satisfy your curiosity."

"You knew the murdered man, Robert Forsyth?"

The Vicar assented confidently. "Oh yes, well! I thought that I had made that clear. His niece worships at Saint Veronica's. Poor Forsyth himself came occasionally—always at the Harvest Festival, for instance. I am inclined to think, though, that he came 'to plough the fields and holler'. A lot of them like to do that, you know, just once or twice a year." The Rev. C.A. Sellon smiled again.

"How long have you known him?"

The Vicar pursed his lips. "Oh, a matter of two years or so. Soon after he moved to Upchalke. He came to live there, you know, about a couple of years ago. His niece started to come to church and—well, you can guess the rest." The Vicar again concluded on a note of amiability.

Mr. Bathurst nodded equally agreeably. "Who told you his name was Robert Forsyth?"

"Why, he did, of course. Who else would have?" The Vicar's eyes contracted in surprise.

Mr. Bathurst stuck to his guns. "So that if he had told you his name was Rudyard Kipling or Little Red Riding Hood, you would have accepted the truth of it just the same? I'm sorry, sir, and I hope you'll forgive me, but you follow my meaning, don't you?"

The vicar's paleness gave way to a flush. "Er—yes—I do . . . but I scarcely considered it—"

Mr. Bathurst intervened. "Exactly, sir. You accepted him as Robert Forsyth because he told you that was his name. Just as many hundreds of people are accepted in exactly the same way. But, if you'll pardon my saying so, sir, your real mistake, as far as the man's identity was concerned, was to certify that Robert Forsyth was alive when, before you met this particular man, you had never encountered the genuine Robert Forsyth, and were taking the man, whose identity you were establishing for the County Borough of Easthampton, entirely on trust. Upon his absolutely uncorroborated word."

The Vicar stared as he heard the terms of Anthony Bathurst's verbal indictment. "Yes, yes," he said haltingly. "I see your point, now that you put it in that way, but I assure you it never occurred to me as a possibility—even that there might be . . ." He waved his hands rather helplessly.

Anthony shrugged his shoulders. "Well, there it is, sir. I'm afraid there's no doubt about it. The man whose identity you vouched for every quarter was a fraud."

"Dear me, how terrible! And I trusted him. Why, his niece was attending a Bazaar Committee on the very evening that he was killed."

"And how long before that did you last see the dead man?"

"I believe—on the previous day. When he brought me his most recent Life Certificate for my signature. He always came to me at the beginning of each quarter for that purpose . . . as you are—er—apparently aware." The Vicar coughed behind his hand.

"About the day before, eh? As close up as that?"

The Vicar had been thinking. "Yes . . . it was about the day before. It must have been. I'll tell you how I can remember. My dog was ill at the time—about the beginning of October. I've a Sealyham and the vet., Mr. McCracken, was attending him. I remember talking to

Forsyth—the man I knew as Forsyth—about the dog. Well, I must be getting along now. I've a good many other calls to make. I hope that I've helped you, gentlemen. I do really. Good-bye, Major Marriner. Good-bye, sir." The Vicar of St. Veronica's shook hands.

"What was the length of the stolen harpoon, sir?" asked Anthony.

"About four feet, I should say."

"Barb-headed?"

"Oh yes, barb-headed."

"Thank you, Vicar."

The Vicar took his departure. Anthony and Marriner exchanged further opinions. They eventually reached a certain measure of agreement; especially with regard to the present location of the lost harpoon.

"Oh, and by the way, Bathurst," said the Chief Constable, "I ought to tell you before I forget it—I've interviewed that girl with regard to the scarf with which Mrs. Bryant was strangled."

"Heather Barton?"

"Yes, Heather Barton. That's the name. She *admits* that the scarf belongs to her, but she says a she left it on the divan in the smoke-lounge at the 'Tracy Arms' when she went out that morning, where the murderer, she says, must have found it."

"I don't believe—" began Mr. Bathurst.

"You don't believe her?"

Anthony shook his head. "That isn't what I was about to say. I don't believe that I've ever handled a case where two murders have been committed and the weapon supplied in each instance. In a way, our killer has been almost waited upon hand and foot. Extraordinary thing, you know, that."

"Yes," replied Major Marriner, "I suppose it is, though I haven't the slightest idea as to how you work that out."

"I didn't," said Mr. Bathurst quietly, "it was worked out for me. Which, you will admit, makes a great difference."

Major Marriner looked thoughtful.

When he looked up, Anthony Bathurst was smiling at him whimsically.

Chapter XIX
NEWS FROM LANNING

BATHURST'S train ran into Lanning about one o'clock in the afternoon of a very delightful autumn day. He had his plans all prepared. His first port of call were the public offices of the Lanning Urban District Council. Here he repaired to the Rating section. The inquiry that he presented was referred by a junior clerk to the Registration department. Mr. Bathurst made his way down a long, bare corridor. A middle-aged lady with a pleasant manner and a high-pitched voice listened to his request.

"Forsyth," she repeated after him. "Horace Samuel Forsyth. And about two years ago. Yes, I can turn that up for you. But it *may* take a little time." She turned and spoke over her shoulder. "Miss Langridge, please. Bring me a register for the year before last, will you please?"

Anthony waited patiently. The middle-aged lady showed an inclination to become conversational. Anthony answered pleasantly. The dutiful Miss Langridge appeared with a copy of the required register.

"You've no idea of the address, I suppose?"

"It means looking for the name down all the roads and streets," she said. "But they're in alphabetical order, that's something. We'll look in Cassell Ward first. That's the most residential one, perhaps."

"Thank you," murmured Mr. Bathurst. He watched her trim finger run down the pages.

The girl with the truly Sussex name stood by attentively. The middle-aged lady flicked the pages of the register one by one. Suddenly she stopped.

"Here's a Forsyth," she said quietly. "Robert Chester Forsyth, living at an address in Runge Hall Lane—'The Antlers' is the name of the place. That wouldn't be the one, of course?"

Mr. Bathurst shook his head. "No, that's not my man. As I said, my chap's called Horace Samuel."

The lady smiled. "A relation, I suppose?"

"I am not sure," returned Anthony, "but I hope to know for certain before very long."

"I see."

The middle-aged lady resumed her search. She reached the end of what was evidently the register for Cassell Ward.

"Polehook Ward, Miss Langridge, please."

Miss Langridge handed up Register Number Two. The Registration Supervisor repeated her previous activity. Again unsuccessfully. Anthony began to feel a little anxious. But his confidence speedily returned to him. He knew that he must be right if he had read the case as he knew it must be read.

"Clayhall Ward, Miss Langridge, please."

The third register was handed over to the elder lady. More pages were flicked assiduously. Then came the turning-point.

"Here it is," announced the supervisor.

She reversed the book for Mr. Bathurst's examination. He looked at the place which her finger indicated.

"Forsyth, Horace Samuel, 58 Russell Crescent."

Anthony nodded and deliberately looked at the line below. What he read there caused him to nod to himself with satisfaction. "Forsyth, Winifred Nina." Here, then, were they whom he wanted. He made a pretence of committing the address to paper. The supervisor intervened.

"They're not certain to be still there, you know," she declared, with a warning note in her voice. "I'll make sure for you." She turned and spoke again to her assistant.

Miss Langridge produced several other registers. The supervisors—Miss Hayes, as Miss Langridge addressed her—turned her attention to them. Eventually she reported upon her findings.

"Your friend left this address somewhere about the autumn of two years ago."

"Yes, that's just about when he did leave."

"He doesn't appear in the register after the one you're looking at, so that he must have gone away from that house. I can find the exact time, or almost the exact time, when he left, if it would help you."

Anthony shook his head with a smile. "No, thank you very much. You have given me all I want, thank you."

The lady smiled in return. "Very well. Miss Langridge, put these all back in their places, please."

The pile of registers disappeared. Anthony thought of the other name that was occupying his thoughts. "Peter Stone". But he realized that to institute a search for this would be utterly futile and a complete waste of time. It was without doubt an alias, and therefore, from this point of view, meaningless. He therefore thanked the middle-aged lady again and took his departure. Outside the Lanning public offices he made for a policeman whom he had previously observed on traffic duty. He waited for a convenient moment to approach him.

"Russell Crescent? Could you kindly direct me?"

The constable pointed down the main street. "Straight down there, sir. Third right and then second left."

Anthony thanked him suitably and made his way as the man had directed him. About a quarter of an hour's sharp walking brought him to the road that he desired. Anthony noticed with satisfaction that the name "Russell Crescent" showed in a prominent position. He found which was the even-numbered side and walked down it slowly. When he reached the house that had once been inhabited by Horace Samuel Forsyth, he halted for a second or two before passing it. It was an ordinary, small house of the villa type. It was occupied, but the people who lived in the house now held no interest for Anthony. He was more concerned with those, say, at either Number 56 or Number 60. Anthony determined to take a chance with the former. He walked through the open gate-way and knocked at the front door. An elderly man of middle height answered the summons. Anthony immediately assessed him as a pensioner of some kind. He had a bald, egg-shaped head, dark, deep-set eyes, and a fierce moustache spiked at each end. He was smoking a short-stemmed pipe and wore a grey pullover arrangement. He wore no coat over this and looked somewhat suspiciously at Mr. Bathurst.

"Yes?" he interrogated.

"I'm sorry to trouble you," opened Anthony, "but I've called in connection with a gentleman who used, I believe, to be a neighbour of yours. I think that he resided at Number 58. A man named Forsyth. Perhaps you remember him?"

The man in the grey pullover grunted. "Well, supposing I do, what about it?"

Anthony smiled at him. The man countered by putting his foot rather aggressively over the step.

"I should like to ask you one or two questions concerning Mr. Forsyth."

The man leered cunningly. "And what will it be worth to me to answer 'em? Don't tell me that I shall lose nothing by it, because I've heard that tale before. I'd sooner deal with something that'll put the joint on the Sunday dinner-table."

Anthony shook his head. "I'm afraid that I can't promise you anything in that direction—either of New Zealand or Argentine. Only this."

He put a card in front of the man. The gentleman in the pull-over took it and peered at is suspiciously. Then, having taken in its significance, he nodded slowly and spat with skilful aim and precision on a spot upon his doorstep a few inches from Mr. Bathurst's foot.

"I see. That's how it is, is it? Some jiggery-pokery somewhere. Well, if that's the case, you'd better come inside, sir."

Anthony noticed how his manner had changed since he had seen the visiting-card. He took Mr. Bathurst into a small best room.

"My name's Bishop," he said. "Sit down there, sir."

Anthony took his seat.

"Now what is it that you wanted to ask me, sir?"

"You knew Forsyth, your neighbour, I suppose, pretty well, eh?"

"We were never bosom cronies, so to speak. My missus and his didn't altogether 'it it off, you see. Used to give each other a bit of what the cat cleans its—cleans itself with—over the garden fence. You know what I mean, sir, I've no doubt."

Anthony nodded his sympathy. "You remember when Forsyth moved from here?"

Anthony was amazed to see the effect that his last question had upon his companion, Mr. Bishop. That gentleman's eyes almost dropped from his head.

"When he . . . *moved* . . . did you say, guv'nor?"

"Yes. He did move from here, didn't he?"

"From next door, you mean, don't you?"

"Yes of course. From next door."

"Well, if you call going out in a box feet first, moving—you've about got it."

Bishop removed his pipe from his mouth and almost prodded Mr. Bathurst with it. Anthony knew that he must exercise caution.

"Oh, so Forsyth died here, did he? I didn't know that."

Anthony's thoughts raced perilously. This was a new departure with a vengeance! But, of course, now that he examined it as a fact, he became immediately aware that he should have examined it previously as a possibility.

"When was this, Mr. Bishop?" he asked quietly. "Can you give me any idea as to the date?"

"Yes, easy. October—two years ago."

"What did he die of?"

Bishop paused. "Well, now you mention that, it was a bit mysterious. We all of us here thought so at the time, because we never really heard that he was ill. Not a whisper of it. But, according to his missus's story, he caught a chill one evening coming home from the pictures and pneumonia set in. He was took in about a couple of days. When the undertaker brought the coffin to the house next door, it give me quite a shock. Do you know, I'd got tripe for supper that night, done in milk, with onions, and the sight of that coffin fair put me off of it."

Anthony's brain was taking in as much as it possibly could in the circumstances.

"Of course, of course! Did he have many friends in the district?"

Bishop spat into his fireplace. His skill of direction did not desert him and his length was still perfect.

"None that I knew of. Kept himself very much to himself, I can tell you. But if I may ask the question, what's the trouble? What's behind it? What's the reason of your sniffin' round? Somebody due for a gammon and two? You can 'ave what you like, you know, on the last morning."

Anthony was puzzled. Bishop essayed explanation.

"A bloke due for the nine-o'clock walk can choose his breakfast that morning, even to a nice filleted plaice. Didn't you know that?"

Anthony saw the point and apologized for his appalling ignorance.

"Oh no," he replied, "nothing really like that. Just a matter of tracing some property. It's a bit of a problem sometimes, believe me."

Mr. Bishop seemed satisfied. Anthony felt that he could do no good by staying here. It seemed to him, now that he had heard Bishop's story, that another line of inquiry was demanded at "The Antlers", Runge Hall Lane. He thanked Mr. Bishop as the latter escorted him to the door and quickly made his way back to the main road of Lanning.

He walked towards the newer part of the town, feeling sure that Runge Hall Lane would lie in this direction. An inquiry told him that he was right in his assumption and he soon found himself turning down Runge Hall Lane. He hoped that the new tenant of the premises had been satisfied with the name of Forsyth's choice—"The Antlers".

As Anthony had expected, the property generally was of the modern bungalow type. Suddenly his eyes gleamed with satisfaction. He saw the name that he was desirous of seeing on a dark-green painted gate—"The Antlers". Anthony at once entered the gate of the bungalow to the left of it. He knocked, and a rather severe-looking lady came to the door. Anthony put a request into words.

"I am sorry," she said primly, "but I am unable to help you. I have only lived here since the end of May last. I suggest that the people on the other side of 'The Antlers' may be able to supply you with the information that you want. I believe that they have resided there for several years."

Anthony thanked her appropriately, and the lady closed the door upon him decisively. He passed "The Antlers" again and repeated his procedure at the bungalow on the other side of it. This time a young man in the early twenties came to answer him. Anthony saw at once that he was both intelligent and approachable. Anthony again formulated his request.

"I'll ask Bill—that's my father," he grinned. "He's pottering about in the garden somewhere. He's got an idea he can grow champion dahlias. And as it keeps him quiet, we let him go on thinking so. Come in, will you, and take a pew."

He put Anthony into a well-appointed room and made an exit on a chorus of "Bills". His return was speedy. He was accompanied by a stout, grey-headed man with twinkling eyes in a rosy face.

"I've told Bill what you want to know, and here he is. If he talks too much, stop him every five minutes. That's what I have to do."

Bill, like his son, was geniality itself.

"I knew Robert Forsyth fairly well, through, of course, living next door to him. He lived here for some years. I remember him dying. His relation, the other Forsyth—I think he must have been a cousin or something—asked me to go in there when he was lying dead. A very decent old chap in every way. I went to his funeral up in the old churchyard. The gravedigger and a woman and I, and I think another man, were the only people there. He had few friends. Forsyth, the relation, called here and found him dead in his chair one night. Heart. And he had never been under the doctor all the time he was here. There was no inquest. A doctor was sent for and he agreed to issue a certificate, I believe. He was satisfied that the old man went under as the result of a heart attack. The relation, of course, identified him and gave all the necessary particulars."

"What relation was he? Have you any idea?"

Bill shook his head. "No. I never troubled to inquire. It really wasn't any of my business. The old man had told me once or twice, *before* this so-called relation turned up, that, as far as he knew, he had no relations in the world, so I think it was a surprise for him when this fellow *did* put in an appearance here. Still, they got on very well together, I say, and I fancy a bit of company cheered the man up."

Mr. Bathurst put a strange and unexpected question.

"Did you see the coffin when you attended the funeral?"

Bill stared at him. "Of course I did. How could I help . . ."

Mr. Bathurst amplified his question.

"Close to? That's what I should have said in the first instance."

"Oh no. I only saw the coffin in the hearse and when it was lowered to the grave. I was never really close to it."

"And the funeral took place from the other Forsyth's house? That is so, is it not?"

Bill nodded. "Quite right."

"And yet that *other* Forsyth, you say, wasn't present at your neighbour Forsyth's funeral? Although the funeral was from his house? Rather remarkable, don't you think? Or at the least unusual?"

"I entirely agree—and I even mentioned the fact to one or two people at the time. But I heard—I forget who told me, it's two years ago now, you see—that the man, the relation, was ill. Too ill to get there. I wasn't really concerned at the time—and there you are."

Bill smiled at Anthony Bathurst as he concluded his account of the Forsyth funeral. Then he seemed to think of something else.

"And what's behind your visit, sir? Bit o' money at stake?"

"Yes. We might call it that. You've certainly got the right idea. Thanks awfully." Anthony extended his hand to each of the two men who grasped it warmly. "A flying visit to Somerset House," continued Mr. Bathurst, "may solve the major portion of my difficulties. Again thanks to you!"

Bill and Bill's son smiled as one man. "Only too pleased," they said together. "After all—"

"What?" inquired Anthony.

"After all, we are here to help each other, aren't we?" Again shone the joint Bill smile.

"Are we?" said Mr. Bathurst. "I must confess that I often wonder."

Bill and his son watched his departure and then turned enthusiastically towards each other.

"Good show that—what!"

CHAPTER XX
THE TRAIL AT LAST

ANTHONY Bathurst spoke on the telephone to Sir Austin Kemble, the Commissioner of Police, New Scotland Yard. The commissioner, it seemed, had definite points of view. Major Marriner's name was mentioned on several occasions. Anthony smiled as he replied more than once.

"I agree, sir, all the time. But—and I must point this out, in fairness to *all* the men down here at Chalke—it's the most complicated case that I ever tackled. What? . . . Oh no, sir, not at all. On the contrary I have every hope. Yes—and before long. Say within a fortnight." He paused and listened again to the Commissioner. "I know, sir. But you have *(a)* the *two* Forsyths, *(b)* the Life Certificate complication, *(c)* the second murder . . . yes . . . dreadful that, I know . . . and *(d)* the wretched stag cryptogram . . . and there's the whole bag of tricks at your service. The last-named baffles me completely, but again I have hopes! Listen, sir!" Anthony put his lips close to the mouthpiece and almost whispered to the Commissioner. Mr. Bathurst concluded: "So you see, Sir Austin, the criminal first—the solution afterwards. Or first that which is natural, secondly that which is spiritual. We must leave matters at that. Good-bye."

Anthony replaced the receiver. The news that he had just received from the Somerset House inquiry suited him admirably. He knew now that he was right so far and the thought pleased him.

Before he returned to the "Tracy Arms" at Upchalke he wanted to settle one more factor in the case. He referred again to the terms of the letter sent to "Peter Stone" by "Throstle"—the letter that had been concealed by the coal-scuttle-shaped biscuit-box on the mantelpiece of the Bryants—the letter the postmark of which had been Lanning. Anthony considered the sentences of the letter that intrigued him beyond all others. "It only proves how marvellously lucky we were to see the picture when we did. Had it been on the Thursday instead of the Wednesday—well, what about it then? And just because an afternoon turned out wet." Anthony nodded to himself corroboratively. The word "picture" referred to a cinema; of that fact he hadn't the slightest doubt. Everything pointed to it. The wet afternoon. That drove Peter Stone and his partner Throstle into the cinema. The difference that was hinted at concerning two days that were successive, Wednesday and Thursday, concerned most certainly the customary mid-week change of programme. Anthony began to rub his hands. Thank God there was but one cinema in Lanning! For he was certain that Lanning was the place that had known the wet afternoon. A much larger town plus its attendant conditions would have materially added to his difficulties.

Robert Forsyth had been murdered on October the 3rd. It was pretty certain that Peter Stone had wasted little time with regard to his temporary migration from Lanning to Upchalke. Anthony remembered another phrase in Throstle's letter. "When you came to your quick decision and left here." He referred to the calendar contained in his pocket diary. It would have been, he thought, in all probability, one of the two last Wednesdays in September. Stone had gone to the Bryants, "more like the end of September". Lanning! South coast. Not too far away from London. The weather should have been much the same there as it had been in town. Mr. Bathurst turned to his own daily jottings in his diary. It had been his habit for years to make notes of the weather from day to day. It might well be that the practice would help him now. Anthony turned first to the entry for the last Wednesday in September. What he read there pleased him immensely. "Lovely Day. Sun." That should rule out September's final Wednesday. Anthony turned rather impatiently to the Wednesday of the previous week. Would the luck hold? "Dull morning. Heavy rain afternoon." There was the day that he wanted. He felt sure of it.

How long would it take him to get in touch with the Rothway Cinema, Lanning? Then he remembered that in his suit-case was a copy of the *Lanning Herald* which he had brought back with him but two days previously. Mr. Bathurst found the suit-case, the newspaper, and the telephone number that he desired. He got "Trunks" and eventually the communication. Mr. Bathurst asked certain pertinent questions of the manager. The manager replied that he would have to look the matter up. Would Mr. Bathurst kindly hang on? Mr. Bathurst intimated that he would hang on with pleasure. Considering everything, the wait that was inflicted upon him was not too long. He heard the manager's steps again as they came towards the telephone. Words came to him. Names. Names of pictures. Anthony listened eagerly.

"This was our programme on the afternoon you're asking about. *Pathé Gazette. A Woman's Devotion*. The *Home Magazine. Martin Marlowe's Marriage*."

Anthony made mental notes. Then he asked further questions.

"The Distributing Agency?"

"Yes. Where, for instance, could I see those pictures, assuming that I very much wanted to?"

The manager supplied additional necessary information. Mr. Bathurst thanked him and thoughtfully replaced the receiver. He returned to his chair by the fire. Was the procedure that he was considering worth the trouble? He carefully weighed the pros and cons. After a considerable period of intensive thought, he decided that it most certainly was. If it proved his contention in any way, his feet would then be shod with faith, and he himself buckled with the armour of light. First of all, then, he would speak to the Commissioner, Sir Austin Kemble, and then to these people whose names had just been given to him. The Commissioner would fall into line. Anthony would ask Sir Austin to accompany him to the test, as he had invited Major Revere when he had investigated the strange case of the murder of Vera Merivale. Coincidence there. But how essentially different the two problems!

Anthony Bathurst, Sir Austin Kemble, and Chief Inspector Andrew MacMorran sat in a tiny room and watched a small screen with an equally unpretentious proscenium. The three of them comprised the entire audience.

"No 'standing only' about this show," commented MacMorran.

"What have you?" inquired Sir Austin Kemble. "The entire programme or merely the two actual pictures?"

"The lot, sir," replied Anthony, "in case. You see, I'm handicapped. I don't know what I'm looking for. It may well be that I shall have to see them round twice or even more than that. Perhaps, though, it may save us time if we concentrate on what you have just called the two real pictures." Mr. Bathurst called back to the operator. "Put on *A Woman's Devotion.*"

"Ay," said MacMorran, "I could do with a basinful of that! Talk about night-starvation!"

The operator obeyed instructions, and the three men watched the picture. It was definitely bad in every way, and Anthony found nothing whatever in it that excited his attention. He then instructed the operator follow on with the programme as originally presented. There came several interesting features under the auspices of the *Home Magazine*, and then, after that *Martin Marlowe's Marriage*, which was, if possible even more appalling than its predecessor, *A Woman's Devotion.* A smiling Anthony leant over to speak to the Commissioner.

"If these are a fair specimen of Lanning pictures, this may be the reason why Forsyth the second moved to Upchalke."

The picture dragged on to its sickening conclusion. Anthony realized that he had once again drawn a blank.

"Well," said the Commissioner, "what about it now? Got any inspiration from any of that?"

Anthony shook his head. "No, sir, nothing. Not a glimmer. I'm disappointed. I don't know quite what to—half a minute, though!

There's the *Gazette* yet—we haven't had a look at that. Operator, put on the *Gazette*, will you? It should have been on at the opening, but I told you to miss it."

The *Gazette* started, with its usual varied and topical incidents. Anthony, it must be confessed, was now watching rather lazily. He feared that in some way he had missed the boat. But suddenly he felt himself galvanized into life. He saw the name Chalke show on the screen. And then the caption: "More than 'Three Fishers' at Chalke. Commencement of Annual Angling Festival. Scenes on the Harbour." Anthony craned forward in his excitement. The Commissioner realized from Mr. Bathurst's attitude that something was afoot and craned forward likewise. Anthony saw the harbour and a line of prospective anglers standing at the side of the harbour wall. A boat rode on the waves at the end of the harbour. Anthony thought that he could almost read the name on the bows. Was it *Vaar*? Just as he was making up his mind, the scene disappeared and gave way to its successor. The contestants for the Angling Championship were being introduced one by one. Anthony listened to the names with acute interest. The entries totalled between twenty and thirty. Each came forward and smiled at the audience. The announcer then stated that the competition was about to begin. Rods were poised and lines cast into the water. The announcer then made a few more general remarks.

Then came Anthony's triumphant moment. Standing by the last angler to the left of the line was a man. Up to now only his back had been visible. Suddenly this man turned, and his features for the first time could be seen properly. Immediately Anthony knew who it was. Every line of his face Anthony recognized. It was the man who had been murdered in the bungalow at Upchalke. The man who had been accepted as Robert Forsyth, the ex-rate-collector of the County Borough of Easthampton, until Wilfred Hatherley's story had set rolling the ball of doubt. Anthony remembered the photograph which he and Hatherley had looked at in the offices of the *Chalke Daily Gazette*. He recalled, too, the occasion of the annual dinner of the Upchalke Skittles Club held at the "Tracy Arms", and the thin-faced, spare-lined, hollow-cheeked man whose photograph had been pointed out to Hatherley and him as that of the murdered Robert Forsyth. This man in the picture that had just faded was the same man without the shadow of a doubt. He grasped Sir Austin Kemble by the arm and called out to the operator.

"That's all, thank you."

The Commissioner looked at him inquiringly.

"Tell me," he said simply. "What did you see?"

Anthony noticed the whimsical expression on MacMorran's face.

"So you've backed another winner, eh, Mr. Bathurst?"

Anthony grinned at him in return. "Operator!" he called again. "Show that Angling Festival at Chalke again, will you, please? Look at this again, Sir Austin. And you, Andrew. I'll tell you what it's all about when the time comes."

The three men sank back in their seats again and carefully watched what they had already seen before. At the appropriate moment, Anthony gave the necessary warning.

"That man there. Turning round to us. You saw his back before. Take a good look at him."

Sir Austin Kemble and Chief Inspector Andrew MacMorran leant forward and stared hard at the man of Anthony Bathurst's indication. The picture faded again. The operator stopped. Anthony spoke very quietly.

"That man at whom you've just looked, gentlemen, is the man who was murdered in the bungalow at Upchalke."

"Forsyth?"

"Forsyth, if you like, Sir Austin."

"Incredible! And even now I don't know that I see why you have—"

"I'll tell you what happened, sir. The murderer traced his victim through seeing him in that harbour scene just as we saw a moment ago. He discovered, in that way, where he could find his victim. I suggest that he may even have been searching for him for some considerable time."

Anthony regarded his two companions with a smile. Sir Austin spoke.

"Which means this: that *now* you can—"

Anthony intervened. "Which means that *now* I know I'm right about so many things."

"I see. Whereas before . . ."

"Whereas before I was uncertain. Yes—that's the position, Sir Austin."

"What do we do now, then? That seems to me to be the pre-eminent problem. Delays are dangerous. Even as it is, too much time has elapsed for me to feel entirely comfortable."

"The confusion as to the identity meant that delay was inevitable from the outset, sir. That was much more our misfortune than our fault. But I feel sure that the guilty person is marking time now the same as we are. He's waiting—as we are waiting."

"For what?"

"I think, sir, until he solves the stag's message. He won't move again until he's done that."

"How do you know he hasn't done that already?"

Anthony considered the question for some little time before replying. He noticed how intently MacMorran was gazing at him.

"I don't think that he has," replied Mr. Bathurst, "for this reason. The murder of Mrs. Bryant. There is no doubt at all that the two crimes are connected and, that fact conceded, the murderer of the second Forsyth is still close to the scene of his first crime. And he will remain there until he gets what he's after—what he's been after for years, probably. That's how I see things, Sir Austin."

Anthony flicked the ash from his cigarette. Sir Austin Kemble nodded his head with slow approval.

"Yes, on the whole, I'm with you. And what *is* he after, Bathurst? Tell me that, if you can."

"I don't know, sir. The doggerel has it—'My Royal Burden Straight to find.' What is a Royal Burden?"

"The crown," promptly replied the Commissioner.

"That is one, certainly," returned Anthony Bathurst, "but only one. There are others. I don't think it's the crown that they're after this time, when I remember the people that were concerned in that little problem that my commentator has handed down under the title of *The Sussex Cuckoo*. No, I think that the quarry this time is something more intrinsically valuable than the Crown of England."

"The Crown Jewels, perhaps," volunteered MacMorran perkily.

"Colonel Blood's dead, Andrew. And things are different now by a long chalk. No, I don't fancy it's the Crown Jewels either."

"But you say you don't know *what* it is." This last was almost a remonstrance from Sir Austin Kemble.

"I won't deny it, sir. But if you will allow me to say so—'tomorrow is also a day'. Give me another week."

Sir Austin Kemble regarded him critically.

"You feel confident that within a week—"

"Yes, sir. I've at last reached a stage when I can concentrate. I feel like a man who's learning Greek. I've at last mastered the alphabet. From now onward, I can see my way."

Chief Inspector MacMorran looked at Anthony with admiration. "Then I guess that means trouble for somebody," he contributed.

Chapter XXI
THE WOODCARVER'S SHOP

WHEN Anthony returned again to the environment of Upchalke he was acutely conscious of a marked change in the attitude of various people towards him. Upon consideration, he was not altogether surprised. He knew that he had shown his hand too openly and in that way declared his identity to some extent. Fentiman had, no doubt, drawn certain conclusions and, that accomplished, had not been backward in opening his mouth. Fentiman himself, Mrs. Fentiman, Mulrenan, Miss Glen, Skipwith, and Burns, and even Hatherley, who was still there, obviously with permission of Mr. Frederick Sharpe-Lodge, showed unmistakably through their various reactions that they were not prepared to accept Anthony on exactly the same terms as they had accepted him before. McCracken seemed to eye him now with a kind of jocular whimsicality. Only Stromm appeared to be unchanged, but Anthony understood this without difficulty. Stromm was not a local and therefore extraneous, as it were, to the circle of suspicious curiosity. Fentiman was inclined to be communicative, but Anthony could see that there was now definite design in all that the man said and did. Fentiman was clearly out for information, and Anthony felt by no means disposed to give it to him.

On the afternoon of the first day of his return to Upchalke Mr. Bathurst decided to take another chance. The idea had been in his mind for some time, and today he determined to put it to the test. Immediately after lunch, therefore, he left the "Tracy Arms" and took the walk by the river into Chalke. His objective was a certain shop on the outskirts of Chalke, almost opposite to Repton Straight. Its special feature, according to its advertisement and the goods that it displayed in the windows, was wood-carving. Various carved objects such as wooden coal-scuttles, wheelbarrows, arks, pipes, bowls, and, particularly for Anthony's interest, animals of all kinds were shown on shelves for sale to the public. Anthony reached the shop and walked to the window. Lions, dogs, goats, elephants, cows, horses, cats—all carved in a lightish wood, were all there priced at different values. Anthony took a cigarette from his case, lit it carefully, and strolled leisurely into the shop. A small man, a strange little ferret-like man with greyish whiskers, grey eyes, and white eyelashes, rose from a sitting position behind the counter and looked at him with an amused expression.

"Good afternoon, sir," he said.

"Good afternoon," replied Mr. Bathurst.

"What can I do for you, sir?"

Anthony smiled. "Well, at the moment, I'm not quite sure. But I'm interested in woodcarving generally and in yours especially."

The little gnomish man rubbed his hands on his apron and leant forward over the counter. His elbows, as he rested on them, looked to have sharp points.

"I'm very pleased to hear you say that, sir. Between you and me and the gatepost, I'm by way of being proud of my carving. It's the finest in the West Country, bar none. We're famous everywhere, even in the Colonies. Lymum ware is bought and sold all over the British Empire. People come in here and tell me things—you wouldn't believe the outlandish places where they run across some of my little specimens."

"I can quite believe it," declared Anthony Bathurst.

"Yes, sir. As you say, sir. Well, it's no good me doin' all the talkin'. What may be your pleasure, sir?"

"Well, I've been having a look at your windows, and I'm rather taken with a good deal of your carved stuff. First class, all of it. I don't know that I've ever seen better—of its kind."

"I'm delighted, sir." The ferret-like eyes almost danced with excitement.

Anthony went on with his plan of campaign. "The animals have caught my fancy most of all. Excellent, every one of them. The elephants are extraordinarily good. Have you any types that you don't show in your windows?"

For a moment Anthony thought the proprietor of the world-famous Lymum ware was taken aback.

"What was the particular kind that you would be wanting, sir? I dare say that I might be able to—"

Anthony interrupted him. "I was thinking that your list of animals was not entirely representative. For instance, I couldn't see any stags in your window—there's nothing at all of the stag family."

The man shook his head, but in corroboration rather than in contradiction.

"No, sir. I mean that I haven't any carved stags in the present stock, but of course, as I said, if you were very desirous—"

"Well, I was, rather—the stag seems to me to give such splendid opportunities for your work. Far more than many of those that you are showing. The intricacies of the antlers, for example—there's a chance there for very fine artistic work."

"Oh yes, sir, I agree with you. But we have turned out stags before now. At the present we just happen to be without any—that's the position. If you care to place an order with me, sir, and let me know just when you want the article delivered, I'll give you my word, sir, that I shan't disappoint you. I can assure you that we take orders for all varieties."

"I was thinking of a stag carved in, say, something like ebony. Could you manage that for me, do you think?"

Anthony saw a peculiar look come into the little man's eyes.

"Well, now, sir, that's what I call a most remarkable coincidence."

"A coincidence? How's that?"

"Why, this—it wouldn't be the first time that Lymum ware turned out a carved imitation ebony stag."

Anthony's heart gave a little leap. His long shot might yet come off! He purposely minimized his display of interest.

"Oh, really! Two minds with but a single thought, eh? Two collectors whose hearts beat as one?"

"In a way, sir. I suppose it would be that. It's some time ago that it happened, but your words just now brought it all back to me."

"Not a recent affair, then?"

The little man shook his head. "No. Let me see, now. Over a couple of years ago, I should think—from memory. But I remember it because I took the order in the first place and also saw that it was carried out. What would be the size of the animal that you would be wanting, sir?"

Anthony thought of the stags that had been in the Forsyth bungalow and approximated measurements. At any rate, a carved ebony stag would be a memento for him of the case. If only Sir Austin Kemble were with him! Anthony smiled to himself at the idea and answered the little man's questions to the best of his ability. The details of his reply were carefully noted in a book. Anthony tacked back to the point which interested him most of all.

"I've just been thinking, was this other collector that you mention a local man by any chance? If not, it's just on the cards that it might be a man whom I know."

Thereat came disappointment.

"I never knew the customer's name, sir. He dropped into the shop, very much as you yourself have done, gave the order that he wanted, executed, left a deposit, and then called back for collection on a date that we arranged. That was all there was to it. As we should say in the trade, just a cash transaction and no personal account opened."

When he heard this, Anthony realized that he had learned here all that he was destined to learn. Pity! Nevertheless he had definitely made ground. He was certain now that Lymum ware *had* played a part in the pattern of things. That the original Forsyth stag had been brought to this very shop in which he was now standing in order that an exact copy might be made from it. Another idea suddenly struck him.

"This stag that you made two years ago—was it made from a copy or constructed from measurements supplied?"

"Not from another figure, sir. Just from measurements that were given to me."

"Thank you," said Mr. Bathurst quietly. "I'll call for my stag, then, on—what day will suit you?"

The little man looked at a calendar intently. The calendar hung behind the counter.

"In ten days' time, sir, if that will suit you."

"It will suit me admirably," replied Mr. Bathurst.

CHAPTER XXII
THE CHURCHYARD OF
ST. VERONICA'S

ANTHONY Lotherington Bathurst halted and looked at the Parish Church of St. Veronica's that stood almost on the edge of a cliff that was crumbling. He saw that it was of Norman origin and Perpendicular development. He had read that beyond the cliff, less than a century ago, fifty yards of land had extended seaward from the Churchyard. Before the Marine Parade had been built, this stretch of land, known as the Hillocks, had been the great place for promenade. For where could better vantage-ground have been found for view or sea-breeze? Anthony thought that St. Veronica's must have been originally a small cruciform church, with a central tower. Later, it was obvious, the building had been converted into a much larger edifice with a tower at the west end.

Anthony, it must be conceded, was more than curious regarding the Rev. Charles Ashmore Sellon. He went closer so that he could read the notice-board that published certain information. Anthony noted the Vicar's qualifications. Then he went into the church. Under the tower stood a magnificent Norman arch, and in the porch were pillars of the same period. These pillars carried history and becoming ornament in their capitals. Anthony observed that the middle pillar of the south aisle had, amongst its foliage, four shields, of which three appeared to be original. They bore respectively two staves in saltire which terminated in *fleur-de-lis* with large crescent in the fess point, three lions heads and the letters H.M. festooned together—ascribed, Mr. Bathurst discovered shortly afterwards, to Lady Helen Marradick, the Lady Bountiful of the district in the year 1588.

The next pillar, eastward by the Vicar's stall, bore on one face a large fret, the badge of the Bryanstons, the famous Bryanston Tangle, indicative possibly of a gift or benefaction of the great Bryanston family. An old lectern supported a chained Bible. A magnificent mural painting was over the chancel steps. The church boasted a wagon roof, a Jacobean pulpit, a memorial window in the north wall to the beautiful Beryl Hartley, and a most gorgeous tapestry in the gallery (1490) that depicted the marriage of Henry VII and Elizabeth of York under the title of "The Union of the Roses".

Anthony passed on to another corner of the church. He read that a number of old coins found during the work of restoration were now contained within the old lectern. Also that the church had eight bells and seven hundred and twenty-two sittings.

It was at this moment that Mr. Bathurst had his greatest stroke of fortune. He left the church dedicated to St. Veronica by the big main door, and made his way into the spacious, strangely shaped church-yard. Immediately to his left he halted by a most unusual-looking tomb. Instead of the ordinary headstone there had been erected a tall column. The appearance of this was so abnormal that it at once excited Mr. Bathurst's keen interest. On the column, reading down-wards, there were inscribed the following words. Anthony walked towards it in order that he could the more easily read them.

Sacred to the memories

of the

REV. STEPHEN CONWAY,

Vicar of this Parish, 1849-1867,

and his brother,

REV. HUGH CONWAY,

whose untiring devotion and patient self-denial on the night of Oct. 25th, 1859, will live for ever in the hearts of all those who were privileged to know them. STEPHEN CONWAY, *born* July 8th, 1819; *died* June 22nd, 1867.

HUGH CONWAY, *born* Feb. 21st, 1814; *died* April 18th, 1873.

"And underneath are the everlasting arms."

This monument and memorial erected by the relatives and friends of the 465 human souls who perished in the terrible disaster on the night of Oct. 25th, in the year 1859 as written above, to whom the Rev. Stephen Conway wrote no fewer than one thousand and seventy-five letters.

As he read the lines, Anthony stood there almost petrified by the significance of the sculptured words. "When Death with Icy Wings did stalk, For twice two hundred human souls." Here was a definite pointer, here in front of him, with regard to the message from the antlers of the stag. The terrible disaster on the night of October 25th, 1859. Here it was, the clue that he had been seeking for so long and which had now come to him, tossed almost wantonly by the fingers of Fortune. But what was the disaster and what had it to do with Robert Forsyth and the men who had gathered round him? What had it to do with the murdered woman, Bryant? Anthony stood there, in front of the tomb of the Conways, his brow deeply furrowed in thought. There was one thing—now that he had progressed thus far, the remainder of the way should not be difficult.

He began to make his way slowly along the churchyard path. A sudden turning brought him to an angle made by the church wall. He noticed from obvious signs that this portion of the wall had been more recently erected than the remainder. A few more steps brought him face to face with two huge mounds. Anthony advanced eagerly to the first grave.

In memory of those named below who lost their lives in the wreck of the *Royal Stag* in Chalke Bay on the night of October 25th, 1859.

The words on the stone at the head of the second grave held an added sadness.

In memory of the unclaimed bodies, buried in this common grave, of those persons drowned in Chalke Bay on the night of October 25th, 1859, when the *Royal Stag*, homeward-bound from Australia, foundered.

"In death they are not divided."

Anthony's breath came more quickly now. The Royal Stag! Stag! The antlers! The ebony stag! And the vital clue that he had sought had been close at hand all the time. The irony of fate! But the ball had been placed on his toe at last.

Anthony walked quickly from the churchyard in the direction of the Chalke Free Library. He would be able to obtain information there for a certainty. Arrived there, he walked straight to the Reference Library and asked for Picton's *Manual of Sea Disasters of the Nineteenth Century*. Seeing that Chalke was implicated, the local authority would be bound to stock a copy. Mr. Bathurst's assumption proved to be correct. Picton's *Manual* was produced, Mr. Bathurst signed the necessary receipt and retired to a tranquil corner where he might read in peace. His grey eyes gleamed as he came upon the following report and settled down to digest it.

> The *Royal Stag* was wrecked on the Murray rocks in Chalke Bay on the night of October 25th, 1859. The *Royal Stag* was a full-rigged ship of 3000 tons burthen, with auxiliary screw, belonging to Yardley, Gibb and Co. of Liverpool. She had left Melbourne on August 26th, 1859, with 322 passengers and 188 officers and men. She carried a light cargo of wool and hides and approximately £850,000 partly in gold ingots and partly in gold coin.

Anthony nodded to himself as he read. He was beginning to understand now why Forsyth had died with a harpoon through his chest. Strange, that, seeing that the Rev. Stephen Conway had once been vicar here. He went on with his reading.

> The wreck was due to the terrible storm which raged round the coast on the night of the disaster. The *Royal Stag* struck a terrific on-shore wind against which her screw and engines were entirely powerless, and though strenuous endeavours were made to anchor, the anchor dragged until the ill-fated ship struck on the sharp, tooth-edged Murray rocks in Chalke Bay about 3 a.m., finally breaking up at 8.22 a.m., when no less an 465 persons lost their lives. Of the 510 people on board, only 45 lived to tell of the wreck. Many of the panic-

stricken, frenzied passengers were drowned owing to the fact that they were carrying heavy belts of gold-dust round their respective waists. The bodies of the victims were buried in the little churchyards along the coast in the various bays in which they ultimately came ashore, but the great majority rest in the churchyard of St. Veronica's, Chalke. In this churchyard, also, all the unidentified bodies were buried in a common grave, which grave is now within the precincts of the church. It is impossible to speak in too high terms of the Rev. Stephen Conway, the Vicar of St. Veronica's, and his brother, the Rev. Hugh Conway, who was staying at the Vicarage on the night of the disaster. Words cannot adequately convey an idea of their untiring devotion and self-denial during the fearful scenes they were called upon to undergo. At the time of the wreck, the Vicar, never sparing himself, took into his personal charge no fewer than 222 bodies, and made a complete catalogue of the personal effects found upon each in the hope that it might be found possible at some future date to establish certain identifications. Captain Garfield O'Connor, the commander, was the last man to be seen on board alive; and one seaman, a Maltese, by name Samuel Forsetti, escaped miraculously, actually swimming ashore with a rope. £300,000 value of the gold that the *Royal Stag* carried was subsequently salved by divers, but the depth of the water in certain parts of the bay and the strong-running cross-currents made operations difficult and there must still remain great wealth round the Murray rocks in Chalke Bay which may or may not be wrested from the sea at some future time. Golden sovereigns (carried by the *Royal Stag* from Australia) were picked up in large quantities for many months afterwards on the sands near the scene of the wreck, and from time to time—indeed, up to the year 1920—pieces of wreckage have drifted ashore on the Chalke coast which have been identified as having belonged to the unhappy *Royal Stag*. A contemporary writer has written the following passage concerning the wreck. "So tremendous was the force of the seas that struck the *Royal Stag*, and so mighty were the walls of waves, that one great ingot of gold was beaten deep into a strong and heavy piece of the ship's solid ironwork, in which also eight loose sovereigns were found as firmly embedded as though the iron had been liquid when the ins had been forced into it." A curious walking-stick found among the wreckage and believed to have belonged to Capt. O'Connor, the commander, was for many years in the possession of the Rev. William Futchells, Rector of Poplar, and for a period in 1899, following upon his death, was on view in the window of a shop in Brunswick Road, Poplar.

Anthony Bathurst put down his book and endeavoured to collect his many devastating thoughts into something like order. Gold. Coins and ingots. Half a million unaccounted for—according to Picton's *Manual*. In Chalke Bay somewhere. Of course it had been an ebony stag! And the dwelling-places of the Forsyths had each been named "The Antlers". A Maltese, Samuel Forsetti by name, had escaped by a miracle and swum ashore. Anthony picked up the book again and looked at the name. It attracted him. Pity that the account omitted to give Forsetti's age. That fact might have helped Mr. Bathurst considerably. He wrote down once again, on the back of a used envelope that he took from his pocket, the lines of the memorized message.

> When Death with Icy Wings did stalk,
> For twice two hundred human souls,
> I drew the Serpents from their Holes,
> To meet a Waterloo at Chalke.
> Try then the Sails that never fly,
> My Royal Burden Straight to find,
> For One shall Live if One shall Die,
> If Out of Sight—*not* Out of Mind.

And then, having written the eight lines, Mr. Bathurst added the line of letters that had been on the reverse side of the piece of paper. Z/J/AHEI. In this last connection, an idea had already occurred to Anthony and what he had read but a few moments ago had revived the association. Substituting numbers for letters according to the ordination of the alphabet, Mr. Bathurst immediately had the following line of figures: 26/10/1859. Here was the date of the disaster of the *Royal Stag*, for if she had met the storm on the night of the 25th October, she had certainly not struck the Murray rocks until the morning of the 26th. Anthony, therefore, was satisfied. Much was becoming plain, and he must now again examine the eight lines of the message. Anthony looked again at Picton's *Manual* and then decided that he need have no more of it. He therefore returned it to the library attendant, at the same time making a request for Pliny's *Natural History*. He was desirous now of testing yet another idea. The attendant obligingly handed over the second volume. Anthony Bathurst returned to his chair, opened the work of Mr. Pliny, and turned up "Stag". For some moments he read on without finding what he wanted. But at length his patience was rewarded. Mr. Bathurst reached a passage which he read with avid interest.

> The reason why a stag symbolizes Christ is from the ancient idea that it draws serpents from their holes by its breath, and then tramples them to death.

Then followed a footnote to this effect.

> In Christian art the stag is always depicted as the attribute of St. Julian Hospitaller, St. Felix of Valois, and St. Aidan. When the stag is shown as having a crucifix between its horns, it alludes to the legend of St. Hubert, and when it is portrayed as luminous, it belongs to St. Eustachius.

Anthony Bathurst closed the labours of Pliny and rubbed his hands. Here was certainty confirmed and corroborated lock, stock and barrel. This meant now that the first three lines of the message were deciphered. And yet one more, Anthony saw, if he but looked ahead a little distance. "My Royal Burden Straight to find" obviously referred to the gold cargo that the *Royal Stag* carried, much of which still lay deep around the Murray rocks in Chalke Bay. But did it? That was the question. What had happened since 1859 to bring this train of murder? The remaining lines, unhappily, still meant nothing, or almost nothing, to him. What was meant by the allusion to "Waterloo", and then again, to the "Sails that never fly"? Anthony took his copy of Pliny back to the "Reference" counter and smiled at the bespectacled, frozen-faced attendant.

"Thank you," he said to her. "I am obliged."

"It must be true," he remarked to himself on his way out, "that beauty lies in the eye of the beholder otherwise we should all be submerged in a sea of troubles and by opposing *not* end them."

Mr. Bathurst walked slowly back to the strange atmosphere that now distinguished the "Tracy Arms".

Chapter XXIII
THE NET BEGINS TO CLOSE

To his surprise the first people to meet him in the lounge, upon his arrival, were Wilfred Hatherley and his chief, Mr. Sharpe-Lodge. Anthony Bathurst advanced to them with a question on his lips.

"What? Back again, gentlemen? And to what do we owe the reason of this further visit?"

Sharpe-Lodge answered him with an air of furtive mystery. "There has been a second murder, Mr. Lotherington. A second crime of violence has been committed. Why? But, of course, I waste my time. For you know of these things better than I myself."

Anthony chose the words of his reply deliberately.

"I know of the second murder. I was here, on the premises, when the woman was killed. But I know no more of it than that. Regrets if I disappoint you. Where were you yourself—and Mr. Hatherley?"

"We went back to our work at Easthampton. It was necessary. My advice was wanted, on a matter of the mechanization of accounts, due to the trouble up at Milburne. I took Hatherley with me. When I heard of this last terrible development, I immediately instructed Hatherley and we returned. I run away from nothing, sir. I have never run away from anything. Nor do I shirk anything that may even be broadly regarded as my responsibility." As he spoke, he turned and looked at Anthony with his curious, bird-like stare. "You don't catch me, you know," he added. "I'm afraid that I'm too old a bird for that to happen—when I credit Plant, I never fail to debit Stock. Do I, Hatherley?"

"Never, sir."

"You can vouch personally for that?"

"I can vouch personally for that."

Hatherley's replies were comically solemn but clearly sincere. Anthony thought of the paper that had been stolen from the drawer in his bedroom on the evening when he had dined on the *Vaar* with Vass and Captain Stromm. Somebody had known that he was with Stromm that night, without a doubt. At the same time there was the risk which had always been present since the theft of the paper. The risk that the murderer might solve the hidden meaning that it held, gain his objective, and then disappear silently from their midst. Disappear as silently as he had come. Anthony determined to take a chance.

"You can clear your minds of the idea that the murders, or even the first murder, cast any reflection upon the County Borough of Easthampton itself."

Sharpe-Lodge jerked his head to one side. "Now isn't that considerate of you? Mighty kind, I call that."

Anthony smiled at him. "Why do you say that? Did you already know?" Mr. Bathurst's tone was bland and his inflexion ingenuous.

Sharpe-Lodge seemed a trifle aggressive. "The Reverend Sellon, the Vicar of St. Veronica's, Chalke, has been good enough to set my mind at rest on that account. He assures me that he signed the Forsyth Life Certificates in perfectly good faith. I was determined to leave no stone unturned until I had assured myself on that point." Sharpe-Lodge puffed out his unhealthy-looking cheeks in a terrific attempt to attain importance.

"You mean that the Reverend Sellon was merely careless? He accepted a condition that was placed before him without any intelligent inquiry? Oh, I entirely agree. Believe me, Mr. Sharpe-Lodge, those Life Certificates of yours were but the minor means to a major end. Sad though it may be, Easthampton can be regarded as itself again."

Sharp-Lodge coughed behind his hand, and as he did so the door of the bar opened and McCracken came out, accompanied by Mulrenan and Captain Stromm. Fentiman was close on their heels.

The landlord of the "Tracy Arms" appeared to be remonstrating with McCracken.

"Look here, Andrew," he was saying as he came through the door, "that's all very well from your point of view, but I have the reputation of my house to think of. All your talk of what you're going to be in the future doesn't pay my brewer's bills. No, sir! I'm to blame. I should never have listened to you in the first place. I was warned not to."

Mulrenan clapped Fentiman on the back and gave a high-pitched, giggling sort of laugh.

"You and your warnings, Fentiman! You amuse me. If we'd listened to you in the first place—well, I ask you!"

McCracken's face beamed with satisfaction and he was evidently in the highest spirits. As they came abreast of Anthony, their voices ceased, and Mr. Bathurst knew why. Since Marriner had come here on the morning that Mrs. Bryant had been murdered, Anthony had observed several differences regarding personal association and contact. Sharpe-Lodge and Hatherley drifted away with the advent of the others, and Anthony intercepted Captain Stromm. The Swede's hand shot out, and he grasped Anthony's as the other men passed on.

"I thought you'd gone. And I was even a little hurt that you had not, as you say here, wished me good-bye."

Anthony shook his head. "No, I hadn't gone in the way you mean. As you see, I've come back."

Stromm smiled. "I am glad. For my holiday is nearly up. I return home tomorrow."

"By boat?"

"Of course, Mr. Bathurst. Vass has put in again—a special commission. I would go no other way." Stromm lowered his voice. "It is sad—this poor woman here being killed. The police seem to have made little headway. The atmosphere here has changed so since you left us. They all whisper at each other and look at one another—as you say—sideways. Fentiman and McCracken and Mulrenan and all those others. I have been a little bewildered when I have seen it all. That attack on you was bad enough, but nothing like this. It has spoiled the last days of my holiday." He spoke simply but feelingly.

Anthony nodded. He felt that he could understand Stromm's position, and, to a large extent, sympathize with him. Stromm continued in his slow way.

"Although, of course, it will all be a tale for me to tell when I get back to my native land. That is something that can be placed on the other side of the account. For they say that a teller of tales is always a popular fellow." Stromm smiled his slow smile. He beckoned Anthony to come nearer to him. "And if I tell you the truth, Mr. Lothering-ton, and I do, because you have been extremely kind to me during my stay here and I feel that I must do something for you in return, let me put you on your guard." And Captain Stromm lowered his voice. "You have been attacked once already. I know that, because I was with you at the time. I like to think sometimes that I may even have helped you then."

Anthony put his hand impulsively on Stromm's arm.

"You did, Stromm, you did! Have no doubt of it, man!"

Stromm nodded his head slowly. "Thank you. I am very pleased—much more pleased than I can express—to hear you say that to me and to know that you mean it." His face beamed, but he soon grew serious again. "I said that you had been attacked once already. Well, look out for yourself again." Stromm turned his head and looked in the direction of the door through which the other men had just passed. "I have noticed—besides the whispering that I spoke of—that they hold no goodwill towards you. More than once I have caught the sound of your name in their conversation. And it has been accom-panied by ugly looks. Especially from—"

Anthony heard the door open behind them, and Stromm paused abruptly.

"Especially from whom?" demanded Anthony eagerly.

But steps could be heard coming towards them. Stromm was on his guard at once, and started forward away from Anthony before he waved his hand in a gesture of good-bye. The move seemed an eminently natural one, and Anthony understood the reason of his dissimulation.

"When do you sail?" cried Anthony, catching the spirit that Stromm had initiated.

"Tonight!" cried Stromm without turning round again. "Come and see me. Before eight. We'll drink a farewell glass."

Anthony understood what lay behind the captain's words. Stromm would give him the name for which he had just asked him. A clever touch!

"I will," he cried after him, "and thanks a million."

Mulrenan and McCracken passed him as he stood there, and made their way upstairs. Within a short time Anthony Bathurst took the same direction. He walked straight along the corridor to his bedroom. His footsteps made but little sound on the strip of carpet that covered the middle of the way. Before he came to the place where the corridor turned, he heard the sound of a bedroom door shutting. He quickened his pace. Mr. Bathurst came to his bedroom door and opened it. As he entered the room, something at once caught his eye. It was a piece of paper pinned to the pillow at the head of the bed. Anthony Bathurst wasted no time in collecting it. He was amazed to see that it was a message to himself, typewritten in facetious terms.

"Dear Interfering Bathurst,

Yes, it's true, you see! We recognize you in your true colours at long last! Although, of course, we suspected you from the first, you hid your real identity very successfully for a long time, and as a result nearly caught us napping. How unfortunate for you that the murder of the Bryant woman meant that you must leave your ambush and come into the open! Otherwise, who knows what might have happened? Well, here's a piece of information for you. Thanks to your copy of the "stag" cryptogram (that you so kindly left for us in your drawer), you may be pleased to know that neither Forsyth nor Mrs. Bryant died in vain! But you may not be so pleased when you realize that you have met your "Waterloo" at last. Your "Waterloo", be it noted, which is not the right "Waterloo". Ha-ha—what a cinch it was, directly the paper came into our possession. Thank you for so kindly providing it. And the funniest thing about it all is that you haven't the remotest idea as to our identity! How are the mighty fallen, to be sure! At the same time, you're lucky. Lucky to be alive! If it hadn't been for your pal, that hulking Swede, being with you at the wrong moment and upsetting our calculations, we should have got you. Good night, dear, blind, bamboozled Bathurst—go back to London and buy yourself a pair of pink ones serene in the thought that all's fair in love and war, and that you will never be forgotten by—Gunga Din and his mate. Why "Gunga Din"? Well, we ask you, even if you can't solve the message from the "stag", surely you can see that! All the best, my dear Old Bathurst!

G.D.

Anthony smiled as he read it, but the smile held a dangerous quality. Two things became more clear to him than ever before. One, that he must waste no time with regard to any of his preparations, and, two, that he *must* solve the last lines of the "stag" cryptogram within the next few hours. He carefully placed the paper that had been pinned to the pillow in his wallet, and made his exit from the bedroom. A few paces brought him face to face with Heather Barton. She looked bright and smiling, and held out her hand to him.

"I want to thank you, Mr. Bathurst," she said simply, "for your kindness. I took the advice that you gave me the other day and it has worked out splendidly. Nearly all my troubles are past and over."

"I am so pleased," returned Anthony.

She passed on along the corridor. Mr. Bathurst rubbed his chin contemplatively. Then he pulled himself together and went back to the lounge. According to his calculations, he had approximately five hours and a half in which to accomplish the task that he had set himself. He looked at his wrist-watch to confirm his impression and prayed that his luck would hold.

CHAPTER XXIV
A PIECE OF OLD CHALKE

MR. BATHURST'S objective was a bookcase which he had observed, from time to time, standing in a corner of the lounge. True to the tradition of the country, the "Tracy Arms" boasted but a mean, poverty-stricken library, but Anthony had previously noticed that on the top shelf of this bookcase was a book the title of which had held a certain amount of attraction for him—*Old Chalke—Its High-*

ways and Byways. Anthony looked into the bookcase and saw to his relief that the book of his desires was still there. His discoveries with regard to the wreck of the *Royal Stag* had given him a new angle of thought and, in consequence thereof, at least one definite idea. He took the book from its place on the shelf and settled himself down on the big chesterfield in the middle of the smoke-lounge. If ever his wits were to be double-edged, now was that occasion. He would go through this book from cover to cover, and it might be that the vital clue would come to him.

Mr. Bathurst started his desperate pilgrimage on page one. A map of Old Chalke and Environs. Anthony looked it over carefully. It contained no indication such as he wanted. The Charter of Old Chalke, with extracts therefrom. The medieval history of Old Chalke. Its identification with Calcinium which the Antonine Itinerary placed at 168 miles of Londinium. The ancient village of Atchette. The old palaces, in the vicinity, of the Kings of Wessex. The liking of Henry IV, the Bolingbroke of Richard II, for the district and it surroundings.

Anthony read and read again. The agility of his brain, well practised in mental gymnastics, availed him nothing. The first mention in 1199 of the Manor of Chalke. Recorded to have been held by Roger de Dorchester by the sergeanty of a penny per annum and the fourth part of a knight's fee, a Manor which, at that time, consisted of 322 acres. Then the succession to it of Sir Guy de Tanning, that renowned warrior of the time of Edward III, who performed such prodigies of valour at the Siege of Calais, towards which adventure Chalke furnished four ships and sixty-two mariners, a fact symbolized now in the mayoral chain of office. It had been, according to this account, Sir Guy who, with Queen Philippa, had pleaded with the Royal Edward for the lives of the six Calais burghers when Edward, in his royal anger, would have ordered their deaths.

Other famous names followed. Sir Lancelot Tristram, Sir Aloysius Hellarde, Lord Rupert Halcrowe, Christopher Marnocke. Anthony still read on. The setting up of the Court of Quarter Sessions. The visit of Good Queen Bess to Chalke on her way to Truro in 1562. Pictures of Old Chalke market. Tables of Statistical Information over which Mr. Bathurst shuddered and travelled quickly.

Anthony looked at his watch again. To his dismay, an hour had already gone, and he knew that he was four-fifths of the way through the book. He determined to see the matter through to the bitter end. At length, he came to a chapter entitled "Places and Objects of Interest in Old Chalke and the Surrounding District."

Anthony, it must be admitted, was by this time beginning to tire. The Mynch, with its antique lighting-poles. Reddar Gorge. Frewmoor. Oaken Hill and the Silver Capped Island. The beautiful old-world villages of Pyner, Wildellar, Sloane Fitzagon, Great Musgrave, and Albion Redorum. The Wessex Museum with its geological treasures and rare fossils, its old stocks, unique for the fact that they held four malefactors, its Aumbry and Wood Tracery from a thirteenth-century chapel, the Cynewulf memorial, dated A.D. 774, the old, disused mill right near the sea at Chalke Gate, first built in 1682, then burnt down at the beginning of the nineteenth century, and rebuilt in 1815, the year that Wellington defeated Napoleon Bonaparte on the field of Waterloo, in memory of the Duke's great triumph. The ancient lych-gate—Stay . . . Waterloo . . .

Anthony looked up from the book, his heart pounding against his ribs. Waterloo at last! An old, disused mill close to the sea. Excellent! An old, disused mill! His hands closed on the edge of the chesterfield. "Try then the Sails that never fly." A disused mill—the sails of which would never fly again. Of course! Here was the solution and the reason why the Forsyths had come to Chalke from Lanning and met "murder on his way"!

Anthony began to think hard. Even now the murderer had beaten him to it, and he mustn't spare a single second beyond the demands of necessity. More than that even. There was the distinct possibility that he was already too late. He must forgo his appointment with Captain Stromm, valuable though it might have proved. Unless, of course, he could fully act within the period that preceded it. Chalke Gate! He knew in which direction it lay—he had seen the name many times on signposts. Judging by the description of the place that he had just read, this place, Chalke Gate, would be approximately three to four miles away. Inasmuch as it was close to the sea, there would probably be two approaches to it—an inland route and a coast road.

Anthony deliberated. Again he looked at the time, for he found himself confronted with a problem. Should he consult Major Marriner at once, or should he first of all act on his own initiative? But for the presence of the vital factor of time, he strongly inclined towards the latter action. After all, he had nothing proven, nothing clear-cut that he could show to the Chief Constable, and say, *"Le voilà!"* He felt that, although he had such a small time-margin for safety, he must make sure, or, at any rate, *more* sure, of his ground before he could go to Marriner and ask for official action. If, by the last chance of all, he turned out to be wrong—well, the subsequent position would be by no means a pleasant one for him.

Mr. Bathurst replaced *Old Chalke—Its Highways and Byways* within the bookcase, and paced the room. Suddenly he stopped, and threw up his head. He had made his decision. He would go to the old mill himself before he went with his story to Major Marriner. He would see the lie of the land himself before he took any other action. He *must*.

Chapter XXV
THE OLD MILL

Mr. Bathurst closed the door of the smoke-lounge behind him and unobtrusively made his exit from the front door of the "Tracy Arms". If it were possible—and he was moderately certain that it would be so—he intended to travel by the coast road that ran along the top of the cliffs. He climbed to the summit of the hill, over the brow of which he would come eventually to the cliffs.

On his way, he passed McCracken standing in the porch of his establishment. He wore a maroon-coloured pullover with grey flannel trousers, and a pipe stuck aggressively from a corner of his mouth. He smiled at Anthony as he walked past, but did not speak. At the top of the hill he came to the old-world bungalows appropriately modernised with the long front gardens where, not a hundred yards distance apart, Burns and Skipwith lived. Strangely enough, each was in his front garden as Mr. Bathurst went by. Like McCracken, at the foot of the hill, each man smiled at Anthony as he walked by the front gates. Neither of them waved to him; neither spoke.

Anthony pushed on ahead and soon struck the coast road that he desired. At various points wooden barriers had been erected at the cliff's edge to indicate the danger of crumbling headland due to sea erosion. Anthony carefully noted the places. At times, where the vantage-ground was safe, he went close to the edge and looked over at the sea. Yellow, churning water some distance out caught his eye, and he guessed that he was looking at the chain of rocks in Chalke Bay, the Murray rocks, whereon the *Royal Stag* had foundered somewhere like eighty years ago. The cliff road rose and then fell again, but Mr. Bathurst maintained a level pace, and eventually, after just over an hour's walking, he faced a weather-beaten signpost that pointed to "Chalke Gate—½ mile".

To Anthony's pleasure, and also to his relief, here the path across the cliffs descended, and soon he found himself at the top of a flight of rough wooden steps that had been cut in the face of the cliff. Anthony took them and within a few minutes came down on a wild expanse of seashore, immediately behind which was a long, undulating stretch of grassland. Few habitations were in sight, and Anthony guessed that many a keg of brandy and bale of lace had been landed here in the past years without paying due toll and excise to the officers of His or Her Majesty's Revenue. In all respects and conditions, the spot was ideal for adventure.

Anthony turned his back to the breaking sea and scanned the horizon in all directions. His heart leapt, for there, away to the east, his eyes picked out the stationary sails of an old windmill. A quick calculation of distance and intervening obstacles showed him the most convenient route to take to get to it. Across miniature hills and coarse tussocks of wind-blown grass, Anthony slowly worked his way round towards the site of the old mill. He passed nobody, and not a soul was in sight. He realized more and more the meaning of his journey, and endeavoured to visualize the conditions of that dreadful night in October, eighty years ago, when the *Royal Stag* had broken up on the Murray rocks.

When he came to the mill, he saw that it stood in a kind of enclosure. This enclosure was shaped almost in the form of a square and was rounded by a wooden fence about seven feet high, broken and battered in many places. There were the remains of scattered outbuildings and the ancient ruin of a dwelling-house that stood dilapidated and desolate almost in the middle of the enclosed space. From his first half-glance, Anthony saw that this mill, in its best days, must have been an exceedingly prosperous venture. He looked over the fence. There, on the body of the brickwork, he could read "The Waterloo Mill, 1815". Anthony looked up at the sails again. Many years had passed since they had turned to the caress of the wind. Rebuilt in 1815, and given the name "Waterloo" for that reason, Anthony could see that the mill had known little of its appropriate use since the *Royal Stag* had met its end in Chalke Bay. Perhaps even in the year 1859 itself the sails had already ceased to revolve. If that had been so, the original task had been rendered much easier for those who had come here seeking.

Anthony found a suitable gap in the broken fencing and went into the enclosed space. The neglected grass was growing almost knee-high, and to his satisfaction, nowhere could he see any sign of a path or of grass trampled down. He walked right up to the ruined dwelling-house. Decay and dilapidation were in evidence everywhere in and around it. Human habitation must have ceased generations ago. Anthony made a circuit of the building. The "stag" cryptogram had been in the possession of the murderer for some days now, it was true, but there might still be a ray of hope.

Anthony left the ruined dwelling-house and walked in the direction of the outbuildings. These were in similar conditions to everything else that he had seen there—wretched and ramshackle. One had evidently been used as a granary. Floor had been built on floor, and there were the double doors through which the flour sacks had been hoisted for husbanding or for distribution. Mildew and rotting wood showed almost everywhere.

Anthony looked up to the top floor and made a quick calculation of the height. He then walked round to the rear of the granary, and at once something met his eye that caused his heart to beat more rapidly. For amidst this scene of dire desolation there lay a reminder of contemporary association. Anthony Bathurst strode forward and picked it up. It was a gold cigarette-case. Mr. Bathurst opened it. It was, unfortunately, empty. Anthony turned it over in his hand, but it was innocent of initials or, indeed, of any clue that might have assisted him in the matter of establishing an identity. He put the cigarette-case carefully into his pocket. Here was an indication which he couldn't possibly ignore. Mr. Bathurst felt strangely disturbed.

He took a few paces away from the granary, and then he saw something else. Here, on the rough pathway, were the unmistakable marks of the tyres of a car. Anthony followed the car-tracks for a distance of about a hundred and fifty yards. They led him, he felt, to a piece of ground that had probably in the past served the occupier of the "Waterloo Mill" as his garden—probably his kitchen-garden. Suddenly the tyre-marks stopped. There were deep ruts in the ground. Anthony looked ahead, and his heart sank. For there, straight in front of him, was a square patch of ground that had recently been dug. The newly turned earth showed black and soft, in striking contrast to all the ground around it. Anthony knew only too well what these signs meant. He was too late. "The Royal Burden" had been found and might well be miles away while he was standing there. Anthony marvelled at the intelligence and astuteness of the murderer. Then he cursed softly and seriously.

He had but one chance left to him now. To get his man before he had had time to dispose of his haul. He must see Stromm at all costs. The evidence that Stromm had promised would clinch the matter and enable him to proceed with complete confidence. He must get back to Chalke at once, without the slightest delay. He ran back through the long grass to the broken fence. As he ran, he saw something shining on the top of the grass. He dived for it and picked it up. It was an Australian sovereign dated 1858.

Chapter XXVI
CHECKMATE FOR MR. BATHURST

Anthony did the journey back to Chalke in what must have been almost record time. In the town he made straight for a telephone and spoke to Major Marriner. Anthony's tones were grave, and directly he heard them the Chief Constable of Remenham realized that both he and his auxiliary were rapidly nearing the time of crisis.

"You have no doubt, you say, Bathurst?"

"Well . . . very little, sir."

"For God's sake, don't make a mistake. You think that Stromm will give you the name *that you're expecting to hear*? It's astounding—from almost every point of view—whichever way you look at it. I can't altogether take it in now. What?"

"You'll find I'm right, sir, when all the smoke has cleared away. It's been a shock to me, I give you my word. Now, let us go over again what we've arranged. Do you mind repeating it, and I'll check up on it in its various stages? Go ahead, sir, will you?"

Marriner recapitulated Anthony's suggestions. Anthony nodded from time to time.

"Right. Right. That's it. Absolutely in order. Now, that's a load off my mind."

"Good, Bathurst. Now, when shall I see you again?"

Anthony spoke quietly into the mouthpiece. Marriner replied at once.

"I understand. You're sure that you think it better policy not to close in at once? I'm strongly tempted to move with—all right! Just as you wish. Let your friend at court settle it definitely for you. I can understand your feelings in the matter. Goodbye, and, for God's sake, be careful. I don't want Sir Austin Kemble crying out for my dead body to replace yours—even at the price of a spectacular triumph. Cheero."

Anthony replaced the receiver thoughtfully, and slowly retraced his steps to the "Tracy Arms". Sharpe-Lodge met him in the doorway. He was opening a packet of cigarettes as Mr. Bathurst entered.

"Hallo!" he exclaimed. "Have a cigarette? I'm glad to have the chance of another word with you, because I'm leaving early this evening, and I was afraid that I might miss you. I didn't want that to happen. That would have placed the proverbial straw on the camel's back. He can't change his spots, you know."

"No," said Anthony in reply, "but very often, when I consider the question, I don't think that he wants to. Where's your man Hatherley?"

"Gone," returned Sharpe-Lodge. "The Ministry of Health auditors have arrived at Easthampton for the annual audit of the accounts, and Hatherley is required there. I have discovered from past experience that he makes a most admirable and effective conduit-pipe. You know what I mean—'lyaizon' officer. So I had to send him back. Great pity! He was terribly disappointed. Still, there you are—needs must when Machiavelli drives, and it's no good locking the horse in the stable after the door's been opened. It's beyond the pale, and half a loaf's better than no bread."

Sharpe-Lodge emitted a puff of smoke. Anthony nodded rather hopelessly.

"As you observe, Mr. Sharpe-Lodge. Well . . . I must drag myself away. I have a great deal to do. I don't know in what circumstances we shall meet again, but, whatever they are, I shall always remember you. You have assisted me considerably."

"How *are* things in *the* direction?" asked Sharpe-Lodge carelessly.

"Little progress, I fear. From what I hear—and pieces of news *do* filter through from time to time—the police meet a blank wall everywhere. Still, a little later and things may change. You never know, and as you would agree, the darkest hour immediately precedes the dawn. Let's hope that's the case this time."

Anthony shook hands with his companion and went to his room within the "Tracy Arms". "Extraordinary man," he thought to himself, "and with, doubtless, many gifts—not the least of which is personality. Stayed on here later than his assistant, Hatherley. Rather surprising—that!"

Mr. Bathurst made certain preparations for the ordeal which confronted Marriner and him and which was but a few hours off. Dress? He decided, after a certain amount of consideration, on cap, mackintosh, pullover, and grey flannel bags. Luckily he had included all of these when he had packed his suit-case on the morning that he had left town—the morning after he had received the warning by telephone. It would be an advantage to him to travel fairly light, and the clothes that he had selected meant, at any rate, a certain amount of comfort. In addition, Mr. Bathurst placed in his pockets his two usual allies for an adventure of the kind that he contemplated—his revolver and his electric torch. By this time but one doubt assailed him. He was uncertain as to whether the prize, the *Royal Stag's* Australian gold, had been removed entirely, or transferred temporarily to a spot from which it was again to be picked up. Had he known which of these conditions applied for certain, he could have advised Marriner with so much more exactitude. Still, he must chance the possibility of either, and make arrangements on those lines.

Mr. Bathurst carefully placed his things conveniently to hand and then repaired to the dining-room for a little light refreshment. Stromm had said before eight. He would leave here at seven. That would give him ample time for the one vital conversation with Stromm before he acted in conjunction with Marriner. He checked up again carefully on the time factor. There was this to it all the way. Whatever he did himself, the Chief Constable was watching the game at the principal end, so that nothing could go wrong there.

Anthony left the "Tracy Arms" precisely at seven o'clock. As he crossed the threshold, he could hear the clock of St. Veronica's, away over in Chalke, chiming the seventh hour of the afternoon. He travelled by the motor-omnibus that runs between Hatchett and Chalke and which stops just outside the "Tracy Arms". He took this step purposely. This particular bus—"the seven o'clock in", as it was known to all the intimates of the "Tracy Arms"—was invariably well filled and, in this respect, Anthony Bathurst was playing for safety. There is nothing more conducive to personal safety than a bodyguard consisting of many members of the general public.

The bus ran into Chalke uneventfully and Mr. Bathurst alighted at the usual terminus, opposite the saddle-maker's shop. It was fairly dark now and this particular part of Chalke, all along the parade as far as the harbour, was by no means well lighted, especially at this season of the year. Anthony decided to avoid promenade in case his movements were known and he had been trailed, and go by the road at the back of the hotels, which runs past the famous Janet Ford's Cottage and then turns sharply to the entrance to the harbour.

Walking quickly, he reached the harbour approach without hindrance. He took a hurried glance at his watch. The time showed at twenty-two minutes past seven. So far, so good. But from this moment things began to happen. He had scarcely set his foot on the big cobblestones that paved the approach to the harbour when a man stepped from the shadows and accosted him. Mr. Bathurst's hand closed round the butt of his revolver. The old elementary game, of course, of the counterfeit messenger.

"Mr. Lotherington?"

Anthony s heart leapt at the words. He knew now that crisis was close at hand. He must be wary if he were to come through this alive.

"Yes," he countered.

"Captain Stromm sent me down to meet you, sir. You're rather later than he expected. He was worried about you, I think. The *Vaar*'s been shifted to the other side of the harbour and it's very dark down at the end there. Come with me, sir—I'll take you along."

Anthony looked into the man's face. It was a thin face with dark, peering eyes. The man was tall and spare and wore a dirty, torn jacket over a blue jersey. Anthony felt certain that this man was not from the *Vaar* and that he himself was not intended to reach Stromm that night. He tested him.

"Is Captain Vass aboard?"

The man nodded. "Oh yes, sir. The skipper's there."

Anthony thought now that he had seen the man before somewhere. There was something about his face . . .

"Right-o," he declared. "Lead the way. I'll follow you."

Anthony motioned the thin man to walk in front. To his relief, the man accepted the imposed conditions without demur. They went slowly. It was a dark night and the cobblestones of Chalke harbour are large and clumsily laid. Anthony picked his way upon the man in front of him. Now, the wall of Chalke harbour runs a good half-mile into the open sea, through deep, fast-running water, and it was some time before Anthony caught sight of the *Vaar*.

"What time do you sail?" he inquired casually.

"Do we sail?"

"Yes—the *Vaar*. What time?"

The man shook his head. "I don't know, sir. I hadn't heard when Captain Stromm sent me down to meet you."

Anthony wondered more and more and held his revolver more tightly. Suddenly the man almost stopped and his walk appeared strangely hesitant. Anthony's eyes never left him, which fact proved Mr. Bathurst's undoing, for a few paces farther on he tripped headlong over a rope that had been stretched across the harbour from side to side. In a flash the man turned and was on him. Anthony felt the impact of a flying form, saw an upraised arm that held a nasty-looking weapon of sorts, was helpless to avoid it. He lurched sideways as he lay on his shoulder and the stunning blow fell on the side of his head. Dazed and almost powerless, Anthony felt the world slipping from him, as his assailant wrenched at him again, heaved at his prone body, and then sent him headlong into the water. For the third time in his adventurous career, Anthony felt that this must be the end. Piercing thoughts stabbed at his brain as he was falling. If only Marriner would be able to . . .

Chapter XXVII
CAPTAIN STROMM TAKES A HAND

HAPPILY for Anthony Bathurst, Fate intervened. The blow that had been aimed at him with the intention of rendering him unconscious had been only partly effective. His quick lurch away from it was destined to save his life. Instead of having been knocked silly, he had taken his bludgeon, or whatever the weapon had been, on the side of his forehead, which meant that the weapon had caught him a glancing blow that had put him out but temporarily. As it was, his lapse into complete unconsciousness lasted but a few seconds. His falling body struck the water and the cold shock it gave him restored him with a sharp intake of shuddering breath to the conscious state. Under ordinary conditions Anthony was a strong and practised swimmer, but he was weakened and shaken now, apart from the handicap of his clothes, and he knew that he could not last out for long.

A quick mental calculation proved to him that he was considerably nearer the sea-end of the harbour than he was to the shore end. He must try to reach one of the boats there. It would tax his strength and his powers of endurance to the utmost, but he knew that it was his one and only chance of coming through that night alive.

Firstly, to give himself a rest, he turned on to his back and floated. His head was bleeding now and excessively painful. The contact of the salt rather aggravated the pain, but the sting and the smart all helped to sharpen his consciousness and to intensify his realization that if he were going to win through he must fight, and fight hard. Luckily the mackintosh which he was wearing was loose-fitting and quite free round the armpits, so after a few moments' rest Anthony turned from floating and struck out strongly towards the sea. By now the coldness of the water was brought home to him acutely and his head became a thing of dead, dulling, numbing pain. But Anthony kept on, and for a time was able to make fair headway. He swam on but he knew that he was fast reaching the limit of his resources and that unless he soon came to boat of sorts all would be over for him. He continued to swim on, but his strokes gradually became feebler.

When he thought that all was lost, however, he suddenly became aware of a huge black shape that seemed to tower in front of him and then to engulf him. Anthony threw out his hands in what was really a semi-despairing effort to grasp something. Then it flashed through his brain that the black shape was a boat and that, if his luck still held, salvation for him might be at hand. The water tossed him helplessly against the side of the boat. His shoulder and arm were bruised and buffeted by the contact. Then, when at almost his last gasp, he saw that there was a porthole open, and with a desperate effort he launched his body towards it. As it touched the side of the boat Mr. Bathurst flung out his arms again and by a miracle of miracles caught hold of the edge of something. He held on tight, heaved his body forward through the porthole, and then fell headlong to the floor. A wave of suffocating blackness passed over him . . . and Anthony knew no more.

He has never been quite sure as to how long he actually lay there, but when he came to, Captain Vass was bending over him, saying, "Drink this, my dear fellow," and Stromm, smiling genially, was kneeling beside him, propping his head up.

"Where am I?" said Anthony weakly.

"On the *Vaar*," returned Vass, "in a cabin, but how you got here we are none of us yet very certain. All we know is that one of the crew found you lying here unconscious and reported the fact to me. I found Captain Stromm here and between us we have managed to pull you round. But come on, don't talk yet, and don't worry. And get this brandy down your throat."

The grateful spirit speedily warmed and revived Anthony, and within a comparatively short time, with new life in him, he felt capable of certain action.

"I must get these wet clothes off."

"That will be all right," returned Vass. "I will get you some others."

"And then I must get back to the harbour when I have had my word with you, Stromm—that highly important word." He smiled at the Captain.

Vass looked dismayed. "But we are on the open sea, some miles from Chalke harbour. We had been under way an hour before you were found. But tell us—what happened to you? We are both puzzled."

Anthony rapidly told the two men what had occurred.

"Please oblige me, Captain Vass. Send a wireless message to the Chief Constable at Chalke—Major Marriner. Tell him where I am, will you—it's desperately important? He has made an arrest tonight in connection with the murders at Upchalke and I must get back to him, because I hold absolutely vital evidence in the case. At any rate, I must let Marriner know where I am."

Vass beamed over him. "I can do that for you. Indeed, I shall be pleased to do it for you."

"Thank you, Captain Vass; I am your debtor." Anthony turned to Stromm. "They did their best to keep me from reaching you, Stromm, and came within an ace of succeeding, but they failed—and a miss is as good as a mile. I made it! Tell me, Stromm, what was the name that you promised to pass on to me if I came to you tonight?"

Stromm smiled and then spoke to him slowly. . . .

"You are a wonderful man, Lotherington! I am proud to have met you and more than delighted to be able to help you. I am touched by your courage and determination. I will write the name down for you . . . and let me tell you . . . I am pretty certain that my suspicions will be eventually proved correct. Let me find a piece of paper."

Stromm groped in his pocket for suitable writing-paper. At last he found a piece. Anthony waited impatiently for Stromm's information. Stromm thought for a moment and then wrote two words across the paper in a sprawling hand.

"I am not used to writing your English language," he said apologetically, "so you must make allowances, as you say, if the writing is not too clear. But there is the name that you have done so much to get. I would have told you in the hotel, but I thought it might be dangerous for you and perhaps help to put them on their guard." He passed the piece of paper across to Anthony.

Mr. Bathurst read what Stromm had written and a great wave of thankfulness and relief seemed to come across his face.

"Thank God I was right, Stromm!" he cried. "That is the man whom Marriner was to arrest tonight. Your confirmation removes all doubt from my mind."

"I am so pleased," said Captain Stromm.

"And I," said Vass, "will go and send this gentleman's wireless message, and also see about some dry clothing for him. All's well that ends well."

The skipper of the *Vaar* made his departure.

"This man," said Stromm hesitantly, "he will be hanged?"

"I hope so—if he's proved guilty. He deserves it."

"That is a great pity! To be hanged. I am always sorry about a thing like that. A pity! A life . . . and the other lives too—the murdered people—thrown away!" Stromm shook his head philosophically.

A member of the *Vaar*'s crew entered the cabin with an armful of clothing.

"Here you are, Lotherington," said Stromm. "Put this on. Then you will feel a lot better."

Anthony needed no second bidding. Dressed in dry clothes again, he bathed the cut on his head with warm water. Stromm left him to it and Anthony pondered over his recent words. Stromm—of all people—a sentimentalist! Vass knocked on the door.

"My operator has sent over your message and he has just picked up the answer."

"And what is that, Captain Vass?"

"The Chief Constable of Remenham is sending a boat out for you. It will overtake us, so that the *Vaar* need not delay or slow down at all. And I am pleased." Captain Vass smiled with all the cordiality of his nature.

Anthony shook hands with him in appreciative spontaneity. "You're a good chap, Vass, and I shall be eternally grateful to you. You and Stromm have helped me no end. I was afraid just now that my presence on board the *Vaar* was going to prove a nuisance to you, but your news makes me feel much better about things."

"It is a pleasure," returned Vass, obviously delighted by Mr. Bathurst's expression of gratitude. "Anything that I can do I will do most gladly."

"I am sure of that." Anthony looked at his watch as he spoke. "What time do you expect them to pick me up?"

Vass cocked his head to one side in calculation.

"Not for nearly an hour yet, I should say, making allowance for the difference in speeds. We have been under way getting on for two hours now, you see."

Anthony nodded in understanding.

"Now that you are more yourself again," said Captain Vass, "come into my cabin and have another 'spot'. Then we can wait in there for your escort to come along. It will be more pleasant and more comfortable sitting in there."

Anthony accepted the invitation with alacrity, and shortly after they reached the skipper's cabin Vass sent along to Stromm to complete the party. The *Vaar* was now making good headway and he could see that Vass's calculation concerning the overtaking boat could not be a great deal out. Stromm duly came along and they chinked glasses. Eventually Anthony unburdened himself.

"I've a sort of confession to make to you two chaps. In a way, it's only right that I should. But my name isn't Lotherington as I've been leading you to suppose. Lotherington happens to be my second Christian name. It's not my surname. My surname is Bathurst. My full name—Anthony Lotherington Bathurst."

He saw Vass staring at him with a surprised look in his eye.

"Anthony Bathurst! Then I have heard of you! You are the well-known crime-expert—the investigator!"

"That's right. I'm the man. But don't flatter me, skipper—I wouldn't say any too well known."

Vass held out his hand. "Shake, Mr. Bathurst. It's an honour to meet you."

Stromm followed suit—a twinkle in his eye. "It is my ignorance and my misfortune, I suppose, never to have heard of you, Mr. Bathurst, but I, too, am delighted. Although I am a simple man and I shall always remember you as Lotherington—my very good friend Lotherington. You understand?"

"Of course—and what suits you suits me. So Lotherington goes with me, Captain Stromm."

"Why did you hide your identity, may I ask, Mr. Bathurst?" The query came from Captain Vass.

"Well, I came down from Scotland Yard at the special request of the local police to look into the Forsyth murder, and it was agreed among us that I should have a better chance if the locals did not know who I actually was. As Lotherington, I had a much better chance, you see, of picking up valuable information."

"And do you think that it has worked out that way?" asked Stromm.

"Oh, it helped, no doubt . . . although it took us a long time to get our man. Still, the proof of the pudding's in the eating. Thank you, skipper."

Vass again filled the three glasses and merriment and camaraderie flourished in the cabin of the skipper of the *Vaar*. The time went by unheeded and unchecked when suddenly, whilst in the midst of a maritime reminiscence, Vass stopped speaking abruptly and listened. Anthony heard the sound of men's voices shouting to each other. He was able to distinguish sounds. "Ahoy—*Vaar*!"

"There's your boat, Mr. Lotherington—I mean, Bathurst," said Vass. "And that means goodbye, I'm afraid."

Anthony nodded. "I'm afraid so too. But you saved my life tonight, and I'll never forget it."

"I must go on deck."

"I'll come with you. What about your clothes that I'm wearing?"

"Send them on to me at Narvik. 'Care of the *Vaar*' will find me."

Vass, followed by Anthony and Stromm, went on deck. A large motor-boat rode the waves by the side of the *Vaar*. About six men were aboard. Anthony quickly picked out Major Marriner.

"You there, Bathurst?" shouted the Chief Constable. "By Jove, but you've put our hearts in our mouths, I must say."

"I'm here, sir, thanks to helping hands."

Vass went to the rail and shouted down. "Come aboard, sir, and crack a bottle. I'll heave to and drop a ladder."

"O.K.," bawled Marriner, "but I can't stay too long."

He climbed the rope-ladder adroitly and swung himself aboard. After shaking hands with Vass, he walked straight across to Anthony.

"Congratters, Bathurst! Our man is safely under lock and key in Hatchett gaol, you're alive, and the case ended. But, tell me, did Stromm agree with us? Was his name the same as ours?"

"The identical man, sir. I was relieved when he told me, I can tell you."

The Chief Constable turned to Stromm.

"How did you guess? I tell you candidly I didn't. When Bathurst here told me, I was astounded."

Stromm smiled. "He gave himself away to me—three times in all. Can you stay a few more minutes? It will not take longer than that. Yes? Then I will tell you. I should like to tell you."

Vass issued instructions. Major Marriner went to the rail and roared to the crew of the motor-boat.

Chapter XXVIII
NOT WANTED ON THE VOYAGE

"Three times he gave himself away to me," repeated the astute Stromm, delighted beyond measure to hold the stage in this manner. "I will tell you when they were."

"I shall be most interested to hear," interpolated Mr. Bathurst, "if only to compare notes and to see how far you agree with me."

Stromm nodded compliance. "Yes, of course. Well, the first time was when he used Miss Barton's scarf to strangle Mrs. Bryant with. I was behind him in the hall of the 'Tracy Arms' when he first noticed the scarf hanging on the banisters. And I saw him notice it, if you gentlemen can follow what I mean. Yes?" He paused on a note of inquiry.

"Yes. Go on," prompted Anthony.

"Well, when I heard about the scarf having been used for the murder, I felt certain I knew the man. So I settled down to watch him more closely."

"You're a man after my own heart!" cried Anthony with impulsive admiration.

"That's the first point. Now for the other two." Stromm smiled. "The second may not be quite so simple to follow and understand, but it arose out of his—what is your word?—reaction . . . his more recent reaction towards you, yourself, Mr. Lotherington. I beg your pardon—I should have said Mr. Bathurst. Old habits, you see, are hard to break."

Major Marriner smiled broadly. Stromm, unperturbed, carried on.

"He began to watch you. Your every word, your every movement. All his watching and all his wariness were the actions of a guilty man. But what he *didn't* know was this. That all the time that he was watching you—*I* was watching him. Every time that we were together in the 'Tracy Arms'. Talking eating, drinking—anything that you like. Oho—it was good that—that game of cat and mouse—because it was also a game that two could play."

"And *did*," remarked Anthony.

"And did." Stromm repeated the words.

"Now for your third and last point," contributed Anthony. "And then I'll check up with you. Up to the moment, I'll say you're doing well."

Stromm put his finger to the side of his nose. Vass understood what the gesture was intended to convey. That Falk Stromm, late of the Swedish Navy, would recount this story of his exploits on behalf of the British Police Service in all the beer-gardens of Narvik—and, in addition, that the story, such as it would be, would lose nothing in the telling! As he thought these things, Captain Vass smiled hugely to himself. But Stromm was by this time in his stride again.

"The third time was the day before yesterday. He used the telephone in the 'Tracy Arms'. I overheard certain words of his message. I was left in no doubt at all. That was why I told Mr. Loth—Mr. Bathurst here that I was confident I could give him the name of the man. He nearly came to grief getting to me, but he managed it in the end, and Captain Vass and I were very glad to see him, let me tell you."

Stromm's recital finished on the same note as that on which it had begun—with a smile.

"Well," said Anthony, "I'll be frank. I was able to pick up only *one* of your points, but that's neither here nor there. You've taught me a lot, Captain Stromm, and I'm always ready to learn off anybody. We ought to have pooled our brains earlier and worked in double harness. Well, Major Marriner, we must get back to our prisoner. I want to interview him within the next twenty-four hours. There's a lot missing in the story yet. Many gaps—and gaps that only he can fill. Will you make arrangements, Captain Vass? Major Marriner and I must get back."

"I will see to it for you at once," said Captain Vass, as obliging as ever.

"Good."

Vass left them. Captain Stromm shook hands with Anthony and turned to find himself looking down the barrel of Major Marriner's revolver. Spoken words trailed lazily into his brain ". . . for the wilful murder of Horace Samuel Forsyth and Rose Woodburn Bryant . . . warn you . . . anything that you may say . . . used in evidence against you." Now there were handcuffs on his wrists. His fury was speech-less, but his eyes blazed in an angry vendetta—a vendetta none the less vindictive for being helpless.

Vass returned and fell back in amazement. Anthony made quick explanation. The explanation was followed by an inquiry.

"Luggage? Yes. Some in his cabin—some below. Altogether a suit-case and six sacks of potatoes. King Edwards, he said the pota-toes were. He's very fond of them and can't get them in Sweden, so he told me."

"Or in England, either," remarked the Chief Constable, "from now onwards. Get them on deck, will you?"

Vass gave quick and urgent orders. The strange procession formed and within a few minutes the motor-boat that had intercepted the *Vaar* was speeding back to Chalke harbour. One of its passengers sat fierce-eyed, silent, and tight-lipped. Recently expressed words of his own raced monotonously through his brain. "A life thrown away." He writhed impotently in his seat, but the handcuffs held him fast.

Meanwhile Anthony Bathurst exchanged views on many things with the Chief Constable of Remenham. And at the bottom of the boat lay six sacks—not of potatoes, but of good Australian gold!

CHAPTER XXIX
ANTHONY BATHURST FILLS IN THE BLANKS . . .

Sir Austin Kemble, the Commissioner of Police, New Scotland Yard, Major Marriner, Chief Constable of Remenham, and Anthony Lotherington Bathurst sat in the library of the first-named at his private house that nestled charmingly in the Surrey hills. They had dined well and Sir Austin was athirst for information. His other natural appetites in the same direction had been partly satisfied and there was ample time to complete the effect.

"I understand, Bathurst," he said, "from what Major Marriner tells me, that the Crown will be able to attach to the case an adequate motive. I am very pleased to hear that."

"That is quite true, sir," replied Anthony. "To begin with, we have traced the prisoner back to Lanning, where he has lived for some years. He went there, in the first place, of course, to be near Forsyth. By Forsyth, I mean the genuine Forsyth, the retired rate-collector of Easthampton. We won't call our man Stromm any longer—his real name is Gabriel Rock, wherefrom hangs a story."

Major Marriner intervened. "Once we had that name in our possession, we had a definite jumping-off point and very soon matters became highly interesting. But Bathurst will tell you. Go ahead, Bathurst."

Anthony smiled and took up the story again.

"You have already heard, sir, of the wreck, of the *Royal Stag* on October 25th, 1859, the undoubted genesis of the case. Well, Major Marriner and I have instituted intensive inquiries and we have learned that gold to the value of nearly half a million was subsequently salved from the wrecked ship by professional divers who were employed on the work of salvage by the shipowners of Liverpool. During the diving operations, so the Chief Constable had been informed, a considerable portion of the salvage went astray, estimated by some people at £100,000. It was removed from the wreck, but never accounted for properly, and after a time suspicion attached itself to two of the divers who had been at work at the time and were the last men known to have handled it. These men, by name, were a John Forsyth and a Charles Rock, the father of the retired rate-collector and the grandfather of the man awaiting trial."

"But I don't quite understand," intercepted Sir Austin Kemble.

"You will, sir, if you wait patiently," said Mr. Bathurst imperturbably. "Forsyth and Rock were brought in guilty and received heavy sentences, but the missing gold was not found."

"Till the other day, I suppose?"

"Till the other day. Forsyth and Rock had contrived to bury the gold not far from the sea-shore, in the garden, probably, of the old disused 'Waterloo Mill', but were suspected, arrested, and went to prison before they could lay their hands on it again. By a strange stroke of Fate, both died in prison and neither of them ever saw the old mill again. *That* is what we know, what we have so far established." Anthony drained his glass. "For most of the remainder, sir, you must allow me to draw upon my imagination. I've chatted it over with Major Marriner and he agrees with me that what occurred afterwards must have been something after this fashion. The first man of the two imprisoned divers to die was Charles Rock. He passed on certain information to his son, but it contained nothing definite enough for the son to act on it safely. Besides, Forsyth was still alive, with every prospect of liberty in the near future. The information that Rock minor had, such as it was, went from him to our Rock, the grandson, whom I will call Rock minimus. But again the information was too inadequate for successful action. In the meantime, however, John Forsyth had died in prison, leaving behind him the message that we have come to know as the 'stag' cryptogram, the message that Gabriel Rock eventually solved and, as we now know, acted upon. John Forsyth managed to convey this to his son, Robert—who received it, I suggest, concealed in the carved ebony stag. But Robert was a rate-collector, and the risk and the uncertainty of the venture made but little appeal to him, so that he did nothing about it."

"Until he retired," contributed the Chief Constable quietly.

"Yes," echoed Mr. Bathurst. "Robert Forsyth retired to Lanning, to where Gabriel Rock eventually traced him."

"I am a little puzzled," remarked Sir Austin. "Why didn't Rock trace him before—when he was at Easthampton?"

"That was due, I think, sir, to two things. Gabriel Rock's father didn't tell him of his grandfather's past until just before he died, and also, Easthampton was a long way from the West of England, to which part of the country both the Rocks and the Forsyths originally belonged."

"I understand. Proceed, Bathurst, please."

"Gabriel Rock, you see, was a man of more imagination, more initiative, and more industry than either his father or grandfather before him. He had the idea that Forsyth had certain information in his possession which, added to his own, might well put him on the road to the recovery of the stolen gold. So he went to live at Lanning, made Forsyth's acquaintance, cultivated it, and, I think, got certain facts from him without ever learning the terms of the 'stag' cryptogram or the Chalke allusion. Then Fate dealt another strange hand."

"Enter Horace Samuel Forsyth," quoted Major Marriman, "L.U.E."

"That's it," said Anthony, "that's it exactly. Now H.S. Forsyth also lived at Lanning, and the fact that he was a namesake of Robert Forsyth brought the two men together. They probably met one day—quite fortuitously, shall we say, at a shrine of Bacchus—discovered that they were namesakes, were interested thereby, and fostered each other's acquaintance. I have known this happen before, in actual personal experience. So there at Lanning we have the stage all set for ultimate tragedy—Robert Forsyth, Horace Samuel Forsyth, and Gabriel Rock—all 'old chinas' together."

"Excellent," said the Commissioner, rubbing his hands. "Robert contented with his lot, Horace Samuel perhaps a little mercenary over trivial things, and, between the two of them, Gabriel watching and waiting for the clue that would help him to his heart's desire—his grandfather's stolen fortune."

"Your picture is an authentic one, Sir Austin," said Anthony. "I am almost sure of it."

"What happened then?"

"A very simple thing," replied Mr. Bathurst. "Just a little something that is happening somewhere every day. Robert Forsyth died."

"Then the fun began," chuckled the Chief Constable.

"H.S. Forsyth, who was a pretty wide bloke, realized that Robert of that ilk had no relatives to mourn or exult at his decease. He found him dead one night, and, grasping the situation at once, he hit upon a cunning scheme by which Robert's four pounds a week allowance from the Superannuation Fund controlled by the County Borough of Easthampton might be his until the end of his own allotted span. He took charge of all the final arrangements and worked matters thus. *(a)* Representing himself as the next of kin, he registered the death in his own name—Horace Samuel Forsyth. *(b)* He cleared out after arranging for the funeral to be from his own house. Rock was the only man at all interested, and Rock, not wishing to attract attention, was lying low. *(c)* After a few days he returned to Robert's house, went systematically through Robert's papers, and then wrote to Sharpe-Lodge, the Easthampton Treasurer, notifying him of the necessary change of address. His scheme was by now almost perfected. He had decided upon Upchalke because Robert had either talked about the Chalke connection with H.S.F. or he found the clue in the stag and had decided that he might have two strings to his bow as well as one. You never know, he argued, and one fine day he might be able to land the 'stag' gold! Robert's signature was copied faithfully—other correspondence could be typed—and one day when Master Gabriel Rock was passing by the place where Robert had lived, an wondering, no doubt, how he could lay hands on the cryptogram, lo and behold, he found the place empty—furniture and everything gone. Suspicious of what he saw, his next call would be on H.S.F. When he found that *he* had flitted too, friend Gabriel began to put two and two together, and after a time realized most acutely that his next job must be to locate the missing Horace Samuel."

"Just a minute," put in Sir Austin. "How about the doctor's certificate? How did H.S. Forsyth get over that?"

"I've considered that. And I made inquiries at Lanning with regard to it. Robert died suddenly from a heart attack. The doctor who was called was satisfied as to the cause of death, and H.S.F. obligingly supplied the name that suited him."

"I see. Now another point. If Robert had discussed the stag and Chalke with Horace Samuel, why hadn't he done the same with Gabriel Rock?"

"Can't tell you that, sir. I don't know for certain that he *did* talk to Horace Samuel. All I know for certain is that *Rock* was ignorant, otherwise he would have turned up in the Chalke district two years before he did. Still, as I suggested just now, Horace Samuel may have found the carved stag and the clue that it contained after Robert was dead."

"All right. Go on."

"The prologue is just about over," remarked Marriner. "You will soon be on to the play itself."

"Well," continued Anthony, "Rock had to find Horace Samuel before he could do anything. That is obvious. For a time he could have had no success. The wily Horace had covered his tracks far too well. Until Fate dealt another picture-card. One wet afternoon in Lanning—during last September, to be precise—Gabriel and Mrs. Gabriel, caught in the rain in all probability, went to a 'flick'. And suddenly, while they were in the cinema, a piece of the world jumped up and hit them hard between the eyes. *Pathé Gazette* was shown on the screen. Remember it, Sir Austin? You saw it with me and Andrew MacMorran. Gabriel Rock—our friend, as he once called himself, Peter Stone—was probably watching quite nonchalantly when the blow came. A scene from Chalke was put on the screen. You saw it with me and you remember my excitement. For there, standing in the picture, his face easily identifiable, was the man for whom he had been looking for so long! The man with whom he so badly wanted a spot of intensive conversation *re* a little matter of his grandfather's loot. Horace Samuel Forsyth!"

Sir Austin emitted sounds of pleasure. "What a break for him! Of course I understand it all better now."

"The skein is now disentangling itself," proceeded Anthony. "Gabriel went to Chalke, located Horace S. at Upchalke without revealing his own identity, and took lodgings with the Bryants. And he was prepared for an arduous campaign, for in order to take H.S.F. by surprise he disguised himself with a black-haired wig. He had gone for the stag—or, rather for its secret—and what that secret was *he meant to discover*. But I don't think that he intended to murder the man for whom he had come. I'll tell you why later. By this time Horace Samuel has firmly installed himself at Upchalke, *with his wife*, as Robert Forsyth. Who was there to say him nay? And here I come to a serious weakness in the Easthampton Treasurer's Department with regard to what their Treasurer calls 'identification by Life Certificate'. Look at it for yourselves, gentlemen. Horace, recently arrived in the district, goes to the Vicar of St. Veronica's when Easthampton requires the first certificate that Robert is still alive, and says in effect, 'Sign this for me, Vicar, please. It's for my pension.' Now the Vicar's *only* knowledge that the man is Robert has come from the man himself, who has been in that district but a few months! But he blithely signs—because he accepts him as Robert. As we *all* accept one another, more or less. Think of this, Sir Austin. It's a point worth thinking about—and needs attention."

Sir Austin and Marriner nodded.

"I agree," said the Commissioner.

Anthony went on. "Now I have just stated that Horace Samuel was disporting himself at Upchalke *with his wife.*"

Marriner looked up in evident anticipation of what Mr. Bathurst was about to say.

"But that is true to a point only. Robert Forsyth had no wife, and Horace Samuel thought it would be safer at least for him to have none. In case of stray and unexpected visitors who might perhaps pop in on him one day, thinking him to be Robert. So the wife had become 'a niece by marriage', as far as the outside world was concerned. We found Horace's marriage-certificate at the Forsyth bungalow, and when that happened—fortified by all that Hatherley had told me, which was continually being supported—I began to see glimmers of daylight peeping into the case and to feel certain that there had been deliberate substitution."

"I am still bewildered," declared Sir Austin. "You said just now that you don't think Rock intended murder. Why do you say that?"

"Because Rock took no weapon with him when he called on Horace Samuel. In the quarrel that ensued—he alleges self-defence, you know—Rock used the harpoon that Horace Samuel himself had stolen from the Vicar. Rock has never had a lethal weapon. He has used a stolen harpoon and a borrowed scarf."

"Why did Horace steal it?"

"I don't know, sir. Possibly as a weapon of defence to have handy in case it were wanted, or because it attracted him as an old sailor home from the sea. You see, I knew the dead Forsyth had been a sailor and not a rate-collector at a comparatively early stage of the case. Dr. Thorold informed me that the dead man, when he was first called to him, was wearing his left sock inside out! This is an old superstition of the sea, Sir Austin. The sailor does this to keep bad luck away. So there I was—pretty confident quite early that it was not Robert Forsyth who had been murdered."

"Why didn't Rock find the carved stag and the clue inside it?"

"I fancy that he watched Horace Samuel for some days without the man being aware of it. And from what he saw at odd times he knew that the carved ebony stag was a prized possession. I think that H.S.F. had begun to think more seriously, by this time, of the hidden gold. Very likely he had been unable to read the meaning in the message. But he was a downy bird—he had had a second stag constructed for him in case of complications, and he kept the original in the outhouse where we were lucky enough to find it. Rock got hold of the counterfeit and, as you know, smashed it to smithereens in his attempt to find the cryptogram. An attempt which he afterwards repeated—again unsuccessfully—only to steal it from me sometime later."

"Yes, I follow that. What happened then?"

Anthony rose from his chair and smiled.

"Then came the most difficult part of the case, from the standpoint of the investigator. After the murder of Forsyth, Rock strolled down to the harbour—he knew there was a boat there—not back to his lodgings with the Bryants. And this boat—it wasn't the *Vaar*—took him to Sweden, where Vass picked him up later to bring him back for his so-called holiday. Vass, quite reasonably, thought he lived there—he told Vass so, no doubt—and then, gentlemen, by all the laws of logic, whenever I looked towards him, he seemed the one man in the affair who absolutely must be innocent because he appeared to hold the perfect alibi. Vass was so genuine and authentic, and unwittingly, of course, supplied Rock with the right ring, as it were."

Anthony lit his pipe, and they watched him intently as the flame of the match lit up his face. For a few moments there was a silence.

Chapter XXX
. . . AND ROUNDS OFF THE CURVES

Anthony sat down again.

"Shortly after he returned to Upchalke to renew his quest, Rock made my acquaintance. I think that he was curious about me, so he invited me to the *Vaar* and paid carefully selected ruffians to stage an attack on me, out of which he himself emerged with flying colours to establish himself as an ally. For a long period, this blinded me to the truth, but I really think that I may be justifiably forgiven for the lapse."

Marriner and Sir Austin nodded.

Anthony continued.

"About that time he brought off his master stroke."

"How do you mean?"

"He had been carefully trailing me—he knew that Major Marriner had roped me in—and he stole the cryptogram. He had seen me in 'The Antlers', no doubt, and guessed that our search of the place had been more successful than his. So there he was now, as well off as I was—if not better.

"He communicated with his wife at Lanning, Sir Austin—probably from Narvik. She went to Chalke at once. Where the Chief Constable went, she went. She followed you to my place when you came that night sir. 'Phoned me afterwards—and warned me off! Painted a picture of deadly peril."

Anthony laughed at the savour of the reminiscence.

"Go on, Bathurst. You've got me all worked up, my boy. In many respects, it seems to have been the most baffling case that you've ever encountered. What happened next?"

"Well, sir, again he scored over me. He solved the cryptogram before I did, lifted the gold that his grandfather and Forsyth's father had 'conveyed', way back in 1859, from the waste places of the old mill and—because he considered it by far the safest plan that he could possibly adopt—waited for Vass and the *Vaar* to come to Chalke again to make his getaway. But by this time, by a stroke of luck that came to me in the churchyard of Saint Veronica's, I was well on his heels. And, at a most awkward time for him, he ran into his first patch of bad luck."

Anthony stopped again. The look on Sir Austin's face was almost fascinating him.

"What was that?" inquired the Commissioner of Police, round-eyed and with impetuous eagerness.

"Mrs. Bryant came on the stage when he had almost forgotten her. He had not known that she was periodically employed at the 'Tracy Arms' when there were guests staying there—it was a chunk of bad luck for both of them. One day she recognized him. And what was worse from her point of view, he *knew* that she had recognized him!"

"How did she recognize him? His appearance, no doubt, was greatly changed. You say that previously he had worn a black wig, whereas now—"

"I think, Sir Austin, that in all probability she recognized his voice and indiscreetly showed him that she had done so. From that moment she was a doomed woman."

"There's just one thing about that which occurs to me," said Major Marriner, "and that's this. Even if Mrs. Bryant did recognize him, had he such a great deal to fear? Look at it in the cold light of logic. She could prove nothing against him—nothing at all. After all, the only crime that she could allege against him was that he had lodged at her house a short time previously—under another name. What was there in that?"

Anthony shook his head in definite disagreement.

"That is true, sir, but to a point only. If Mrs. Bryant had told, say, Fentiman, her employer, that one of the people staying at the 'Tracy Arms' had recently stayed with her, disguised, and, as you say, under another name, that story of hers would, at the very least, have directed suspicion of a sort towards Rock. Fentiman would have thought the fact strange, would have discussed it with other people, and Rock would, without the least doubt, have been talked about. Will you concede me that?"

Major Marriner nodded rather half-heartedly.

"Ye-es. I'll grant you that. But still, when you come to analyse it all—"

Anthony interrupted. "Just a minute, sir. Proceed again from the position which I had just reached. Rock is being talked about because of his strange conduct. *At the time of a murder*—a murder committed but a short distance from where Rock had been staying. And all this additional to the fact that Rock had disappeared from his rooms with the Bryants *directly after the murder*, without a word, hint, or suggestion beforehand that he might be going, and had never returned. Won't you admit now, sir, that I have put a different complexion on the matter?"

The Chief Constable inclined his head good-humouredly.

"All right, Bathurst. You win! Go on."

"Thank you. Well, you know how he murdered Mrs. Bryant and the weapon that he employed. He had beaten me to the secret of the old mill, and when I heard that he was leaving the 'Tracy Arms' I knew that he had what he had come for and was making a complete getaway. Also he left me a chatty little note which cleverly diverted suspicion from himself. At least, that was the intention. My job now was to get him alive and, if possible, the *Stag*'s Australian gold as well. I arranged matters with the Major here. I was to go on board and, even if we started, the Major was all ready to intercept the *Vaar* somewhere. He had a watch on the harbour and knew the moment that she sailed. Rock did his best to drown me before I got on board the *Vaar*, as I've already told you. I took a chance there, and although I was on my guard, knowing full well that treachery was intended, that rope across the harbour was something for which I wasn't prepared and hadn't bargained. Once aboard, I still had one thing to do."

Anthony rose and began to pace the room.

"What was that?" inquired Sir Austin Kemble.

"Why, this—that when Major Marriner's boat came alongside and hailed the *Vaar*, Rock should still be unsuspecting, and, when the time came for us to take him, come like a lamb to the slaughter. That meant that there must be a fairly valid reason for the Chief Constable's arrival on the scene. As the boat had started with me on board (as it happened, I had no option in the matter), the wireless message that I prevailed on Vass to send out filled the bill comfortably, and Major Marriner was able to come alongside, come aboard, and have the *conversazione* about the counterfeit arrest that he had made on shore without Rock really wondering what it was all about. We kidded him beautifully over his naming of the criminal—whoever he had named would naturally have been the man we had arrested."

Sir Austin had another question.

"Supposing you had gone on board in the first place, normally? What would have happened then—from Major Marriner's standpoint, I mean?"

"He would have come aboard at a certain time on a pretext to see me—urgently. With the same story of the arrest and with—I hope—a similar result." Anthony turned to them and smiled. "And that, I think, Sir Austin, just about sums the whole matter up."

"Oh no," returned the Commissioner, with a smile, "you're not going to get away with it like that. Even if you think you are. You've given us the facts of the case, I admit, and its various stages; but you've omitted a good deal of your own show. Let's have the deductions that you made—or, at any rate, the more important deductions."

Anthony looked inquiringly at Major Marriner. The latter's face was impassive. It gave Mr. Bathurst no indication whatever of what he was thinking or feeling. Mr. Bathurst realized that Sir Austin must have his way.

"Well, sir, I was helped tremendously, of course, right at the beginning of the investigation by the information that was given to me by Hatherley. He established the fact that the dead man wasn't the man he purported to be. That is to say, apart from any question of deliberate substitution. This, you will agree, made a splendid jumping-off point."

Sir Austin nodded. "Of course."

Anthony continued, "I think that the first *vital* deduction that I made came from the tongs."

"The tongs? Good gracious! How did that occur?"

"There was *no blood on the tongs*," responded Anthony gravely.

Sir Austin looked startled at the reply.

"No blood on the tongs? Explain, please."

Mr. Bathurst resumed his seat. "I will. When Dr. Thorold was called to the body, he found the tongs lying on the table. Now, it's unusual for tongs to be on the table, and the doctor imagined that the murderer had used them to break up the imitation ebony stag.

I didn't accept this theory—and I'll tell you why. The harpoon had made an appallingly ghastly wound in the dead man's body. As Major Marriner told us when he first presented us with the problem, the place was almost a shambles. There was blood everywhere. There must have been some on Rock and on Rock's clothing, and I thought that if he had used the tongs directly after the murder it was almost a certainty that there would have been traces of blood on them. Similarly, if they had been lying on the table *at the time of the murder*. I looked at those tongs and then I looked at the casement windows, and I came to the conclusion that the tongs were on the table—because it had been impossible for the murderer to put them anywhere else."

Mr. Bathurst paused dramatically. Sir Austin and Major Marriner both stared at him with undisguised interest.

"You will remember," he went on, "that when Mrs. Forsyth returned to the bungalow after attending the meeting of the Bazaar Committee, the front door was bolted as she had left it and the back door was both locked and bolted. And when Jimmie Ward got through the open scullery-window, he found also that the key was missing from the lock of the back door. From whichever way you looked at it, an extremely puzzling state of affairs!" Anthony turned to look at his two companions. "Rock's idea was, I think first and last, to mystify the police. He knew the topography of the bungalow pretty well. He had been watching the place for some days and had prowled round the garden, I suggest, more than once. After he had killed Forsyth, he washed his hands, I fancy, in the sink in the scullery and cleaned his clothing. He had previously noticed the tongs lying on the hearth in the room where the murder had taken place. This gave him the idea to which I just referred.

"Carrying the tongs, he made his exit by the back door. He took the key and then locked the back door from the outside, placing the key in his pocket. His next move was to procure the pair of steps from the outhouse, put them against the window, climb to the top of them, lean through the open window, tongs extended in his hand to the full length of his arm, bend down, and with the tongs catch hold of the top of the bolt and draw it, thus securely bolting the door and— *voilà!*—making us all wonder how and why. He then returned the pair of steps to the outhouse, walked round the side of the bungalow to the open window of the living-room, and carefully returned the tongs—and the only place where he could reach to put them was the table! Have you followed my line of reasoning, gentlemen?"

"Yes, but it was a *general* deduction. I appreciate it, of course; but how about the pointers towards the guilty party?"

Anthony considered the question carefully for a moment or so.

"Well, it was a difficult problem, sir. Complicated by the unusual task that we encountered right at the outset. The mystery of the dead man himself, which we were forced to solve, or partly solve, before we could sort things out, as it were, with regard to the motive for the murder itself."

Major Marriner gave a sign of acquiescence.

"I know how right Bathurst is with regard to that. Only too well. At the commencement there were difficulties at every turn. Hather-ley put Bathurst on the right track to begin with, and then, of course, there was the discovery of the second Forsyth's marriage-certificate."

"Yes," contributed Anthony, resuming his recital, "that put me well on the road. In reply to your question, Sir Austin, about point-ers to the guilty party, I was groping in the dark far too long for any bouquets to be thrown at me. Nobody knows that better than I. Although, perhaps, there was just a little excuse for me. The alibi of the man whom we now know as Rock seemed so absolutely water-tight. My first tiny seed of suspicion concerning him was planted by no less a person than Captain Vass. That, perhaps, surprises you?"

"It does, rather," returned the Commissioner.

Anthony grinned at the candid admission.

"Thought it might. I'll tell you what it was. When I went to dine with Vass on the *Vaar*, as Rock's guest, amongst other things he told me that Rock had been 'ill' all the time on the voyage over. A severe cold. This cold had kept him confined to his bunk throughout the voyage. When I first heard it, it seemed commonplace news and I paid no attention to it; but afterwards, when certain ideas were beginning to take root in my brain, it gradually became more important and assumed very different dimensions."

"What was the point?" queried Sir Austin.

"The language. Vass spoke excellent English; but Rock, posing as a Swedish naval officer, had very little Swedish, and he had, in order to avoid a certain amount of suspicion and curiosity, to conceal that fact as much as possible. So he feigned illness—a sudden chill—and kept himself in his bunk all the time. When he took me along with him to dine with Vass, the conversation was bound to be in English because of my being there. Therefore, during that time, he would be comparatively safe."

"All that makes me wonder," mused Sir Austin Kemble, "why did he cultivate your acquaintance so? Why do you think, Bathurst?"

"To be close to me and to know, because of that, more or less what I was doing; and then, as well, to allay any suspicion I might have harboured concerning him. He was able to stage the attack on me by the harbour and, by reason of what he did there, ingratiate himself in my favour. Oh, he knew his book, did Gabriel Rock!"

"So that's when you began to suspect him. Tell me how it ultimately developed."

"It became a reality, sir, when Mrs. Bryant was strangled."

"How do you mean? I don't know that I—"

"Well, it was moderately obvious that Mrs. Bryant was murdered because she knew something, and therefore must be prevented from circulating that knowledge. That was almost the only way by which she could have entered into the plot. As you know, I called on her husband. I learnt about the lodger, the dark-haired lodger, who disappeared from Upchalke directly after Forsyth's murder. A letter for this man had been left behind. It was a moral certainty, immediately I heard of him, that this lodger merited very special attention. Now what was he, Sir Austin?"

"Er . . . in what way do you mean?"

"Well . . . was he a native or a stranger?"

"Er . . . I suppose you'd call him a stranger, wouldn't you?"

"Exactly . . . and that's the conclusion to which I came. This piece of evidence that I collected at the Bryants' seemed to me to eliminate everybody with the exception of Rock, Hatherley, and Sharpe-Lodge. Mrs. Bryant knew all the others who had been in contact with the crime. Even Mulrenan, who early on enjoyed my attention for some little time, had been to the 'Tracy Arms' in the past and was far from being a stranger to her. So there I was, you see, thinking very hard in terms of the gallant captain."

"And you were right," declared Major Marriner. "When I got your last message and those final arrangements of yours I was inclined to hesitate as to action, but then the truth came to me in a flash and I saw all the points that you had made quite clearly."

"Well . . . that's that," said Sir Austin Kemble, in final comment. "Oh, by the way, Bathurst, I meant to tell you . . . the Lancashire police picked up Mrs. Forsyth this morning, at Bootle."

"Winifred Nina?"

"Yes. From what I hear, she knew of her husband's fraudulent action with regard to the genuine Forsyth's superannuation allowances, but I doubt whether we can touch her in any way. There's nothing she can be justifiably charged with. She was hardly an accessory to the fraud . . . and there's no doubt that she had to do as her husband ordered her."

"I beg your pardon?" said Mr. Bathurst.

Sir Austin repeated his previous statement.

"She had to do as she was told. That's what I said. Like most married women."

"If I were you, sir," replied Mr. Bathurst, "I'd go to bed. You're over-tired."

"What do you mean?"

"Well, sir, I can think of no other satisfactory explanation."

Sir Austin Kemble stared at him before stretching out his hand for the tantalus.

"Bathurst," he said solemnly, "there are times when I'd sooner drink whisky than listen to you . . . and this, my boy, is one of 'em. All the best! And to you, Marriner."

THE END